TOUCH OF BLOOD

CURSE OF THE GUARDIANS BOOK TWO

TAYLOR ASTON WHITE

DARK WOLF
PUBLISHING

Edited by Alexander Small
Cover by MiblArt

www.taylorastonwhite.com
Official Taylor Aston White Newsletter

SUMMARY

He's never wanted anyone... until her.

After being condemned to the fighting Pits as a child, Kace was forced to do horrifying things to survive. Now, as an adult with a curse that intensifies his rage, he keeps himself away from anything that can break his carefully constructed control. So when he meets Eva, the only woman who has ever ignited such raw, violent passion, he has no choice but to stay away.

Eva didn't think much when her vampire ex-boyfriend showed up asking for her back. Except she wasn't interested, and the man she had once loved wasn't taking no for an answer. Defended by a tall, moody and definitely dangerous man her ex left, and she thought that was the end of it...

Until she wakes up dead.

Thrown into an unfamiliar world, Eva only has one hope to free herself from her new master, and it just happens to be the same man she's been warned to stay away from.

SIGN UP to Taylor's newsletter to receive exclusive updates on upcoming releases!

AUTHOR NOTES / DISCLAIMER

Touch of Blood is a very slow burn, but spicy paranormal romance that's worth the tension. The story contains dark themes, explicit content, graphic violence, profanity, and topics that may be sensitive to some readers.

Trigger warnings:
Graphic gore/death, torture, sexual assault (not on page), sexually explicit scenes, kidnapping, blood play.

This book is written in British English, including spelling and grammar and contains dark, graphic details.

BREED INDEX

Celestrial - Also known as 'angels.' Can lose their powers and wings, known as 'falling'

Magic class - Unknown

Origin realm - Unknown

Other - Once a celestrial has fallen, they're rumoured to be as weak as humans, but none have openly confirmed (See Fallen Angel)

Daemon - Druids who choose to ascend into black magic. In return for more power, they sacrifice their bodies and sanity

Magic class - Black

Origin realm - The Nether (also known as Hell)

Other - Once imprisoned in The Nether, they now freely move between realms

Druid - Born male, druid genes are inherited from the fathers

Magic class - Natural/Arcane. Can be strengthened with Ley Lines

Origin realm - Earth Side

Other - Breed governed by the Archdruid. When they come of age they must tattoo a syphon, known as a glyph, around their wrists to better control their arcane

Guardian - Druids who were cursed to share their soul with a 'beast.' Their bodies, including their 'beast' form, are designed to battle Daemons, with increased strength, agility and ability to survive severe damage

Magic class - Natural/Arcane. Can be strengthened with Ley Lines and glyphs

Origin realm - Earth Side

Beast - Unknown

Other - The Archdruid made the deal with Hadriel, the Fallen Angel who powers The Nether, creating the curse in return for soldiers

Fae - Umbrella term for anyone from Far Side. Includes faeries, selkies, pixies etc. Split into two castes, light (Seelie) and dark (Unseelie)

Magic class - Wild Magic

Origin realm - Asherah of Far (also known as Far Side)

Other - Never say thank you, and be wary of gifts (Fae stuff seem to have a mind of their own)

Fallen Angels - Celestrials that have 'fallen'

Magic class - Unknown

Origin realm - Unknown, but now reside on Earth Side

Other - Hide themselves amongst humans, always trying to regain their wings

Ghoul - Name for a failed vampire transition. Primal instincts only

Magic class - N/A
Origin realm - Earth Side
Other - Killed on sight

Human - Class themselves as the 'original' species on Earth Side. They have no access to their chi
Magic class - N/A
Origin realm - Earth Side
Other - Make over 60% of the population

Shifter - Born with a animal spirit, able to transform into said animal
Magic class - N/A
Origin realm - Earth Side
Other - Are not infectious, despite rumours. Usually live in groups/packs with a strict hierarchy

Witch - Humans who were gifted the ability to access their chi. Magic originated from the four elements, diluting through generations
Magic class - Arcane (balls of concentrated chi), Natural (plants) and Black (blood/death)
Origin realm - Earth Side
Other - Rumoured that it was Fae royalty who originally gifted humans magic

Vampire - Humans who've been infected by the Vampira virus
Magic class - N/A
Origin realm - Earth Side
Other - Low success rate, resulting in death and/or Ghouls. If turn is successful they must feed from a live source, surviving on proteins found in fresh blood

SHADOW-VEYN INDEX

Shadow-Veyn are wild creatures easily influenced by Daemons. They hide themselves from the general populace with glamour, but lower class cannot hide their shadows (hence their name)

Magic class - N/A

Origin realm - The Nether (Hell)

Other - Along with Daemons, they're no longer imprisoned in The Nether. Feed upon flesh, and as of yet, no evidence that they breed

Classifications -

A - Small. Weak. Used as scouts

B - Venomous. Covered in black fur

C - Can heal using dark vapour

D - Scales as strong as armour, as well as fur

E - Defined by sheer size, and extra bones along spine

TOUCH
OF BLOOD

CURSE OF THE GUARDIANS
BOOK TWO

TAYLOR ASTON WHITE

CHAPTER I
EVA

There were worse things than a crazy ex. Bitten by a fire ant probably sucked, for example. Bungee-jumping off a bridge only to realise at the last second the rope hadn't been tied securely. Going back to your date's place to find less than three inches in the downstairs department was a pretty crap situation too, but maybe not as bad as a crazy ex. More disappointing than anything.

Lucas, the ex who currently distracted her was in the audience, watching her with those hungry eyes that she used to love, but now nothing but disgust tightened her stomach. Eva missed a move, her dance partner Caleb glaring a warning before he pulled her against his bare chest, compensating for her mistake.

Shit! she scolded herself. *Get yourself together!*

Concentrating, she let the beat settle into her bones, losing herself in the music. The dance was pure passion, about sex and the intimacy between two people who were not meant for one another. They told a story of love and hate, the emotions exaggerated in fluid movements across the stage.

She didn't need to look onto the floor to know there

were people watching, their gaze a heightened sensation against her own, exposed skin as she rolled her body alongside Caleb's. It was sensual and expressive, and one of the many reasons she loved to dance.

Eva danced for The Dollhouse five times a week, both with partners and solo. It was advertised as an upmarket dance and burlesque bar, and while there were poles for some of the dancers to shimmy along, they classed themselves as just another theatre in the West End. There were no personal performances, and definitely no extras offered like other establishments.

The patrons couldn't touch the dancers unless they were invited onto the stage, which sometimes they were, but only if consent was exchanged. The manager was a stickler for rules, and anyone abusing said rules were immediately ejected from the premises and banned for life. It was a safe place for her to express herself and dance, and the money wasn't too bad either. It wasn't caviar and gold watches, but it wasn't stressing over the next meal either.

The room erupted into applause, her breathing heavy as she folded her body into a low bow, long hair brushing the stage. She didn't linger, not wanting to see whether Lucas still sat at the end of bar, dark eyes watching her every move. She couldn't believe she wasted six months with him, even after everyone had warned her. The red flags were obvious now, but they weren't as clear back then through rose-tinted glasses. He had greeted her with shoes shinier than her entire life, and then left her with some nasty bites and a bruised ego.

"What the fuck, Eva," Caleb grunted with a frown, the glitter on his face melted from sweat. "What was that about? You never miss a move."

Eva plastered on a fake smile. "Sorry, my ankle twisted," she lied. "It's been a long night." Their duo was her last dance of her shift, and wanting to change before she confronted the man who had wanted to share her as if she were a toy, she turned toward the dressing rooms. Crystal, Tasha and Pearl were pouting into three of the five available mirrors, the racks of costumes splitting the backroom into sections.

"Hey babe, you staying for a few drinks?" one of the girls asked. Eva wasn't sure who, her back turned as she shimmied out of her skirt.

"It's Saturday," Tasha moaned, the slight whine in her voice giving her away. "You have to stay for at least one!"

Eva pulled up her jeans before quickly yanking on her t-shirt, not caring that glitter and makeup smeared across the fabric. "Can't tonight, rain check?"

She wanted a long hot bubble bath, but because her shitty flat didn't have a bath she would settle for a scalding shower instead.

Scrubbing her face clean with a baby wipe, she grabbed her bag. She was sure her skin would hate her, but right then she just needed to get it over with. She hadn't seen Lucas since she had told him to leave and never look back... after he had hurt her for the second time. The first time had been an accident apparently, but once it had happened again within the same week she kicked him to the curb.

"Where are you?" she muttered as she parted the crowd. None of the patrons approached her, not only because of the rules but because she looked entirely different without the costume and makeup. Her brown hair had been released from its constraint, the heavy waves hitting her mid-back while her lips were no longer painted a scarlet red. Bar the glitter, which was a fucker to get out of anything anyway, she looked plain, unexciting compared to the sparkly men and women who danced on stage.

She spotted Lucas at the bar, exactly where he was

earlier. His smirk deepened when his eyes met hers, his fangs peeking through his lips.

"What are you doing here?" she snapped, wanting him to leave quickly and without a scene. "I told you to leave me alone, no stalking and definitely no turning up at my work unannounced."

"Baby, is that how you really talk to someone you love?" When she didn't respond he stood, pressing into her space. "I want another chance, I can't stop thinking about you."

"That's a joke, right?" Anger darkened her tone. "It's literally the definition of insanity."

"Excuse me?" His eyes narrowed at her in hostility.

"Doing the same thing over and over again and expecting different results. You hurt me, twice, and then marked me as a snack for all your Vamp buddies." The latter something she had found out *after* she had already left him, but it still hurt to know she had been nothing to him but a vein. *Fucking arsehole.*

"You're being dramatic," he said, rubbing the top of his gold ring, his own initials carved into the flat surface. "I wasn't really going to share you."

"Share me? I'm not a possession you arsehole!"

Lucas rolled his eyes, and Eva had to take a steady breath to stop from exploding.

"Look, I got carried away with a feeding, I didn't mean to hurt you. It's not my fault you excite me," he added with a shrug. "This is as much your fault as it is mine."

Eva kept her voice low, not wanting to be overheard. "And I told you exactly where to go last time you asked for another chance. Fuck off Lucas, I'm not interested in being your little chew toy."

"You stupid bitch." The words shot out like bullets, his hand snapping out to grip her upper arm tight enough to bruise. "Are you fucking that other dancer?"

Watching his face twist into rage reminded her exactly how he had tried to control every aspect of her life. She hadn't realised, and almost lost her friendships and her job and possibly even her fucking life because of his jealousy.

Where the bloody hell were the bouncers?

"You'll never get anyone better than me," he continued. "You're just a slut who can..."

His fingers tightened before he was wrenched to the side, followed by a crack as he crashed against the wall beside them. Eva blinked, the whole movement so fast it took a second for her brain to catch up to the situation. Lucas snarled, clawing at the arm that held him against the wall, his feet dangling beneath him as if her were a child, and not an adult of six feet.

Oh shit!

"Apologise," the man growled, pressing closer until he was almost nose to nose. "Now."

Lucas snarled, his expression blocked by the stranger's wide shoulders. "Fuck you!" he managed to squeeze out, the sound strangled.

A deep chuckle. "Careful, fang face."

They were starting to gain an audience, something she didn't want. She needed this job and was already on a warning from when she punched a bartender for groping her. He had been fired, but apparently it wasn't good business for one of the dancers to knock out other staff.

"Put him down," she said calmly despite the anger that bubbled, touching the stranger's shoulder. "He's not worth it." She ignored the muscles that bunched at her contact, immediately pulling her hand back.

The man's head turned to the side, and she sucked in a breath when she recognised the square jaw, strong nose, and dangerously dark forest green eyes.

"Kace?"

5

Lucas dropped to his feet so suddenly he nearly collapsed, very unlike his usual vampiric grace. He caught himself on the bar, his hand leaving a perfect imprint of his palm. She would be blamed for that, she just knew it.

"You know this guy? What, you fucking him too?"

Kace let his silence answer for him, his head dipped so that his beautiful red hair hid the expression in his eyes. She had never seen a shade like it, so deep it was like dark mahogany mixed with the heart of a ruby.

The silence stretched, Lucas's face tightening.

Wait...

Kace had remained silent on purpose.

Men!

"Who I fuck is none of your business anymore!" Not that she had anything to do with Kace, the man was as moody as the moon. She had only met him a handful of times, and that was when he was guarding her best friend's flat that just happened to be beside her own.

Lucas launched forward, fist blurring towards Kace's jaw in a strike that would kill most people. Vampires had double the strength of humans, and she knew from experience how vicious Lucas could be once he was worked up. She was lucky she'd only left the relationship with a few scrapes and bruises.

A gasp escaped her throat, but Kace barely grunted as he caught the fist in his larger hand.

Lucas frowned. "What the?!"

"Hey Red, we got a problem?" Marshall, one of the bouncers bounded over. "This guy giving you trouble?" The man was built like a mountain, over six foot and an impressive set of shoulders that made most misbehaving clientele hesitate. But when he moved closer, she realised Kace was taller, somehow more intimidating with arms roped in sleek muscle that looked like they were built for speed rather than just strength.

"I've got it," Kace muttered, tightening his grip until Lucas hissed.

Marshall smirked, folding his thick arms over his chest. "Make sure you clean up after yourself, I ain't gonna deal with whatever's left." His attention turned to Eva. "You okay, sweetheart?"

Eva managed a nod, scrambling after Kace who had marched Lucas towards the emergency exit. "Wait!"

Kace ignored her, yanking Lucas with him as if he were a disobedient child. He paused as soon as the door swung open, the alley beyond illuminated by the harsh streetlight overhead. His grip loosened, enough for Lucas to break free. "Fuck off," he snarled.

Lucas hissed, eyes bleeding to black as his fangs elongated past his lips. "Or what?"

Kace smiled, a cruel twist of his lips.

Lucas froze in a way that was unique to vampires, his body so still he appeared as a statue. There was no breathing, no flutter of an eyelid or even a twitch of muscle. The only movement was his eyes, which flicked between Kace and herself.

His smirk was dark, calculated when he finally moved. "I'll see you around, babe," he said as he turned towards the mouth of the alley. He disappeared into the street beyond, and only then did Eva allow herself to relax, just a little.

"What was that? Why did you have to make it so much worse, *Red?*" She purposely used the nickname. "Don't bother helping next time."

His eyes snapped to hers, then dropped to the mark on her upper arm that already ached, her pale skin easily bruised. "Sure."

Just a one-word response, and it heightened her already simmering anger.

"What the hell?" She moved closer, noticing how he stepped back at the same time. "What are you even doing here?"

"I didn't realise you owned the city," he said, the words edging towards a growl. "I'll remember to ask permission next time I want to speak to an acquaintance."

Eva let out a frustrated scream. "You're such an arsehole! Don't bother helping next time."

A snigger. "Noted."

His dark green eyes held a glimmer of unpredictability, like a predator sizing up his prey. It was even more frustrating that they fascinated her, even as his manner pissed her off.

"Careful," he said, his tone deepening at her attention. "We don't want a repeat of last time."

Eva blinked, and the memory of his lips against hers, of his tongue dominating her mouth in powerful thrusts that made her try and pull him closer flashed inside her mind. She couldn't remember the conversation right then, or what had even led to the situation, but she had melted at the touch. She was an embarrassing puddle when he lifted her, his fingers beneath her skirt within seconds. And then his tongue...

Eva swallowed her moan, hoping the burn from her cheeks didn't give her away. It had all happened in the hall, where anyone could see him on his knees with her leg slung over his shoulder.

Luckily, Kyra had come home and interrupted what clearly would have been a huge mistake. That was all it was, a giant, humongous error in her judgment. She clearly hadn't been thinking straight when she wrapped her hand around his...

Oh my god, stop it Eva!

Kace stepped forward, his voice dropping as the harsh light above cast shadows across his sharp cheekbones. "Or is that exactly what you want?"

The man infuriated her, so why did her traitorous thighs press together in anticipation?

Eva fought an embarrassing moan. She needed to get laid, but not by the man who stood with a permanent scowl before her.

"You wish," she said in a suspiciously husky tone. "You couldn't handle me."

Fuck. Me. Sideways. It had sounded like a challenge, and that was not her intention. What the fuck was with her attraction to hot, dangerous guys?

His eyes narrowed, and she hoped like god that he couldn't read her mind.

"So yeah, erm, thanks for that," she said quickly, clearing her throat.

"Is that Vamp going to cause you problems?" Kace dropped his gaze, and Eva swore she felt it burn across her skin.

"No I doubt I'll see him again. He'll find someone else to play with and then forget about me." She needed a shower. Cold. "I'm going home now. So... bye."

She didn't wait, just jogged out front towards to her car. It was late, and even in a city that never really slept it didn't take her long to get to her building, parking in a space that was surprisingly close to the entrance.

Even the distance hadn't dampened her embarrassment, nor the arousal that just made it that much worse.

"What's wrong with me?" she groaned, settling her head against the leather of the steering wheel. Kace was a mystery, a grumpy arsehole who scowled at her more than smiled. So why was her body ready to climb him like a mountain?

'To be fair, you threatened him with a wok the first time you met.' Kyra's voice drifted into her head so clear it was like she was sitting beside her. She hadn't seen her friend in weeks, which meant they were due to schedule their bad TV and takeaway night. It was something they used to do all the time, but since Kyra had moved away a few months ago and was busy doing whatever job she did for The Magicka, they never seemed to have the same free time. It sucked, but she was happy for her friend. She deserved happiness more than anyone.

Maybe I can ask her about Kace? she thought to herself as she began to climb the stairs to her floor before quickly squashing the notion. *No, that was a bad idea.* She didn't need complicated, moody men in her life. Even ones who were as damn sexy as him. No, it looked like it was just her and her battery-operated boyfriend. B.O.B would never judge her angry sex fantasy about a tall, irritating man who she knew nothing about.

With a dramatic sigh she opened her front door, the automatic light in the corner flicking to life when she moved inside. She was acting like a woman in heat.

As if she was psychic, a text popped up from Kyra. *'Girl night tomorrow? I need a break from all this testosterone!'*

Eva grinned, typing her reply out quickly. *'Please tell me that all that testosterone is at least giving you the best orgasms of your life?'* She could imagine her best friends face, Kyra very easily embarrassed when it came to sex. *'Don't keep me waiting,'* she quickly added before Kyra could respond. *'I need to live vicariously though you!'* It had been a while since she went out and had the chance to meet someone, her work taking precedence over her social life.

Phone clutched in hand, Eva glanced up at the family

photograph on the wall, touching her fingertips to the glass like she did every time she came home. "Evening guys," she said to her parents. "I know, I know, I'm home later than normal. You wouldn't believe the drama."

She knew it was crazy that she spoke to her parents' picture, but she had found comfort in it for the few years she was forced into care. She'd been alone for over ten years, her parents dying when she was just a teenager. She enjoyed telling them everything about her day, well, everything except men. Even in death she didn't think they would want to know it had been a dry spell.

Dropping her keys on the side table she headed straight for the kitchen in the back, placing the leftover lasagne into the microwave and setting the timer before grabbing one of her homemade muffins.

If it could be baked, Eva would make it. It was different to dance, but it was something else she loved to explore and experiment with. It was just a bonus that at the end she got something delicious to eat, well, most of the time it was delicious. Sitting herself on the counter she began to nibble the edge, watching the countdown glow just as her phone buzzed.

'Firstly, Xee told me not to kiss and tell. Secondly, you're tragic. It's a good thing I love you!'

Eva smirked, her finger moving quickly over the touchscreen as she began to reply. A loud bang caused her to jump, her phone dropping from her hand to crash on to the floor.

"You stupid cunt," Lucas snarled, hands wrapping around her arms in an iron grip. "Do you really think you could ever be with anyone other than me?" He threw her across the room, her stomach connecting to the sofa hard enough that the whole thing knocked onto its back, taking her with it. He kicked at her ankle, and Eva let out a scream as she felt the bone break before he reached down to grip her throat, pulling her up as if she weighed nothing, her lungs screaming for air.

Eva pulled at his fingers, scratched down his arms but nothing moved his clutch. His face was void of the humanity so many vampires wore, his once warm brown eyes completely black with rage, his lips pulled back to reveal large fangs.

"I marked you from the beginning," he spat at her. "And now I'm going to make you mine, forever."

His fingers finally released, allowing her to take in a much needed breath, but the respite wasn't long lived. His fangs struck, the pain paralyzing before she felt the familiar burn of his venom. She pushed at his shoulders, trying to break the seal but with every passing second she weakened.

For fuck's sake.

She was going to die, and she was still covered in glitter.

CHAPTER 2
KACE

TWO MONTHS LATER

Kace relaxed into his stance, fists clenched as he waited with the patience of a predator. His opponent huffed out an unsteady breath, red-faced and sweating so much it would obscure his vision soon enough.

His ribs ached, but not broken from the numerous hits he had allowed to land. His knuckles bled through the wraps he was made to wear, not that he received much protection from the thin fabric. He could heal almost any damage faster than any other Breed, a gift from his curse, he supposed.

Finish him! his beast roared inside his mind, needing to feel the warmth of the opponent's blood against his skin. They both needed the cages, a safer way for him to exert some of the extra aggression he carried without hurting anyone. Well, hurting anyone he wasn't fighting.

The Vault was a shady business deep within the Undercity, run by an equally shady guy, that consisted of illegal hand-to-hand fights, no holds barred. There were no weight limit or restrictions, you could fight anyone you wanted for the right money. Admission to the place was cheap enough it encouraged attendance, but the real money was in the bets.

He always bet on himself, and because he didn't lose, unless it was on purpose, he had a nice little nest egg. His brothers all contributed in different ways to the Guardians. One controlled several multimillion-pound companies as well as a little bar. Another was a computer genius with sought after hacking skills, and there was even one who made and sold some of the best weapons on the continent.

Kace, in contrast, beat the shit out of people.

His opponent's muscle tensed, the kick coming less than a second later. Kace caught it with little effort, frustration making him growl. He wanted a real fight, not one where he could predict every move before his challenger even thought of them.

The Fae had blue pearlescent scales along the edges of his face, and more of a snout than a humanoid jaw. He couldn't tell which type of Fae he was, only that his strength was close to a mid-predator shifter, but weaker than a vampire. A Vamp would have broken at least three bones, fuck, even a shifter would have caused more damage than Crocodile Face.

Sometimes he needed the pain, needed a reminder that he was alive, that he had survived. He needed the discomfort to remind him not to kill.

Kace's fist shot out, connecting to Croc's cheekbone with a satisfying crunch. He had pulled his punch at the last second, wanting the fight to last long enough that he started to feel the slight calmness of exhaustion. It was the only thing that settled his beast, that stopped the bastard who shared his soul from riding him for more violence, for more death. All his brothers carried the same burden of their own shared souls, and yet he had to be landed with the one homicidal maniac.

A heavy snarl vibrated between his ears, fur pushing beneath his skin as his beast tested the boundaries of control. Only a year or so ago his beast would have won, and would have forced a shift into his alternative shape. Even after all the training he still lost himself in extreme situations, or when he couldn't be bothered to act civil.

His beast knew three things, violence, hunger and sex.

Sometimes that's all he wanted too.

The furious snarl inside his head cut off, and Kace turned to see what caught the maniac's attention. A heavy kick landed on his stomach, but other than an uncomfortable exhale of air he continued to stare through the chains of the cage, unable to look away from a woman that looked very similar to the same one that haunted his fucking dreams, and had drawn over and over again.

Darkness drawn to the light.

What the fuck?

EVA

Eva watched Kace dominate, his movements quick and precise despite his size. Her throat burned, hunger almost overwhelming even as she fought the repulsion of Lucas's hand on her thigh, his thumb brushing higher and higher beneath the skirt he forced her to wear.

If he recognised the red-headed fighter he hadn't acknowledged it.

"Come on, come on!" he grunted beneath his breath, a betting slip held tightly in his other fist.

It was the first time she'd been allowed outside since she had woken up dead. She wasn't even sure how long it had been since the overwhelming pain had pulled her from a groggy sleep, her body cold and a hunger so endless she had attacked Lucas with a strength that surprised her.

She remembered his laugh when she bit into his arm, content to tear and maim until his blood had hit her tongue and she swallowed until the ache in her stomach lessened. She remembered how his laugh changed into a sensual moan, his fingers gripping her closer until the same blood in her mouth had turned to ash.

She had released him as quickly as she had attacked, crawling away with a body faster than before, but not as fast as Lucas, or as strong.

She had learned pretty quickly vampires required regular blood, otherwise they weakened until they were almost back to human. Which was the only reason Lucas was able to keep her as long as he had, his grip tight to stop her from running away.

She missed warmth, her new body unable to regulate temperature when starved, a bloody walking corpse.

"You stupid fucking bastard!" Lucas cried beside her, his fingers pressing hard enough her bone creaked at the force. "Hit him back!"

Eva made no noise, not even a whimper at the increasing pain. It was a distraction from the aching in her throat, at the continuous control it took not to grab one of the shouting men beside her and to sink her fangs into their flesh until she was full.

Two months ago that thought would have made her recoil in disgust, but now her new improved canines punched down as blood splattered the floor of the cage, so sharp they pierced into her bottom lip. Her stomach grumbled, a sweet tasting saliva filling her mouth as her fangs throbbed…

Eva froze as Kace turned, a frown pulling his brow as his eyes met hers. It was only a split second, not long enough for her to react before he returned to his opponent. But long enough for any hope she had to shrivel and die like her soul.

Fuck! Fuck! Fuckety-fuck!

What was she thinking? She barely recognised herself in the mirror, her skin a shade paler than her already fair skin. Her blue irises she had inherited from her mother had darkened to black, which was apparently a sign of rage, or intense hunger. She was both.

Lucas had explained she wouldn't truly die from starvation, but it would teach her a lesson. He wanted her to beg, to obey.

She would rather die.

Eva felt the beat inside her chest, which was a comforting surprise considering Lucas had enjoyed joking about how his Breed had no hearts. She wasn't truly dead, not when she still had a heartbeat, still breathed and felt pain. She just wasn't human anymore.

"I can hear your heart from here," Lucas growled.

So could she, the boom, boom, boom overstimulating against her heightened senses. Her hearing was able to pick up every conversation in the large room, the voices all muddled together unless she concentrated. Even her sight had improved, everything seeming brighter, more defined. It was distracting, her mind unable to focus.

"Filter your senses and calm down before someone notices."

She opened her mouth, a sharp retort ready but no sound came out. Only the infinite burning that had stolen her voice, every swallow excruciating.

"I think I prefer you like this," Lucas said before he returned to the fight.

Fuck you, you small-dicked piece of shit! If only her gaze could cut.

She looked around for someone else, anyone else. No one turned, not even a flicker of care as they watched the cage. The place was busy, the wooden benches that circled the fight so full, many people stood at the back. There was a betting office, the front covered in a metal lattice with a small section cut out at the bottom. Boys, maybe early to mid-teens ran the bets between the office and some of the punters, carefully manoeuvring the chaos.

Cheers, as well as cries of despair as the fight continued with brutal speed, the smack of flesh on flesh igniting the crowd. The man next to her stood, arms wide as he roared. Another joined him, and then another until a whole row obscured the view.

Okay, okay, okay! she chanted inside her head. *This is it!*

She didn't know when she would get another chance.

She had to time it just right.

Eva shoved forward, hard enough to jolt the man who stood by the bench in front. He turned faster than she anticipated, hissing out a rumble as she pointed beside her. Without hesitation the man pushed Lucas, the movement causing the grip on her leg to slip. She shot to her feet, ignoring the weakness as she moved through the crowd. Her limbs felt heavy, her movements awkward as she was still to get used to her new body.

The exit was blocked, so she headed towards the centre. If she needed to make a scene she would. If she needed to climb over the damn cage and join in the fight she would.

She hadn't been paying attention to the match, the noises and scents overwhelming as she pushed herself through the rippling crowd. They heaved forward, and she was caught in the wave, crushed by the cool mesh of the cage.

"Get back!" A man barked, banging something hard against the metal links to create an audible clang. "Everyone take a step fucking back or risk being kicked out!"

The pressure eased, and as she looked up Kace landed the final blow. His opponent collapsed only inches from her, his face swollen and covered in bruises.

A hand encircled her throat, hot breath touching her ear. "Fucking bitch!" Lucas snarled as he pulled her away. "Why did you go and ruin it?"

Eva staggered, but his grip kept her from falling.

No! she screamed inside her head, twisting until a fang nicked the skin on his arm. Blood touched her tongue, the satisfaction turning to disgust when he smirked.

"Eva?" Kace growled, his eyes turning a shade of silver as he crouched down with a frown, fingers pressing through the holes.

Lucas froze, eyes widening before he shoved them both towards the exit, getting lost in the mass. Cool air kissed her skin, the scent of rain and ozone carried by the harsh wind as Lucas guided them towards the side and away from the crowd.

It was late, the streetlights not reaching the shadows within the alley as rough brick scraped across her back, the pressure increasing on the front of her neck. It stole her breath, her lungs like cement. It was uncomfortable, but not life threatening as she no longer required as much oxygen to survive. She had learned that pretty quickly too.

"Fucking whore," Lucas screeched, his fist hitting the wall beside her hard enough to leave an indent. "No one else will want you, I'll make sure of it."

His blood still coated her bottom lip, the taste divine yet she refused to savour it as she spat.

His fingers tightened, jaw flexing.

"Mr Whitlock?"

Lucas turned with a snarl as three men appeared, their hands resting on the guns at their hips. "What the fuck do you want?"

The man in the middle stepped forward, a pair of sunglasses covering the majority of his face. The other two stood relaxed, expressions schooled into militant boredom. "Mr Whitlock, if you could please accompany us to the waiting car. Your presence is required."

Lucas released his grip, muscles tensed. His movement blurred, but as he stepped away he was met with one of the men.

"Think about your decision, Mr Whitlock," Sunglasses said calmly, his voice matching his disinterest. "He will be most displeased if you don't attend." All three wore dark jeans and long-sleeved shirts, casual but also uniform. Mr Sunglasses lifted up his sleeves, revealing a tattoo of a tightly coiled snake.

Eva shrank back against the coarse brick, trying to make herself look as small and nonthreatening as possible. She flicked her gaze to the right, looking deeper into the shadows and the possible escape beyond. Her sight may have improved, but not enough to see into the pitch black.

"I'll get him his money," Lucas said quickly, eyes dropping to the snake marking. "Tell Dutch not to worry, I'll get it."

"Oh we know you will, Mr Whitlock," Mr Sunglasses said as he gestured to Eva with his chin. "She's pretty, a new pet?"

Eva tensed, hands curling into claws as she felt her fangs punch down. She turned back to the shadows. Would she make it if she ran?

As if he could read her thoughts Mr Sunglasses

smirked. "Try it." His hand touched the gun on his hip in warning.

Fuck.

"Now if you will both come with me, we have a car waiting."

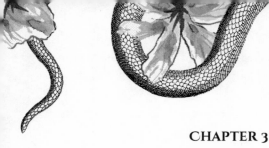

CHAPTER 3

KACE

K ace searched through the crowd that remained, the woman that looked like Eva, but couldn't be, nowhere to be seen. His beast, which would usually be resting at this point, was prominent, agitated.

"You okay?" Jax asked as he took a seat beside him, his hand absently reaching up to touch the scar that sliced down his left eye. *'Or do you need to go again?'* he finished, the ability to share thoughts unique to the Guardians.

Jax was offering another fight, which meant he could sense his tension. He probably was one of the only people who could really beat him, his brother being a master of almost every discipline. He was a smooth blade compared to Kace, whose style was more of a blunt hammer.

"Do you remember Kyra's neighbour?" he asked instead, tugging at the fabric wrapped around his knuckles. The skin beneath was broken, and he savoured the slight sting as the open wounds hit the air.

"The brunette?" Jax frowned, not that he had many other expressions. "What about her?"

"I could have sworn she was in the crowd." Except the woman who his beast had pinned as Eva wasn't human.

Her hair was the same, not simply brunette, but a golden brown with streaks of caramel blonde. Her skin had been paler, the bruises beneath her eyes deep enough to cause concern. Not to mention her eyes. Those of a fucking vampire.

"Isn't she the one who threatened you?" Jax added with a raised brow.

Kace grunted, not needing to confirm Eva's blatant disregard for him. She had been this sunshine with an attitude, her threats amusing, considering she was trying to protect her friend. She was loyal, he understood that even if she was stupid enough to poke at someone bigger and stronger. Something about him must have pissed her off because she went from threatening him to the silent treatment, and when that didn't get the desired reaction, she had changed to teasing.

It wasn't a secret that he had the worst control out of the Guardians, and it had taken him years not to burst from his own skin at any inconvenience. And then Eva happened.

He remembered the exact words she had said before he finally snapped, just like he remembered everything when it came to her. It was a moment of weakness, and usually when his beast forced control he would wake up to the stench of blood and death. Fighting kept his beast tamed, calm enough he could think past the constant rage, and then Eva had teased and he saw red.

She should have been dead, but instead he had pressed her heavily against her front door, his lips crushing hers hard enough to bruise, to punish. She had been just as shocked as he was, but then she had melted at his touch, pulling him closer. His beast had purred, fucking purred as he lifted her up, settling her against his growing cock. He hadn't even realised he'd reached beneath her obscenely short skirt and at the edge of lace until she'd moaned, her

23

pussy soaked, begging for his fingers. Then there was the way she'd tasted...

He was grateful when they were interrupted, because he wasn't sure if he would have been able to stop at just one touch, at one taste. His beast was fascinated, and for that reason alone he had kept his distance. He no longer shifted when he was pissed off, but he couldn't trust his beast around anyone, especially not her.

"Hey man, did you hear me?"

Kace blinked as Jax nudged his shoulder, one of the handful of people he allowed to touch him.

"I said if you did see Eva, you need to speak to Xee and Kyra."

"Why?"

"Because Kyra hasn't seen her in months," he continued. "Apparently Eva texts, but she's still worried."

Months? Kace thought.

"Sure, I'll mention it," he muttered out loud. "You hear anything tonight?" He preferred to attend the cages alone, but his brothers sometimes came to watch and listen.

Lower members of the Undercity came to bet on the fights, speaking about business out in the open. It was a great place to find intel, and to learn of territorial disputes between the Lords that secretly ran the city. They controlled everything from the governors to the Metropolitan Police Force, the Lords infiltrated everything.

Jax nodded. "I need to speak to Titus and Sythe, but I'm hearing whispers of a re-opening." He met Kace's eyes head-on, his gaze unwavering.

He didn't elaborate, and Kace didn't need him too. The Pits were supposed to have been shut down by The Council, but he knew something as profitable as forced gladiator fighting would never stay closed for long. The memories of his time on the sands were vibrant, as if they happened mere days ago and not almost two decades.

The difference between his childhood and now was he fought because he wanted to, and not because he had no choice but to survive.

"You heading home?" Jax asked when he remained silent, concern edging his tone. the Guardians all knew his history, as he knew theirs. They may not have been related by blood, but their traumas and shared curse made them brothers anyway.

"I'll meet you back there," Kace said, waiting until Jax had left along with the majority of the crowd before he allowed himself to brush his hand along the cool metal of the cage. The wax that had been thrown haphazardly across the links had started to peel, protecting his opponent from the metal. Luckily, Croc Face didn't seem effected, iron usually an irritant to the Fae folk. Although, the cage was more to protect the spectators than them. Hudson, the owner, had tried numerous different materials, but a metal mixture was the best without resorting to magic. Spells, enchantments and hexes were blocked from the whole establishment, the crudely designed sphere that hung from the ceiling whining as it absorbed any attempt to fix the fights.

Attention pricked along his spine, but he kept himself calm despite the agitation of his beast. The familiar scent of cheap cherry perfume mixed with desperation wrapped around him, and he didn't need to turn to know it was Ria who had approached.

"Hey, big man," she purred, fingers brushing gently along his shoulder, and before he had even realised he had her pressed against the cage, arm angled behind her back.

"Do. Not. Touch. Me." Kace released her as quickly as he had struck, her eyes vacant as usual.

Ria's smile grew, giving no indication she could feel anything other than the drugs that coursed through her veins. Her hair was tousled, dyed a bright red that matched her medically enhanced lips. It only emphasised the hollowness of her cheeks, and the harsh bites along her throat. "Aw, come on Red. The winner always gets a reward," she said, her other hand reaching forward despite his growl of warning.

"Ria, fuck off," Marshall rumbled from the other side of the cage. "How did you even get in here?"

Ria slowly blinked, her dead gaze swinging to him. "You weren't complaining the other night, was you Marsh? Not when I was on my knees."

Marshall crossed his heavy arms. "You wanna face the boss? You know exactly how he'll react when he finds you trying to work his place."

"I wouldn't have charged." Ria pursed her lips, hesitating a second before she walked away.

"Don't fucking judge me, arsehole," Marshall snarled as he took a seat beside Kace, teeth bared. "I've been trying to get her clean."

"By letting her suck your cock?" Kace settled beside him, careful to keep the gap of air between them. "How noble."

"Fuck you, Red," Marshall grunted, lifting his middle finger.

Kace smirked, brushing the hair from his eyes. "What are you doing here? We're not scheduled for training."

Marshall frowned, pulling out a pack of cigarettes. "We got a new kid, young, only ten." Tapping the bottom of the box he pulled a cigarette out, lighting it in one smooth, practiced movement. "Hudson said he turned up the other night."

That caught Kace's attention. "Hud doesn't usually deal with the new kids."

Hudson ran The Vault, but once a week allowed Kace and Marshall to close the place to help the kids who lived on the streets, as well as ones in difficult home situations.

You got to respect a criminal with some morals.

Many of the kids who came to them were young boys, starved, addicted and abused. Kace and Marshall didn't give a fuck whether the kid was human, Fae, shifter or an octopus. They taught them how to defend and take care of themselves, how to deal with their trauma, if any, and manage the bitter rage that had settled in their guts without giving in to complete destruction.

They were forgotten in society, and without intervention they would find themselves recruited into gangs, behind bars, or even worse, dead. Some of the homeless boys stayed and helped Hudson run The Vault, and in return they had a safe place to stay and get clean as long as they followed the rules.

No weapons. No deceit. No betrayal.

It sometimes took months to convince some of the kids that they weren't there to hurt them, because that was all they knew. Kace understood their reactions personally, which was why he had uncharacteristic tolerance with them and their fucking attitudes.

"Where's the kid?" Kace asked, Hudson nowhere in sight as the boys tidied up the mess left by the crowd. Braiden, who was only eleven, smiled shyly, eyes dropping to the ground while Arnav waved from his position in the betting office.

Marshall shrugged. "How the fuck am I supposed to know? I've only just gotten here." He pulled a long drag, holding in the smoke before he released his breath like a dragon.

Hunter stalked across the space, a bottle of water in hand. He tossed it to Kace, who caught it without looking up. "Why did you play with that faerie like that?" he asked with his usual pissed-off teenage, yet to be man voice. "You could have ended him in the first round if you wasn't so distracted by that chick." His Prussian blue eyes were piercing as he mirrored Kace's posture, sitting down in a chair opposite.

Hunter's face was slim, but not as skeletal as it had been when he had first arrived at The Vault six months ago. All the hints of childhood had been erased by his sharp jaw and high cheekbones, and it was only the fact he still had to grow into his shoulders and hands that indicated he was underage. He was pretty, and the thought of him being an easy target burned like acid.

"What chick?" Marshall asked, leaning back as he stretched his legs out, crossing his ankles. "I thought you were Ace from the amount of attention you give anyone."

Kace licked along his bottom lip, narrowing his eyes at Hunter. "You saw her?"

"Yeah?" An almost hesitant reply, his thick brows creasing together. "Who was she?"

Kace ignored the question. "What would you have done in the cage?"

Hunter straightened, eyes brightening. "I would have ended him in the first round."

"Sure you would, Bud," Marshall laughed. "And do you think that would have made you feel better? Made you feel strong and powerful?"

The hesitation was back, Hunter fidgeting with the hem of his t-shirt. "Erm..."

Kace took a swig of the water. "We're not teaching you to fight in the cages, Hunter."

Hunter shot to his feet. "I'm not a child, I've been practicing and..."

"You're not ready," Kace interrupted. "Fighting here isn't about glory, it's about expression, release and finding a way to manage your emotions through discipline and control."

"You're a fucking hypocrite, Red. You think you hide your rage, but we all see it simmering away when you fight." He stormed off, and Kace let him go.

"He's going to kill himself," Marshall muttered. "Or someone else."

Kace waited until Hunter was out of sight, ignoring the chair he had kicked across the room. "He's only fourteen, he'll get there." Hunter was strong, but he had allowed his animal to take more of the abuse than the boy, not that his pride would admit anything had actually happened. No, the truth had been in his face, in his broken expression. Detachment made it worse, and in Hunter's case it had made his animal wild, which was dangerous for any shifter.

It proved Kace was indeed a hypocrite, because his own beast was just as feral. Not that anyone there knew of his beast, only the teasing glimpses when his irises changed. He wasn't a shifter, but a druid who could shift from one shape to another. Something that shouldn't exist.

Kace turned towards the office before Hudson appeared in the doorframe, his hands slick with red while he casually rolled his sleeves back down. The owner of The Vault was in his forties, with a slightly aged face and the beginnings of salt and pepper hair. Despite being human, Hudson's presence was a magnetic force. Power radiated from him in waves, his dark eyes harsh and deadly.

"So, where's the kid?" Marshall asked when he approached.

Hudson pursed his lips, fury evident in the set of his jaw. "Hospital."

Kace growled, clenching his fists. "They dead?"

They both knew what he asked, because anyone who hurt the kids ended up six-feet under. No exceptions. They were a safe haven, and any kid who entered gained immediate protection. No one could cause them harm, not even their parents without answering to Kace.

Hudson flicked his gaze to him, his anger palpable. It teased his beast, the tension only growing until fur brushed gently beneath tight skin.

"Of course." A savage smile, one that broke the façade of the professional businessman he liked to portray. Deep down he was as fucked up as them.

Marshall sucked in another long drag. "I'll organise his transfer once he's healthy."

Hudson nodded, wiping the blood from his hands on to the dark fabric of his suit. "We've had some interesting people in here tonight. They were watching all the fighters a little too closely for my liking."

"There are whispers of the Pits re-opening," Kace said, his tone sharp enough to cut.

"It's a rumour, but it was only a matter of time," Hudson grunted.

Kace rolled his shoulders, releasing some of the tension. "You recognise them?" The Pits didn't recruit, they stole. There gave you no choice once you were forced on to the claret sands. It was kill or be killed.

"Nope, but it's easy enough to suspect which Lord they worked for if they were here for the Pits." Hudson narrowed his eyes on Marshall's cigarette. "Marsh, make a note anyone who associates with the Vipers is barred from entering the grounds. Even if they have a cute little snake tattoo on their arse, they don't get in. I don't want to risk any of my fighters."

Marshall nodded. "On it, Boss."

Kace let out a steady breath. "They're going to be a problem." The cage helped with his beast, and while he could find respite elsewhere he wouldn't have the same power he had at The Vault. He and Hudson had a deal, which gave Kace full control. Control that he needed. The Pits reopening risked that.

"It's still only a rumour, but if it is indeed the Pits then you're right." A chime beeped, and without another word Hudson headed back to his office, phone pressed to his ear. "What the fuck do you want?" he barked into the receiver, the door slamming shut behind him.

Marshall let out a low whistle. "Hud doesn't usually do the wet work, it must have been bad."

No, it was usually Marshall who carried out the punishments for Hudson. It had only been eight or so months since they had opened the place to the kids, and in that time Marsh had taken it on himself to be the judge, jury and executioner to anyone who caused them harm. Kace had craved the violence, but purposely kept himself separate. His brothers knew of his darker side, knew that he barely walked the edge of sanity. His continuous rage burned like fire in his veins, and he was sure that if he took it further it would finally push him over the edge into oblivion.

Kace clicked his knuckles. "Nobody messes with our kids."

CHAPTER 4

EVA

Eva barely controlled the cold terror that was like phantom fingers around her throat, pressing slowly until her lungs hardened to granite. Lucas sat beside her, his knee jumping nervously. He had grovelled and begged, only stopping when one of the men hit him with the butt of their gun.

She had never seen him nervous. Lucas always had an air of authority, and it was one of the things that had attracted her to him in the first place. She quickly learned that beneath the power that he wore like armour was a cruel man who enjoyed hurting those he deemed weaker than himself. She would never have called herself weak, despite being human, and yet she still fell beneath his fists.

She was thankful in that moment that both her parents were dead, because she couldn't have dealt with their utter disappointment that she hadn't seen Lucas for what he truly was.

A door clicked behind them, and it took everything in her not to turn. She faced the desk with a straight spine, her hands carefully clasped in her lap. Lucas rattled at the small noise, twisting in his chair fully.

"Dutc... Augustine." He swallowed, stuttering. "I'll... I'll get the money. I'll..."

"Oh, you'll get me that money," the man called Augustine interrupted. He stepped around Eva, taking the air along with him as he sat in the large leather chair that seemed to dominate the space. He had made them wait for over an hour, and then made them wait a little longer as he smirked behind the desk, fingers tapping along the wood.

"I see you expected Dutch, but I've taken a special interest in those that steal from me."

Lucas let out a strangled sound. "It must be a mistake, a stupid fucking mistake that..."

Augustine lifted his hand, and Lucas immediately shut up. He wore a black suit, the shirt beneath the same shade while a tattoo of a snake curled around his exposed throat, the head ending on his jaw. Humour danced in his deep brown eyes, and they brightened slightly when they settled on Eva.

She made no noise, but was unable to look away from the scrutiny behind his gaze. She had no idea who, or what he was, and yet he demanded everyone's full attention.

"Did you not think we wouldn't notice?" he asked, directing his question to Lucas.

Lucas stuttered, eyes widening. "I'll, I'll get you the money. One of my guys must have made a mistake or..."

"A mistake is dropping a bag," Augustine interrupted. "Or possibly miscounting. Fifty-grand worth of untracked notes is more than a fucking mistake." The man rested back in his chair, head tilted slightly as he finally returned his attention to Lucas. His brown hair was cut short, a shadow tight along his skull. "Your job was to run the money. A fucking monkey could do that."

"Augustine, please. I'll find out who fucked us over..."

Eva felt a prickle of sensation at the back of her neck,

and then a gun whipped Lucas across his face with an audible crack. His head barely moved, but a red welt appeared immediately, bright against his pale skin.

"Us?" Augustine said, his upper lip curled into a snarl. He reached down, slowly pulling out a large wooden stake, fisting it in his hand. "You lost *me* money, not us."

"Wait, wait, wait!" Lucas shouted, hands held out in surrender. "Take my girl as partial payment!"

Eva shot to her feet, fangs piercing into her lip, the pain a split-second before her own blood coated her tongue. The chair toppled behind her, and as she turned a heavy hand landed on her shoulder.

"Sit," Mr Sunglasses said into her ear. "Now."

Eva let out a hiss, the only noise she could make it seemed. What was she, a dog?

"No bitch is worth fifty-grand," Augustine sniggered. "Not even with lips made to suck a cock."

Horror froze Eva's limbs, her breathing fast enough to hyperventilate. Which for a vampire, was apparently the normal rhythm of a human.

"She's a Venus Darkling," Lucas added quickly. "Trust me, it's the reason I changed her. Even as a human her blood was higher tier, I knew she would have a Venus gift."

You motherfucker! Eva cursed inside her mind, her throat barely able to make a growl.

Augustine seemed to read her well enough, his chuckle ominous. "How old is she?"

Lucas visibly relaxed. "Just over two months."

"A fledgling?" Augustine said, brows shooting up his forehead. "When was she last fed?"

"Four weeks ago."

"That's some impressive control," he murmured, his fingers still playing on the sharp point of the stake. "Venus Darklings are rare, addictive if I remember correctly."

Lucas licked his lips. "She's magnificent, you need to taste. I starve her to keep her compliant, but even her venom is..." He struggled to find the right words. "Her venom is worth her bite."

"Floyd," Augustine nodded to Mr Sunglasses. "Taste her."

Wait, what?! Eva weakly fought her hold, the hand tightening for a brief second before her head was wrenched to the side, lips sealing over her skin. The pain of multiple teeth was sharp, and then she felt a strong suction that caused fire to burn through her veins. Tears marked their way down her cheeks, increasing with every painful pull of his mouth.

"Floyd, that's enough."

Eva tried to move, her arms heavy as she weakly shoved at the hold.

"Floyd!" Augustine barked, standing up. "Now!"

He released her with a reluctant growl, and she collapsed down into her chair. She watched Augustine smile through the hair that had fallen over her face, his lips twisted.

"I can clearly see you enjoyed her," Augustine snickered. "How did she taste?"

Eva followed Augustine's gaze, her veins freezing at the sight of the tent in the front of Floyd's jeans. Lust burned in his eyes when they met hers, despite the lack of emotion on his face, his sunglasses perched on the top of his head.

"Nothing like I've ever tasted before."

Eva reached up to the wound, feeling the ridges left by his teeth.

"A Venus fucking Darkling," Augustine said. "Lucas you've kept an interesting secret, it almost makes me want to forgive your blatant attempt of stealing."

"I wasn't..."

"Does she know what she is?" Augustine continued as if Lucas hadn't interrupted.

Eva lifted her middle finger, answering for herself.

Stop it you fucking idiot! she scolded herself. *You're making it worse!*

"It hurts to be starved, doesn't it?" he said directly to her. "You feel weak, and then you have this intense ache as your own body tries to digest itself. It's both painful and uncomfortable."

"She needed to be punished," Lucas explained. "She hasn't quite grasped that I made her, which makes me her master. She has to do what I say, it's the law."

Augustine nodded, and a forearm was pressed against her mouth. Her fangs struck, and before she could cause damage she moaned as blood poured, the pain in her throat decreasing with every swallow. The blood tasted of earth, timber and fur, Floyd rigid behind her, his warm body pressing closer.

Eva released her fangs, twisting in his grip with an added strength. "Get the fuck off me!" she snarled, her voice hoarse as she shoved him back. She was able to break his hold before she was forced over the desk, the edge pressed against her stomach and her arms pinned to her back.

"Such spirit in someone so small," Augustine said, reaching forward to brush the hair away from her face with the tip of the stake. "I'll take her."

The pressure released, only for her to be pulled back to her chair.

"I'm not some..." A slap across her cheek, hard enough her head snapped to the side.

Lucas shuffled forward, knee still jumping. "Only for the night. She's my fledgling."

Augustine raised his brow. "Is she legal?"

Lucas hesitated.

"Then she's not registered as yours. I will take her as a gift between us, but you still owe me the fifty."

"What?! That's bullshit!"

Augustine flexed his fingers. "I never planned to let you leave here alive, so go before I change my mind."

"Lucas?" she whispered, unable to believe she was actually begging him.

I must have been a terrible person in my previous life, because it's the only explanation to this shit show of my existence.

He looked towards her with eyes that had bled to black, his jaw set.

"What are you doing? Don't you dare go!"

Lucas was possessive, surely he wouldn't leave her?

He stood, and with one final baleful glare he moved towards the door, leaving her with two strangers while blood trickled down her skin.

KACE

Kace felt like a stalker. Even more so in the quietness of the early morning when everyone was fast asleep. The hallway was virtually black, the wall light so weak it barely kept the shadows at bay, and that included the ones that crept along Eva's door.

What the fuck was he doing?

He had no business being in the building now that Kyra had moved into the house with the Guardians, officially soulbound to his brother, Xander. He didn't like many people, but he liked Kyra. Although, she kept trying to save him. He wasn't sure what she was saving him from exactly, it wasn't like he could get rid of his beast, their souls cursed together. Not that he could truly blame his issues on his beast, no, he blamed his grandfather for that.

Fuck.

He definitely had no business standing outside the front door to Eva's, the woman a cyclone of sunshine and attitude. And yet he couldn't stop himself from rapping his knuckles against the door. He needed to... what? See her? Make sure she was okay? He barely knew the fucking woman. Just because he'd made her come on his tongue doesn't mean he had the right to knock on her door.

He lifted his fist again, knocking harder until the door rattled on its hinges.

The flat to his left cracked open, the neighbour wearing only boxer shorts storming into the hallway. "What the fuck, man? It's two in the morning!" he said before he skidded to a halt, blinking sleep from his eyes. "Shit, sorry man. I don't want any trouble."

Kace turned, using the limited light to his advantage. "The girl who lives here," he said, gesturing to the door. "Have you seen her?"

"Not in months, I overheard the landlord complaining about no rent or something."

Shit. "Thanks," he said, dismissing the man who couldn't get his door shut and locked fast enough. Alone in the hallway once more he faced Eva's, shoulders tight with frustration.

She hadn't been seen in months.

His heavy boot hit the wood, the door swinging open with little effort. The noise echoed down the hallway, but he doubted anyone would investigate after the neighbour's confrontation. Stepping inside, he knocked the door closed behind him, the lock shattered into pieces. An automatic light flickered to life in the corner, illuminating the small open plan living room with attached kitchen.

Kace stilled, his beast scratching at his insides as he took in the overturned sofa and blood splattered across the carpet. Rot and dust were a prominent stench, stronger in the kitchen where the microwave door was partially open, flies buzzing inside.

Rage burned through him, the need to destroy something strengthening as he spotted a photograph on the wall, one with a much younger looking Eva and what looked to be her parents. She wore a pink ballerinas outfit complete with tutu, her slippers hung loosely around her neck.

Her bedroom seemed undisturbed, the bed neatly made and clothes filling the inbuilt wardrobe. Jewellery sat openly on the windowsill, expensive pieces beside even more photographs. Some were of Eva and Kyra laughing at the camera, while others were more of her parents. The only photo not framed was one solely of Eva, her head thrown back, eyes closed as she danced. The camera captured her elegant movement, the delicate curve of her arched spine and the way she pointed her toes in explicit detail. Golden brown hair framed her face, her pink lips curved in a quiet, private smile.

It was intimate, and Kace couldn't stop himself from tucking the photograph into the back of his jeans like some deranged stalker.

Where the fuck is she? The thought snarled through his mind, and he wasn't sure whether it was his own or that of his beast, the bastard usually communicating through various growls and roars unless inciting violence.

Chest heavy he turned back to the living room, a set of keys glinting in the corner on a side table. He grabbed them, but before he could leave he hesitated.

What the fuck was he doing?

Eva wasn't his problem.

"For fuck's sake," he muttered, pulling the frames from the walls before moving back to the bedroom. Inside the wardrobe he found a bag, shoving every photograph and piece of jewellery he could find. He didn't bother with clothes, or shoes or anything else that wasn't sentimental and could be easily replaced. Hitching the bag onto his shoulder he closed the front door as much as it would allow before heading to the neighbour's. His knock boomed, and it didn't take long before the door opened a sliver, light leaking into the hall.

"Who manages the building?" Kace asked, ignoring the man's slight gasp when he noticed the flecks of blood that patterned across his face, or the bruise blossoming beneath his left eye. Croc Face hadn't hit that hard, but he didn't really care what he looked like, not when every mark would be gone before midday. "Answer the question."

"The landlord," the man said with a squeak. "He deals with everything. He doesn't live here, though."

Kace concentrated on breathing, mouth open as anger curled his fists, the keys cutting into skin. He reached into his pocket, pulling out the cash he had earned at The Vault. "This is rent to cover flat fifty-two. Make sure it's given to the landlord tomorrow." His voice came out harsh, his beast creating a deep rumble.

The man tensed as if he was about to slam the door, and a pressure settled in Kace's chest, a storm that needed to be released. The security chain snapped when he pressed forward, the man stumbling back.

"Shit, okay!" The man held his hands up. "I'll give it to him in the morning, I promise."

Kace carefully handed the money over, his other hand snapping out to grip the man's wrist before he could pull

40

back. "Anything happens to her place, or anything inside I will hold you personally accountable. Understood?"

The man paled, but nodded as Kace released him. He said nothing as he turned back to the hall, heading towards the stairs as the door slammed behind him. The air was cool when he stepped outside, the usual sounds of the city carried by the bitter wind.

Eva's car was parked around the side of the building, the white BMW covered in various notes asking it to be moved. The scrawls started out polite, the lettering getting more and more aggressive as additional notes were added over time. Scrunching them up in his fist he unlocked the driver's side door, reaching down to pull the seat to its furthest position back, barely allowing himself to squeeze inside and put the bag onto the passenger seat.

The glove compartment was empty other than a few protein bars and a log book, the inside musty and damp. Unsure what the fuck he was doing he placed the key into the ignition, and when nothing happened he cursed.

Kace let out a steady, controlled breath, his beast riding him hard. If he didn't calm down he would need a physical distraction, again.

Fuck this shit.

Grabbing his phone he dialled Sythe, his brother answering on the second ring.

"You know it's almost three am, right?" Sythe muttered. "Where are you? And don't tell me you're out getting laid, because we both know the only thing you date is your hand."

"I need you to come help me jump start a car outside Kyra's old building," Kace replied with a growl.

A pregnant pause. "I have so many questions, but first, what the fuck, K?"

Kace clenched his fists, savouring the pain as his nails

dug in. "Don't ask, just get over here before..." He caught himself, the vulnerability only heightening his lack of control. "Are you coming?"

There was no hesitation from his brother. "Be there in twenty."

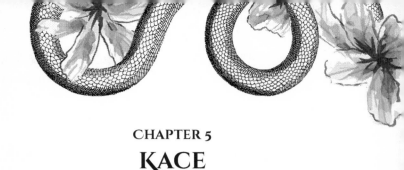

CHAPTER 5
KACE

Sythe let out a low whistle as Kace parked Eva's car in the underground garage, hiding it at the back. "Do you know what this is?" he asked, essentially salivating as he brushed his fingers down the side.

Kace glared at his brother over the roof. "A car."

"It's a classic BMW E30," Sythe muttered, shaking his head. "Late eighties. You want to tell me why I helped you steal this beauty?"

"No."

"Cool, great chat. See if I'll help you steal shit next time you call me at three in the fucking morning." Sythe pushed at the strands of his dark hair, warm caramel eyes narrowed. "K, talk to me," he said, voice softening.

Kace dropped his gaze, knowing his beast was teasing at his irises. He needed to calm down, to hit something before he showed how close to the edge he was. What the fuck was happening? He hadn't been this bad in a while, especially not after spending the last few hours in the cage.

"You know we're here right," Sythe continued. "If you need it."

A knot formed in the pit of his stomach. "I know." He

had no choice but to be okay, otherwise he may as well admit defeat and succumb to the fucking curse. One-hundred years to find someone to soulbind with, or be dragged down into The Nether, the secure prison commonly referred to as Hell. All to become a personal guard dog to the same prick who bound them with the beasts in the first place.

The Guardians were all cursed in their early teens, which meant they had roughly eighty-five years left. Not like he believed he would make it that long, no, he knew there was only one option and that was six-feet under. He just hoped that there would be some sort of reprieve to the constant anger in death, but knowing his luck there wouldn't be.

He had accepted he could never give himself fully to another being, to allow himself to be vulnerable enough that he could ever bind another soul to his. So death was the only option, because no fucking way would he accept an eternity as the beast.

"I'm fine," he replied, hoping his voice didn't strain.

Sythe frowned, but didn't acknowledge the lie as Kace moved further into the basement, hand raised in a goodbye. He had his own room upstairs in the main house, but he preferred the peace and quiet surrounded by the cold concrete. He had the space to lose control without risking the others, especially now there were two females living there who weren't as resilient to the damage he could do when in a rage.

He hadn't blacked out in well over a year, but it was still a constant anxiety. Putting distance between himself and everyone else helped.

The place he had claimed as his own was situated in the corner of the basement just below the garage. It consisted of a pallet of blankets and a mattress, nothing more, nothing less. It was stark compared to the opulent bedroom several floors above, with its large bed, soft rugs and a sparkling bathroom. It was large enough, a room just off his workshop with plenty of space around the mattress. It was clean, which was more than he had growing up.

Kace paused at the door, glaring at the soft pillow that had been placed neatly on the sheets and the vase of flowers perched on a new side table, one that matched the dresser. Valerian, chamomile, yarrow and lavender; flowers and scents specifically designed to calm your mind. He wouldn't have known what the flowers were three months ago even if someone had placed a gun to his head, but Kyra was an encyclopaedia of everything floral and green.

It also meant she had been there, in his space despite warning Xee to keep his mate away. Kyra had saved his life, and for that he was in her debt. But that didn't mean he wanted to be best friends, or for her to tidy up his shit including the homemade explosives he liked to tinker with. Luckily his desk was undisturbed, his drawings exactly where he left them. Amongst the designs of exploding crystals were his other sketches, and they were something he never wanted another soul to see. Images of his nightmares, memories that he tried to suppress through drawings. He would fill a sketchbook of the horrors he suffered, and then burn the book and start again.

Kace stripped out of his clothes, the cool concrete numbing against his bare feet. Something fluttered to the ground, and it took a second for him to realise what it was. He stared at the photograph, his thumb rubbing over the image of Eva dancing. The fire in his chest expanded, anger burning hotter as it seared deep into his gut.

He wasn't sure why he had taken it, or why he placed it carefully beside the vase and flowers.

Not wanting to overthink he turned towards the wet

room at the other side of the floor, stepping beneath the freezing cold spray of the shower. It did nothing to lessen the flames.

Placing his palms flat on the tiles, he leaned his weight against his arms as his head hung low. The water cascaded over his body, a torture in itself as he breathed in long, drawn out inhales and exhales.

Fuck.

Scrubbing a hand down his face he washed himself in quick, precise movements until the water at his feet ran clear. He didn't bother with the towel, the air turning the water droplets to ice as he moved back towards his room.

He couldn't sleep, not when the beast was riding him so hard. Instead, he grabbed some leathers and a weapon he kept in the corner and pulled them on with a quick tug. He wasn't on rotation, but hunting seemed like a genius idea right when he craved violence. He could deal with little sleep, his body used to the insomnia that had haunted him for as long as he could remember.

The house was quiet when he stepped out of the lift on the upper level, dark as he made his way to the garage exit. He didn't want to be seen, didn't want to show the control he had worked so hard on was fracturing at an alarming rate.

"How did I know you were going to sneak out," a voice grunted from the darkness. An orange light illuminated Xander's face, the glow lasting a second before smoke billowed out from his nose.

"Speak of the devil," Kace growled, "what the fuck are you doing out here, Xee?"

"Not the devil," Xander said, ignoring the question. "He's in his place sulking because he lost at poker, again."

Lucifer wasn't the devil, not when they knew exactly who had inspired those myths. While the human mythologies depicted various editions of the male who controlled Hell, Hadriel was a fallen angel who powered The Nether. Which, to be fair wasn't that much different according to Lucy, who had once been trapped down below.

Souls weren't taken there to be punished in death, no it was a realm created to hold the cruellest magic bearers, and once was the home to all Daemons and Shadow-Veyn. Now they had escaped and were causing fucking havoc up on Earth Side, and that was why he was headed back into the city centre with a blade in hand.

"I asked you to keep Kyra away," Kace said, glancing at the rising sun in the distance.

"You've met my mate, right?" Another drag of his cigarette. "You'll learn that women don't listen to fucking anyone."

"I can't have her there, just in case. You know it's a risk."

Xander stubbed out his cigarette before crossing his arms. "You won't hurt her, you're better."

Kace's laugh was hollow, forced. He wanted to agree, but Xander wasn't the one who had woken from a red rage covered in blood with no memory of what had happened. His beast rarely shared the information, which meant it had been bad.

"Your control has improved," Xander continued. "You've been working with Jax and..."

"Just, keep her away, at least from down there." Kace clenched his fist, shoulders tight with frustration. It was a place he needed to be alone, to feel like he wasn't a threat. "I've got to go, I need to..."

Fuck, where was his motorbike?

Xander stepped into his path. "Jax said you saw Eva, why didn't you come straight to me?"

"Jax has a big fucking mouth."

"This isn't a joke. Kyra hasn't been able to contact her in months, she's worried."

"How is that my problem?" Kace snapped.

Xander pinned him with a hostile glare. "Stop being such a fucking prick for one minute."

"Can't, it's a personality trait."

"What did you see?" Xander asked with a growl, his usual patience nowhere to be seen. "How did she look?"

"I'm not even sure I saw her, and if I had solid information I would have shared it." Kace calmed his pulse. "You're clearly not that concerned for Eva if she's been missing for months, and you haven't fucking found her."

"I'm not just going to just break into her flat and force her to see Kyra. She's been messaging, so clearly she isn't missing, just being distant."

"You sound like terrible friends."

Xander's eyes narrowed. "Fuck you, K. You're sneaking out almost every night, should we be concerned?"

Kace straightened his spine.

What the fuck was this? An intervention?

"You want to just come out and say exactly whatever you're thinking?"

Xander cursed under his breath, his anger dissipating. "You know that wasn't what I meant and you know it. You're nothing like your grandfather."

Kace barely controlled his flinch. His grandfather was the man who had raised him from birth, and then became a Daemon before selling him to the fighting Pits at age six. "I didn't realise I had to ask permission to go for late night walks."

Xander snarled before his gaze flickered to something over his shoulder. Kace fought the urge to look, even though if it was a spook, he wouldn't be able to see it anyway. He wouldn't be surprised if he was haunted by the hundreds he had killed, murdered.

"You think I want to ascend? Live up to the family name?" Kace grinned, the smile on the edge of feral. "I'm sure that's what everyone is waiting for, right?"

Xander shook his head, his expression desolate, which made everything fucking worse. "You're your own worst enemy, K."

The beast pressed against his insides, his skin tightening. He didn't bother Xander with an answer as he headed into the privacy of the surrounding grove, needing to be alone before he split at the seams.

CHAPTER 6
EVA

Eva stared at her hands, the skin almost entirely healed despite the tattoos being only hours old. She had been pinned to a table, forced to accept the twin vipers that coiled around each wrist like manacles, the snakes' tongues reaching towards her middle fingers. Within the scales were patterns, but she had no idea what they meant, if anything.

She was human, she had never studied the curves and lines of symbols and spells.

She *was* a human, but not anymore.

Eva flexed her hands, watching the scales of the vipers ripple along her skin.

They had branded her.

Fucking branded!

She had never hated anyone in her life, but right then she hated Lucas. Hated the fact he had taken away her life, taken away her choices.

The security's gaze burned across her exposed skin, the short slip of a dress she had no choice but to wear barely reaching her mid-thigh.

Eva lifted her middle finger, not sure what she was

expecting when his upper lip twitched, but otherwise gave no reaction. He was built like a tank, thick arms exposed as he relaxed casually against the door, a very similar tattoo of a snake curled around his bicep.

She blew out a breath, uncomfortable sitting on the edge of the bed with a strange man staring at her. Her legs were bare, as were her feet as if taking away her shoes would stop her from running away. She had covered them with a soft green blanket, the fabric clearly expensive from the softness of the texture and the French brand on the label. She couldn't move around the bedroom without him moving a step behind, watching over her. What did he expect her to do? Jump out of the window?

Eva flicked her gaze to the large window framed in even more green. She had already looked, and despite it not actually opening more than an inch, they were at least thirty floors up. She doubted even now she was a vampire she could survive that fall.

The security chuckled, as if reading her thoughts.

Eva just repeated her hand gesture, the sound cutting off with a growl. She had tried to make conversation, and had learned quickly that it was futile. Not that she believed the meathead would offer her a riveting discussion, but she at least wanted to ask who decided to decorate the bedroom in various shades of green. No other colour, just green.

A safehouse. That was how Augustine had described it. Designed to be impenetrable against people entering, and exiting. So she had destroyed the bedroom. She had ripped the curtains from their poles, torn the sheets from the bed and pulled out every drawer and tossed the contents onto the floor. The wardrobe had received similar treatment, the clothes inside only marginally more diverse than the decor. Green or black, mostly with snake motifs. She couldn't say they weren't dedicated to the theme.

The security man before meathead had watched her silently as she had torn through everything she could touch. It was only when she had shattered the mirror, picking up one of the larger shards to use as a weapon did he intervene.

She was taken out of the room to be branded, and when she came back everything was in perfect order once more. Nothing out of place.

The security guard pressed a finger to his ear, a frown pinching his brows. "Your presence has been requested," he grunted at her a second later. "Now."

Eva considered ignoring him, the compulsion to fight his demand almost overwhelming. His smile was crooked, his fists seemed the size of her face when he approached.

"I'm coming," she snapped, draping the blanket around her shoulders as she stood.

His eyes narrowed, yanking the cover from her grasp with little effort before pushing her out the door.

What the hell was the point of vampire strength if I can't even hold a bloody blanket?

Eva hesitated as she stepped outside the bedroom, eyes scanning down the hallway to the mezzanine that looked at the floor below. She knew she was in an expensive apartment that spanned two floors, but she hadn't been allowed to explore. She spotted a familiar landmark through one of the windows, comforted by the fact she was still in London.

"Move it," the security grumbled, shoving her hard enough she stumbled. "Through there."

There was an open door at the end of the hall, and as soon as she stepped through, it slammed closed behind her. Augustine watched her from behind a desk, his posture relaxed as he stretched back in his seat, the top buttons of his shirt open. His eyes dipped to her breasts, and Eva stopped herself from brushing her hair forward to hide as she took the seat opposite, sitting tall.

"I want you to dance for me," he said, his face cold.

"Go fuck yourself." She froze as soon as the words left her tongue, waiting for the reprimand. *Shut up, Eva!*

Augustine's heavy brow lifted, but he said nothing as he leaned forward. The tension grew between them, panic fluttering in her stomach as she tried to swallow past her suddenly dry throat. They were alone in the room, unarmed from what she could see and yet she was more afraid of him than the meatheads with big fists and even bigger guns.

"You're a dancer, right?" he asked after a pause, his gaze hard as he started to undo the cuffs on his shirt. "So dance." He pulled up his sleeves, the hair on his arms dark as the silver cufflinks clinked on the desk.

She didn't think anything nice would come out, so she remained silent.

"You'll learn quickly to follow orders." Augustine smiled, and Eva ignored the shudder that rattled down her spine. "Tell me," he continued. "How much do you understand about your transformation?"

Nothing, she wanted to say, but as her voice was the last thing she seemed to control she kept quiet.

"If you do not reply when spoken to I will cut out your tongue, taking away the option," Augustine said as casual as discussing the weather. "Now, how much do you understand about being a vampire?"

"That I'm dead." Her voice came out a croak. "I no longer have a soul."

"Who says you even had a soul to begin with?" Augustine's laugh was menacing. "You're not dead, just a different Breed. Although, many Vamps enjoy playing on the stereotype. Think of yourself as a human with a couple of upgrades. The only consequence is you have to consume blood to keep those upgrades, otherwise your body metabolises itself which is unpleasant, as you already know."

Eva crossed her arms, holding herself together. "What do you want from me?"

"A brave question," Augustine said with a chuckle. "The amazing thing about vampires is that they can take a great deal of damage, and after a little blood and time they will look as beautiful as the day they were turned. It makes them great toys." His appraisal was slow across her face, even slower down the slope of her throat before moving lower. "There are many ways in which I like to break my toys."

An angry tear burned out of the corner of her eye. "That didn't answer my question."

"Didn't it?" Augustine tilted his head, an animalistic gesture before he unfolded to his full height. "Your blood is an addictive aphrodisiac, so strong it will make most men and women do whatever you ask. It's a rare gift indeed."

"How does that work?"

He moved around the desk, stopping at the edge as she froze in her chair. "A random mutation known as Darkling. No one truly understands what happens to human cells when they're attacked with what we call the vampira virus. The majority of humans die, and those that don't become like us. An even smaller percentage find themselves with an added ability, usually related to their masters. Some may gain the ability to shadow walk, some may be able to produce an aphrodisiac in their venom, and others may even be able to hypnotise the weak of mind. I've even known some of our kind to regrow limbs."

"Hypnotise?" she repeated, remembering the rumours as a child. "I thought that was a myth."

Augustine opened his lips, his twin fangs descending. "All myths have a grain of truth. You'll find many people unwilling to look into your eyes just in case. It's something taught to many law enforcement regardless of how rare the ability is."

He reached forward, and faster than she could react he had gripped both her wrists.

"Strength is relative to when you were a human," he said, his thumb brushing the scales on her arms as she fought to be free. "You've doubled your strength, your muscles stronger and harder because of the added protein in your new diet, but you still won't be as strong as me. Pathetic, really."

"Let me go!" Eva hissed. Up close she could see Augustine's skin, noticing every bump and scar that marked his face. Vampires were supposed to be beautiful, their skin perfect. Yet Augustine's imperfections were noticeable, at least up close.

His fingers dug into her arm, the bone beneath groaning. "All my people are branded with a viper, it shows the others who you belong to."

"I belong to no one!" She jerked free, almost toppling her chair back as he laughed. Eva scrambled to her feet, putting distance between them as she pressed herself along the back wall. "And I definitely don't belong to you."

"You keep telling yourself that. When you died, you were reborn as someone else. As a fledgling you belong to your master until you are deemed strong enough to be your own master. Lucas transformed you without going through the system, which makes you unregistered. As per vampire laws I can claim you as my own, which does, in fact, make you mine."

Augustine took a dramatic step forward, his head cocked to the side.

"Mine to punish."

He stepped closer, his breath mingling with hers.

"Mine to fuck."

Eva hit out, her knuckles hitting Augustine's nose with a satisfying crunch in exactly the same way her father taught her back in school. Her own fangs descended at the first scent of copper, her throat burning and stomach tightening as she fought the need to lick the blood that settled on her fist.

She hadn't heard the door beside her open, or even notice when someone grabbed her in a bruising grip, a cool metal settling against her temple. All she cared about was the blood that coated Augustine's front, her pulse a rhythmic beat inside her skull that overwhelmed everything else.

A weight knocked into the back of her knees, forcing her to the floor.

"Ah, now that's where you're supposed to be," Augustine said with little emotion, his brown eyes darkening as he carefully reset his nose with a gut-wrenching crack. He had stopped bleeding almost immediately after her knuckles had connected, but there was enough blood down his front that Eva's fangs throbbed.

She moaned when he leaned forward to rub his blood on her lips, the sound strangled as soon as she realised the noise was coming from her.

"You're so very young, and yet surprisingly stubborn," Augustine growled, his fingers moving to grip her chin, angling her head. "You're going to be fun to break."

Eva trembled, unable to look away as his pupils swallowed the brown of his irises.

"Now, you will call me Master." Augustine's grip tightened, his smile cruel before his fangs struck the side of her throat.

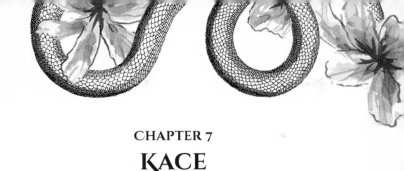

CHAPTER 7

KACE

Kace tracked the trail of blood to the edge of The Bricks, the area notoriously rough compared to the adjacent boroughs. "You guys sense anything?"

Blood on the pavement wasn't exactly uncommon, nor were the shattered hypodermic needles that glittered just beneath the wheel of a smashed up car. Back when Kace was a kid The Bricks was just a single housing estate, but the area had increased along with the mounting mob activity. Drugs were openly dealt in the streets, the area a playground for the city's gangs.

Titus pulled at his shoulder length, supposed-to-be blonde hair, his voice quiet compared to his appearance. "I don't feel anything." He chewed on his bottom lip, twirling the silver ring that pierced through the centre. It matched the one in his left nostril.

"Me neither," Jax said as he came up behind them, the harsh streetlights highlighting his scar. "But something isn't right."

A gust of wind carried a sharp cry, and they all turned towards the noise as one. Despite the late evening, the sound mingled with other shouts and calls. A mother called out for her children to return, while someone else screeched as a thug took off with a watch, hood concealing his face.

No one would stop for a cry, not when it was an everyday occurrence amongst the cacophony of hollers and sirens.

Kace was on edge when they moved forward, ignoring the hostile glares from the locals. There was no greenery, just broken concrete, brick and glass as the buildings became more derelict the further you stepped. It seemed that neither The Council nor the human equivalent cared about The Bricks. It was where Kace was born, where his parents grew up before they abandoned him to his paternal grandfather. All he knew about the people that created him was that he wasn't planned or wanted. His mother had been a teenager who dropped out of school, and his dead-beat father had been a dealer. He had no interest in finding them after all these years, not caring whether they were still alive or dead.

Titus silently dodged the stone that some kid threw from a higher window. It skittered across the road, landing beside a bus stop, the surrounding frame shattered and covered in graffiti. Hexes were drawn in charcoal and chalk along the pavements, dangerous incantations if accidently triggered. While humans accounted for over half the overall population, Breed seemed to accumulate in cities, with London being one of the more popular places to settle in the northern hemisphere.

Titus tugged at his hair once more, some of the strands escaping from his messy bun. "Don't ask," he growled when he noticed both Kace and Jax staring.

"What did you do to Axel?" Kace asked, unable to stop the smirk curving his upper lip. Titus and Axel were cousins, and while they were brought up together, they constantly argued which resulted in childish pranks, including Titus's impressive pink hair.

"Suits you," Jax added with a straight face.

"Fuck off," Titus replied, presenting his middle finger. "I look like candy floss."

Kace couldn't disagree, the pink both bright and somehow soft at the same time. It only highlighted Titus's sharp cheekbones and delicately upturned eyes that he sometimes emphasised with smudged eyeliner.

"Didn't you glue his favourite boots to the floor?" Jax continued, undeterred by Titus's irritation.

"The ceiling," Titus said with a sudden grin. "Took him hours to find them."

Kace chuckled. "You're lucky he hasn't messed with your piercings." He was the only guardian who wore body jewellery, the others not understanding when they all healed at an accelerated rate, their bodies rejecting the metal.

"What can he possibly do? They're hard enough to keep in when my body regularly rejects them, not to mention the amount I've lost when I've shifted. Besides, I doubt he would want to mess with my *other* piercing."

"We don't need to hear about your co..." Kace began before something rippled across his chi, but it was gone in an instant. "Shit."

Jax and Titus had both frozen at the same instant, their irises teasing silver. Kace couldn't sense any Shadow-Veyn, yet his beast was prominent, searching as his awareness stretched.

"Seems the report was legit," Jax said a few seconds later. "I'm guessing everyone felt that?"

"I swiped the pathology reports straight from the data-base," Titus said. "Of course it was legit." Titus had hacked into the official reports of the Metropolitan Police Department. There had been three deaths in The Bricks over the last month, and each one was described as an 'unexplained gruesome homicide.' The notes suspected a shifter attack due to the nature of the deceased, but they had no evidence to back up the comment other than a few claw and teeth marks.

Shadow-Veyn were known to feast on flesh, predatorial animals with only the most basic instincts. Veyn generally kept themselves invisible to the majority of the public, coming out from their glamour to feed. The only warning you had before they struck were their shadows, which was where they received their name.

The glyphs the Guardians had tattooed helped them see Shadow-Veyn despite their glamour, giving them the advantage. Druids in general wore glyphs in their skin to help balance their arcane, the designs a specialised syphon to concentrate the magic without ripping the caster apart. However, the Guardians took the markings to the extreme, their bodies more powerful, designed to withstand more.

Without another word they all headed behind the residential area, the roads narrowing and splitting into tight alleys. Many of the businesses were already closed, the metal shutters locked tight to protect from theft, or some even abandoned outright. A heavy beat vibrated beneath his boots, a club he guessed from the multi-coloured lights that brightened one of the darkened passageways.

Kace whipped his head to the side, his instincts pushing him down one of the many alleys that formed an interconnected maze behind the tall buildings. He pulled on the strength of his beast, reactions sharpening.

"For fuck's sake," Jax cursed as he skidded to a halt, lip lifted in a disgusted snarl. "We got to call in the cleaners."

Kace barely gave the half-eaten corpse his attention. Tension thrummed beneath his skin, the need to kill overpowering everything until it was an almost singular thought. Pulling out a perfectly balanced blade he began to spin and catch, the movement practised and precise as he fought past the haze to finally drop his gaze to the floor.

The body had been torn almost in half, the person's chest split from his left shoulder to his right hip, his organs eaten. His arm was missing, as was part of his foot.

From the flowers that sprung from some of the droplets a few feet away he guessed they were Fae. Strong blooded Fae folk did weird things when they died, and this one was apparently becoming the earth. The blood was fresh, the scent thick amongst the large overflowing skip bins and pile of vomit only a short distance away. Silver cannisters glinted on the pavement, over a dozen all marked with a black 'X.'

Titus gestured to the red flashing light high on the wall, the camera pointed directly at the body. "Don't bother calling the twins," he grunted. "Someone is watching so it's likely already been reported." Just as he finished speaking the camera moved, seeming to zoom in on the knife Kace flipped.

None of them were worried about being caught on camera, even when they had over ten pieces of illegal weaponry between them. Titus would be able to wipe the recording and any evidence they were even there, his brother being a genius when it came to computers.

Jax reached up and snapped the camera clean off the wall, crushing it in his large palm. "Fucking..."

The blade left Kace's hand before the thought even processed, the silver soaring through the darkness to land directly in an eye. The Shadow-Veyn screeched, its trajectory altered as Titus rolled out of the way of a large claw, the nails long and serrated. The creature landed, shaking its head violently to dislodge the knife. The remaining eye rolled freely inside the too-large socket, the iris a bright red compared to the dark green that leaked from its wound.

"What the fuck is that?" Titus asked, but Kace had already pulled out three more knives, the blades soaring with a high-pitched whine. All three hit their targets, but they were nothing compared to the sheer size of the Shadow-Veyn. It stood well over a head above them all, its shoulders wide enough to brush both sides of the alley.

Jax unsheathed his sword, the metal gleaming beneath the streetlights. "Classification E."

"No shit," Titus said as he pulled out his gun. "I meant that's not a fucking hellhound!" Its body was similar to a hound, with a sleek canine form built from pure muscle. Its ears were short, spiked with a barb, while its powerful paws cracked the pavement.

The creature hissed, mouth opening to reveal two rows of razor-sharp teeth. Its face was flatter, more humanoid than the hounds with only a short snout. Bones were exposed beside jet black scales, the hole where its nose was supposed to be a hollow void.

Kace gripped his last knife, his beast pushing for them to shift into their stronger, larger form. He gritted his teeth, the creature turning its attention to him. It was getting easier to remain the man while letting his beast be forefront in his mind. He needed to find a happy medium, one where he wouldn't risk his sanity.

A tongue shot out, split like a snake's as it licked at the blade that stuck out of its shoulder, ignoring the one still in its eye. Dark vapours floated out from its nose, the smoke curling around to flow between each of the exposed ribs at its side, pale in contrast to its dark scales. Sharp bones pricked up like thorns along its spine. It was the main feature that classed it as a Classification E, as well as its sheer fucking size.

Kace felt his tattoos blaze, arcane burning at his finger-tips as voices drifted from behind, reminding him how close they were to innocents. A ball of arcane seared through the air, the concentrated magic hitting the creature dead in the face. The Shadow-Veyn roared, breath full of dead carrion, sewage and rot as the spinal bones flexed, clicking down its back. A split second of tension before it leapt forward, twisting at an impossible angle mid-air to catch itself against the brick wall. The Veyn flipped, landing further down the alley as it slinked away into the darkness.

'*Split and catch it at the other side,*' Jax snarled inside his mind, the mental connection spread to include Titus. '*Push it towards an opening.*'

Kace moved before Jax had even finished, his long legs eating the distance in a matter of seconds while Titus shot in another direction. He could feel the Veyn through the shadows, trying to conceal itself. Arcane continued to burn from his palms, the power sparking down his blade as he raced after it.

Tall buildings speared into the darkened sky, the brick walls closing in. The moon was obscured by clouds when he finally broke out into the open, the Veyn twisting to snarl in the centre square. He was thankful the area was empty, the curtains drawn on the majority of the windows that over-looked the area. It wouldn't matter if they were watched, his job was to destroy them regardless of an audience.

The existence of Shadow-Veyn wasn't a secret, not since one had destroyed tower bridge, the fight live streamed across the world. The Council had decided that if they didn't acknowledge it, it didn't happen which seemed to be pretty common response amongst governing bodies.

The footage had been quickly corrupted, but the city remembered, forums popping up with rumours and specu-lation. Before the Shadow-Veyn had broken out from The

Nether they had a sighting once a month, but since they were able to travel freely between the realms the activity had increased to weekly, along with possessions and general Daemonic fuckery that was the bane of their existence.

Titus appeared opposite, stepping out from beside a closed betting shop with his pistol held forward. Kace didn't need to turn to know Jax exited to his right, circling the Veyn on all sides. It was what they had trained to do, why they were forced to share their souls with individual beasts not too different from the fucking Shadow-Veyns they hunted.

Click. Click. Click.

Bones breaking echoed into the night, the Veyn's ribs opening up at the sides, exposing its vulnerable organs until the scales slithered across in a thin layer. The ribs continued to contort, lifting up in a dramatic curve as the dark vapour flowed between each bone. The vapour seemed to thicken until it coated the entirety of every rib, spreading like a fan until they almost resembled...

"What the fuck!"

A single shot rang out, the bullet hitting the Veyn directly in its newly formed wing. The vapour hadn't solidified, despite how it looked, the bullet soaring through and imbedding itself into the opposite wall.

"Oh shit."

The Veyn snarled, claws digging down as he pushed itself up from the pavement, wingspan continuing to stretch. A gust of wind, strong enough it knocked them all back as the Veyn began to lift off.

Jax erupted from his skin, his beast appearing in a burst of colour. Jax was one of the darker beasts, a blue-black with streaks of silver. His scar was prominent even in that form, the red mark slicing his eye to slightly distort the upper lip of his snout. His markings pulsed with white light, a perfect echo of the tattoos from the man repeated in coarse fur. Similar to the Shadow-Veyn he had prickles along his spine, long needles only slightly thicker than his fur.

Kace stilled, breathing through the urge to shift too. Saliva coated his tongue, the hunger for blood and death strengthening as he held on to the edge of the man by the skin of his teeth. It was a constant static buzz, the only reprieve when he gave in to his beast's bloodthirst.

Jax launched himself across the distance, his tail separating into several distinctive whips. They wrapped around the Veyn, pinning the wings to the ground as Titus and Kace launched their attack. They saw it a second too late, the Veyn's back leg dislocating to bend back at an impossible ankle, the paw knocking Titus back.

"Tee!?" Kace shouted, his knife struggling to slice through the scales as he dodged the other back leg. The blade became lodged in bone, but rather than fight for it he twisted out the way. He caught Titus as he fell to his knees, his chest torn to shreds.

"Fucking ow," Titus hissed through his teeth. "That's a new move." Green mucus oozed from the wounds, his body rejecting the Veyn's poison. It dropped down his front, eating away at the leather before it fell to the floor, hissing like acid at the contact. Whatever coated their claws wasn't as potent as their teeth, the damage already beginning to slow down.

Jax wrestled using his own claws and teeth, concentrating on severing the wings to keep it grounded. They couldn't follow it into the sky, and they definitely couldn't let it escape.

Their beasts were big, twice the size of shifter wolves with thick forearms and paws as powerful as lions. Yet the Veyn dwarfed Jax in size, the biggest they had ever fought.

Click. Click. Click.

The bones snapped back into its chest one by one, the vapour moving to sink in between each individual scale. Jax snapped with his jaws as he struggled to break through the scales that had somehow solidified into armour. The paleness of the ribs disappeared, as did the hollow void of its nose as scales and vapour moved to protect.

Clink.

The dagger Kace had thrown and stuck in the shoulder fell to the floor.

Clink. Clink.

Kace launched himself onto the Veyn's back, being careful of the thorns that protruded from the spine. He caught Jax's attention, the beast harder to communicate with.

'*Keep it steady,*' he shouted telepathically, hoping the beast wasn't beyond words. Kace pulled himself onto the shoulders, having to tighten his thighs either side as he was bucked hard. With no fur he had nothing to hold on with, so he reached down and wrapped his arms around the Veyn's throat, only just able to reach fully around the thick neck.

The Veyn flailed beneath him, pulling back from Jax as he swung his thick body from side to side. Jax tore forward, moving to attack its flank.

Don't shift. Don't shift. Don't shift, Kace chanted to himself, ignore the fur he felt just beneath the surface of his skin. His beast was more powerful, but he could easily become lost in the rage, unpredictable.

Kace tightened his hold around the Veyn's throat, holding it for a few seconds as the thorns lengthened, the pain short but sharp. He released his hold, pulling at one that had pierced through his thigh.

"Fuck!" It was stuck, but kept him steady as he reached around and hit the only blade left, careful not to get too close to its teeth. The knife sunk further into the eye socket, the pained scream of the Veyn reverberating in the open space. His second hit sunk the knife fully into its skull and the death was immediate, the Veyn sagging to the ground with Kace riding its back.

Jax was there a second later, his body slick with sweat as he used one of the discarded knives to slice at the thorn still piercing through Kace's muscle. He pulled it clean out of his leg with one tug, thankful it had missed his femoral artery. It wouldn't scar, his body made to repair methodically as if a machine.

When he was first forced through the ritual of his beast all the evidence of his childhood suffering had been erased, the scars he adorned gone as if he had imagined them. And even now it didn't matter how much damage he suffered to his body, he never marked. It always repaired perfectly, ready for him to try again.

The only exception was Jax, who received his scar after they had been cursed.

"You good?" His leg was steady when he stood, the wound already healing as he stepped back just as the creature began to break down, disintegrating as each piece was absorbed back into the earth.

"Have you seen anything like that?" Jax asked, his voice deeper with the beast despite now being the man. His eyes were mirrored, the same liquid silver that he felt was across his own irises.

"That bastard defied all logic," Titus muttered, still on his knees as he panted through the burn of his chest. "How could it fly?" His wounds were worse than they had initially realised, his blood coating the pavement.

"Since when does magic follow a rule?" Kace asked, rolling his shoulders until they clicked.

Jax crossed his arms, not bothering to cover his nakedness. "It looks like that Veyn was mutating."

Titus groaned as he shakily pulled himself to his feet. "That's all we..." Jax caught him as he collapsed.

"Kace, call for backup," Jax said casually as if Titus wasn't passed out in his arms. "I think I can see his lungs and don't want to move him."

"It's Axel tonight, right?" Kace pulled out his phone. "Hey," he said into the receiver. "We need a pickup..."

"Yeah, I don't think he's able to drive," came the tight response.

"Sam? Why do you have Axel's phone?" Kace asked, lowering his voice, already knowing the answer. "Fuck, how bad is he?"

"Just get here before he does something even fucking stupider," Sam growled down the line. *"And be fast."*

Kace swallowed his own irritation, quickly organising an alternative pickup before returning his phone to his pocket. "Riley and Xee are on their way."

Jax kept quiet, as was his usual response when he was angry. He would have heard the entire conversation.

Kace dragged a hand down his face. "Fuck."

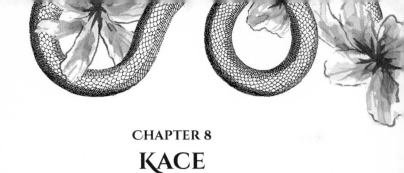

CHAPTER 8

KACE

I t was late, far too late for the bar to be so busy mid-
week, and especially considering it was closer to
morning than the night. The music beat loud enough
to drown out general conversation, the centre filled with
sweaty dancers while many of the tables were filled with
people drinking colourful cocktails in which the bar was
famous.

A few stares as Kace stepped inside, his body rigid as he
made his way through the crowd. People jostled him by
accident, immediately moving when they realised who he
was, and what he was wearing. He had kept the leathers,
Titus's blood now dried as it flaked off with every stride.
Kace breathed through his mouth, concentrating on a point
across the room rather than the bodies that casually pressed
against him.

A hand encircled his waist, a woman pressing herself
along his back before he could step away. Swallowing the
anger and panic he refused to acknowledge her, instead
gently removing her arm before stepping out into the open.
Anywhere else he would have reacted with violence,

making sure the woman and anyone else who thought he was approachable knew not to touch. Ever. Blood Bar was essentially a second home for the Guardians, their faces known enough amongst the regulars as brothers of the owner. He couldn't scare away customers with his hostility, not without pissing Riley off, not that his brother would be really angry if someone touched him without his permission. But it wouldn't exactly go in his favour if he started painting the place with entrails when he was supposed to be fully in control.

If he decided he wanted to take someone up on their offer he would take them out back, face them against the wall and fuck them until they were both spent. And then he would send them away, all with the least amount of touching. It was nothing more than a carnal need, a mutual exchange of rough pleasure with definitely no fucking feelings. He cared little for women, and he never fucked the same one twice. He couldn't risk being close to anyone for too long, just in case.

"You looking for who I think you're looking for?" Payne, the newest bartender said when he approached.

Kace nodded, conscious that there were ears listening.

Payne crossed her arms, her skin a rich ebony that complimented the gold she had painted around her biceps. The fabric of her t-shirt stretched across strong shoulders, the Blood Bar logo a bright red high on her chest. "Sam took him out back." Disappointment darkened the copper of her eyes.

"How bad?"

Payne visibly cringed, and that was answer enough. Lifting a hand in thanks he headed behind the bar to the emergency exit, the door already partially open as familiar voices drifted out.

"Here kitty, kitty," Axel chuckled. "You know you want to come play."

A hiss, followed by an audible smack. "Aye, if you carry on, I'll happily sharpen my claws on your bones."

A pause, Axel's voice deepening. "Is that a promise?"

Kace pushed open the door, the alley outside bathed in shadows. Glass glittered on the cobbled stones, the lights that usually illuminated the alley directly behind the bar recently smashed. Sam's long, pale blonde hair was unbound, the tie gripped in Axel's fist along with a few broken strands.

"What has he taken?" Kace asked when Axel tilted his head towards him, his pupils blown with a smile that stretched his entire face.

"Hey there K, you joining the party?"

Sam glowered, his irises the same amber that they always were, but Kace could tell it was his leopard that prowled behind them. "I don't know, I found him slumped in the fucking toilets." He dragged a hand through his hair, tugging it behind his ears.

Axel returned his attention to the leopard who had worked at the bar for over a year, his smile faltering.

"He's high as a fucking kite," Sam continued. "He won't tell me what he took, but I found a needle."

Kace opened a connection to Axel. '*What the fuck did you take?*'

Axel tilted his head, but he didn't reply. Not that it truly mattered, not when it was unlikely to kill him.

"Sam, can you give us a minute?"

Axel tensed, about to resist when Sam nodded, anger evident in the tension along his body. "I've never seen him like this."

Kace clenched his fist. "I'll deal with it." He waited

until they were alone before he let his frustration tone his voice. "What the fuck do you think you're doing?"

Axel's face twisted into a sneer, his arm coming up to knock Kace back. "You think you're any different from me?" he spat. "We're the fucking same, you and I. You just use your fists to numb yourself while I use something else, something a lot more fun." His words shot like bullets, his pupils covering the entirety of his irises.

"You don't deal with this shit alone, and especially not by getting high! If it's bad, you talk to us."

"Like how you talk about your need for violence?" Axel seemed to shake, a dangerous fury in the set of his jaw. His hair was usually kept military short, but it hadn't been cut recently, nor had his stubble. It should have made him look disorganised, but on Axel it looked fashionably dishevelled.

Kace ground his teeth, fists clenched tightly by his sides. "Don't talk about something you don't understand."

Axel threw his head back in a laugh.

"Does Titus know you're here putting fuck knows what into your body while he gets his lungs torn from his chest?"

Axel's head snapped back down, the glassiness to his eyes lessening.

"His blood sure looked pretty with his pink fucking hair."

Axel let out an unsteady breath, his voice strained. "Titus, he okay?"

"I don't know Axel, I had to leave him with Jax while I came to deal with your fucking arse." His beast was prominent, teeth bared inside his mind at the thought of any of his brothers vulnerable. "You were supposed to be our pick up, and look at you."

Axel shook, fists clenching.

"Now we're going to leave before I let Sam beat the shit

out of you." A pause, colour darkening Axel's expression. "Or is that what you want?"

His smile this time was feral. "Fuck you, brother," he snarled. "Don't think I haven't seen that picture of Eva in your room."

"Why the fuck were you in my room?"

"You're just as broken as me." Axel laughed, the sound void of any humour. "Probably more so." His eyes darted over Kace's shoulder.

"Red?"

Kace tensed at the name, realising he hadn't heard the kid sneak up on him. His beast growled, letting him know that he was aware, but didn't see Hunter as a priority right at that moment.

"Go wait in the car," he told his brother, not waiting for a reply before he turned. "You're a bit young to be hanging around a bar."

Hunter watched Axel warily, not taking his attention off him until he disappeared with an angry huff. "I wanted to speak to you alone."

"How did you know where I was?" He kept his personal life separate from the kids. He didn't want them to know what he was truly capable of. The shifter kids knew something was different, and not just because of his irises. Hunter had once asked him at the beginning what he was, not believing when he had explained he was a druid. He didn't give off Alpha energy like Riley did, but it was something that caught the attention of their animals.

"I followed you once." Hunter wrapped his arms around his chest, his hoodie barely thick enough from the cold. "I'm ready, you can let me fight."

"Yeah?"

Hunter's eyes brightened, his animal teasing his irises.

Kace had never seen Hunter shift, and that was a concern he shared with both Hudson and Marshall. The kid was strangling his animal, and that was dangerous for both himself and those around him. "I've been training really hard. I could fight, maybe earn some money and..."

"When was the last time you used?"

Hunter swallowed, straightening his spine. "Four months. I don't accept anything when I go visit mum."

Kace swallowed his growl. Hunter stayed with Hudson, but he still visited his mother at the drug den he once called home. Hunter wanted to save her, but sometimes people were beyond saving, especially when the woman had tried to use her own son as payment for drugs.

"Red," he said, puffing out his chest. "I'm ready."

There was no hesitation.

Kace grabbed him by the fabric of his hoodie, lifting him up as if he weighed nothing and hauled him far gentler than he should have against the wall. Hunter fought, his fist caught immediately in Kace's spare hand while his kicks barely landed.

"You really think so?" Kace pulled him closer until they were almost nose to nose. He didn't want to hurt him, just scare him enough to realise that if he went into a cage or a ring, he could be killed. *Would* be killed. "You're too impatient."

Hunter breathed heavily, his face red with irritation. He set him down, and when Hunter didn't step away Kace carefully placed his hand on his shoulder. Shifters were a tactile Breed, needing the physical connection to calm their animals. Kace was the opposite, but he couldn't stand there while Hunter was breaking.

"Don't do something stupid because you feel the need to prove yourself."

Hunter rolled his shoulder, dislodging Kace's hand.

"You're not ready. Not yet, but you will be."

Hunter stepped back, pulling his hood up to conceal his face. "Whatever." He disappeared in the same direction as Axel, and before Kace followed he smashed his fist into the brick.

CHAPTER 9
EVA

E va concentrated on the knife beside her plate, the sharp edges tempting beneath the flickering candlelight. It cast slight shadows, and Eva found herself wanting to reach forward as if she could hide in the little marks of darkness.

"Eat," Augustine demanded, watching her while he slowly savoured his breakfast. "We have a busy day." Cutlery scraped across expensive china. "While you may not require physical food to survive, you should appreciate life's pleasures. Now eat." His tone left no room for negotiation.

And still Eva ignored him, looking out the window with a pained hiss. She had been beaten to unconsciousness by Augustine's lackeys, the evidence marking her pale skin. The bruises weren't as dark as she expected they would if she were human, but the twin holes that remained from Augustine's strike were entirely unhealed, painful with every subtle movement.

Vampire healing, what a load of bullshit.

"It seems you haven't learnt your lesson the first time," he said, swirling the dark red liquid in his glass. "Did you want a repeat?"

Eva couldn't bring herself to eat the food, her stomach in knots and hungering for the blood that was only across the table, something that would have made her shudder only months before. "Why am I here?" she asked finally, her voice harsh with the tightness in her throat. This was the third time she had been forced to attend a meal she refused to eat, wearing a dress Augustine had chosen. It was black, skin-tight that barely reached her knees with a slight sweetheart neckline. It bared her arms, as did all of the clothes she had peeked in the wardrobe, showing off the tattoos that were a blatant reminder that she was property.

Augustine settled back in his chair, giving her a measured look. "You need to feed regularly, it's why you haven't healed," he said instead of answering, gesturing to her bite. "Although, I do enjoy seeing my mark on such a beautiful woman. Vampire blood isn't sufficient, we don't have the right enzymes which was why even when you were feeding from that man of yours, you were still weak."

Eva chewed on the inside of her cheek, gaze dropping back to the knife that was so close to her hand.

"Do it and you'll know more pain than you could ever imagine," he said calmly, bringing his blood back to his lips, his eyes flicking behind her.

Eva didn't have time to brace herself before an arm was held across her chest, a wrist pressed against her mouth. Her fangs punched down, ambrosia coating her tongue as she moaned, unable to stop the sound as she sucked on the flesh as if it were a lifeline.

"As you can see," Augustine began with an amused tone. "I control when you eat, and whether you heal."

Eva bit down harder, using the sharp pain as a distraction as she reached for the knife, the edge slicing the arm pressed against her chest before she was shoved forward, a solid weight pinning her against the table. The knife was pulled from her fingers as if she were a child, her movements tight as she tried to fight.

"Enough."

The pressure lasted for a second longer before she was released, the presence behind her stepping back. Slowly sitting up she met Augustine's eyes, proud that she didn't flinch at the unwavering attention. Flesh had ripped when the wrist had been torn away, and Eva spat it across the table. It almost made it the whole way, landing just past the condiments.

Augustine didn't drop the eye contact, a smile creeping along his face. "I wonder what would happen if I gave you to all my men at once? Let them train you until you're my pretty, submissive toy. Then maybe you'll be more agreeable."

Dread speared through Eva, the flash of warmth from the blood turning to ice.

"As if you would allow anyone else to touch something that's yours," a feminine voice chuckled from behind her, so high-pitched it must have been fake.

Eva straightened further, turning her head as the beautiful woman who had tattooed her arms appeared. She was tall and slim, with hair as black as the night. It was perfectly straight, and hit just shy of her lower back.

"Have you told Dutch of your new pet?" Her words were sharp despite the alluring smile that tipped her lips. "You know how jealous he can get."

Augustine's eyes darkened. "Go," he demanded of the security, the door clicking closed a second later. "Why are you here, Hana?" he asked, his question directed at the beautiful woman.

Hana's shoulders tightened, but her face was soft, almost suggestive as she pouted. "I was just curious about your new whore." She reached for Augustine's glass, her tongue a burst of pink as it licked across the rim.

"Careful," he warned, his hands flat on the table. "I don't care whether you're soulbound to my nephew or not."

Hana smirked. "Why did you make me mark her? Why is she so special?" She turned to face Eva, attention piercing from her violet eyes.

Eva tried to remain calm, needing to know the answer too. She found herself staring at Hana's throat, the pulse visible beneath tanned skin. She could even count the beats, her fangs throbbing in time with every thump. It beat faster than her own, her breathing too.

"You're not a vampire," Eva said before she could stop herself.

"Of course I'm not a vampire," Hana said with a flick of her hand, dismissing the comment in disgust. "Augustine, what were you thinking?"

"Since when do I need to explain myself to you?" Augustine snapped, his tone glacial. "She's my fledgling until I say otherwise."

Hana set the glass down hard enough it cracked. "Of course." Her smile was full of poison, aimed at Eva alone. "I guess I'll just watch you break her then." She swayed her hips as she walked towards him, her finger brushing down his arm. "Until you grow bored of her..."

Augustine stood, the table sliding from the force as he wrapped his hand in her long hair. Eva couldn't hear what he whispered in her ear, her body bent at a painful angle as her face flushed a startling red. Hana said nothing as he released, her hands smoothing down the front of her dress as she walked out, lips pressed into a thin line.

"Repeat your question."

Eva blinked, taking a second to realise Augustine had spoken to her.

"Ask me again, why are you here?" he shouted, loud enough it rattled the walls.

"Why am I here?" It came out a whisper.

"Because I take whatever I want." He reached for a remote controller, pointing it at a painting of a ship at sea to her right, the storm violent. The picture flickered, and then changed entirely. "And right now," he continued. "I want you."

Swallowing the nausea that threatened she realised it was CCTV footage. The building was caught at an angle, as if the camera had been placed on the opposite side on a higher floor. She could tell it was early, the familiar lights that usually flashed were off around the marquee designed to blend in with the other theatres. 'The Dollhouse' was written across it, although the camera only caught up to the second 'o.'

"That's a live recording," he commented, voice still threaded with anger as he watched her.

Eva could feel his attention, his eyes searing as they traced across her face. The Dollhouse exploded, the windows shattering as the sign crashed to the pavement below. She could hear the little pops, the screams and the crackles of the fire as it ate through the building as if an accelerant had been used. Minutes passed as the flames danced, brightening up the street as small figures moved out of the way. Only when sirens came did she finally turn away, tears burning down her cheeks.

"You are to be my pretty little bauble," Augustine said, his face void of everything but disdain, his attention still hyper focused. "And when I finally get bored, you will dance and feed my business partners when I tell you to. Your blood will do all the negotiations, and your little pussy is going to seal the deal. So I suggest you keep me amused long enough that I never grow tired."

His chair screeched against the hard flooring, his movements purposely slow as he made his way down the table.

"Every time you disobey me you will be punished," he whispered closer to her. His hand curving along her cheek down to cup her jaw. "At first I will take my disappointment out on you, and when that doesn't work or it gets repetitive, I'll take it out on someone else, just like your friends in The Dollhouse. Nod if you understand."

Liquid salt on her lips, but she nodded as much as his grip would allow.

"Good." His hand brushed lower onto her throat, his fingers touching the bite that had finally begun to heal. "I expect you to be the perfect trophy on my arm. Now go re-do your makeup, you've ruined it."

She jerked herself backwards, turning to the door as it opened.

"Oh and that was just a caution," he said to her back, "I evacuated the building five minutes before the charges were set. Next time there won't be a warning."

CHAPTER 10

KACE

"I have a gift for you," Eva, the beautiful brunette that seemed to hate him on sight said, her naturally thick lips curved into a suspiciously friendly smile. "Call it a truce."

Kace narrowed his eyes while his beast stilled inside his mind, content to just listen to her voice. Kyra's neighbour had ignored him for over a week, barely acknowledging his existence unless he purposely stepped in her way. He wasn't sure why he did it, normally not giving a shit. But he couldn't help himself, wanting to see her reaction when he 'accidently' brushed her arm when she passed him in the hall.

"Well," she prompted when he remained silent. "Do you want to know what it is?" She held something behind her back, and it didn't take a genius to figure out it was probably something baked, especially considering he could scent the chocolate. She had given cookies, cupcakes and other sweet goods to all the other Guardians who had stood guard. Everyone except him.

"No," he said, just to see if her face flushed the same gentle shade of pink she had the first time they had met only a week before. She had threatened to hit him with a frying pan,

82

and in retaliation he had crowded her against the wall, his growl low. He had wanted to intimidate her, to warn her away, but the colour had been soft against her cheeks, her lips opening on a surprised breath.

Eva's eyes darkened, which was not the reaction he had wanted. "I made this," she said, showing him the single cookie held between her finger and thumb. "You know, to help with your condition."

"What condition?" He fought the curiosity that spiked his tone.

"Moodyarseholeitus."

Kace controlled his face, keeping his lips carefully composed into their usual frown. Tension twisted between them, an almost physical abrasion along his skin. "You have an inflated sense of ego as a baker."

"You're insufferable," she said, nibbling the edge of the cookie. "It's a shame you weren't nicer, it really is delicious."

His beast punched through his mind, forcing a growl from deep within his chest. "What are you doing?"

Eva blinked her large eyes innocently. "I'm not doing anything?" Her pink tongue swiped her bottom lip, catching a crumb. "I just wanted us to be civil because I don't know how long you're going to be hanging around, but it seems you're still a moody arsehole."

A red mist descended across his vision, panic hitching his breath before he blinked and found himself across the short space, his hand wrapped around her throat as he pinned her against her own door. He savoured her sharp fear, needing it, the control something he craved.

The cookie dropped to the floor at her gasp, and for some reason he had taken it as an invitation. She was frozen beneath his touch for only the briefest of seconds, her lips tasting of chocolate and fucking heaven before she moaned against his tongue.

It made his cock twitch.

His cock never twitched. Not for anyone.

His hand moved up, sinking into her hair and tugging sharply, causing her to inhale before releasing a groan that he took as only encouragement. He angled her better for his next kiss, the connection bruising, raw as he wanted to punish her with little nips across those delicious lips.

Her hands stroked up his chest, and he expected a hard shove. He braced for it, deciding he wanted to push her a little more until her lips were swollen from his kiss as penance for her ridiculous teasing. What did she expect when she poked the big, bad, beast? Instead, she tugged at his t-shirt, pulling him closer with a moan. His cock jumped this time at the sound, straining against the seam of his jeans.

A purr inside his mind, the sound fucking alien as he lifted her higher, settling her heavier on the door as she instinctively wrapped those shapely legs around his waist. His hands spread across her thighs, on bare skin as the obscenely short skirt she wore hitched around her hips to reveal black lace that barely covered the place he craved to taste.

His fingers stroked closer to the fabric, teasing the edge to feel the damp heat already soaking through. He tore her underwear as if they were paper, her cry captured in his mouth when he speared through the molten folds of her pussy, his thumb circling her clit with just the right amount of pressure that drenched his hand.

When she made a sound between a whimper and a growl he inserted another finger, curling them forward as her internal muscles stretched at the invasion. Her body rocked on his hand as much as her position would allow, her head flung back as she cried, growing wetter until he couldn't take it anymore. Ignoring the sharp pain against his cock, so hard it was about to break in half he dropped to his knees, settling her down unsteadily on her feet before hooking one of her legs over his shoulder.

She screamed at the first stroke of his tongue, and he growled, repeating every lick as she wriggled against his face.

She tasted fucking delicious.

He had never gone down on a female, never caring about his partner enough to concentrate solely on their pleasure. His experience with sex wasn't a good one, a quick release and nothing more. But he now knew what he was missing all these years, how he could feel every ripple as his tongue explored her in both quick and slow strokes, learning from subtle twitches of her muscles and cries of pleasure what pressure she preferred.

Eva liked it harder, giving him little impatient moans when he gentled his caresses into languorous strokes. He found he preferred that too, unable to control himself as her breathing sped up into heavy pants. Her body tensed, and as he moved to suck the little bundle of nerves at the apex of her thighs she exploded, tightening around his fingers that touched deep.

She pushed at his shoulders, hands sweeping down to the front of his jeans as soon as she had the space. He knew he should stop her, especially when his beast was riding him so but he found himself wanting her touch, needing it as much as his next breath. So he didn't stop her when her small hand attempted to wrap around his aching length, thumb brushing across the pre-cum pooled at the head.

A metal squeak. Footsteps ascending.

Kace had removed her from his cock and stepped back to the other side of the hall before the door to the stairs flung open. He remained silent as Kyra walked past towards her flat, frowning at them both. If she noticed the wet sheen along his jaw, or the black lace on the floor she didn't comment.

Not that he cared, because there it was, the gentle shade of pink burning Eva's cheekbones.

Kace opened his eyes to stare at the scarred metal of the lockers, Eva's cries of release still echoing inside his head.

What the fuck was he doing? He was supposed to be preparing, concealing his beast behind a carefully composed mask. Yet, instead he was remembering the most erotic experience of his life, his beast pressing at the confines of his mind to hunt her down and make her finish what *she* had started.

Breathe. In. Two. Three. Out. Two. Three.

Rainbows. Waterfalls. Blood.

He needed to think of anything but Eva, because it did the opposite of keeping him calm. And he needed to be calm when he stepped into the next room, otherwise he wouldn't be able to stop his reaction when he set his eyes on the fresh bruises amongst the kids. Because there would be bruises, and probably even worse injuries that they tried to hide beneath baggy clothes. There always was. And then the rage would come, the endless fire in the centre of his chest that would consume him until he was nothing but an obsidian void capable of nothing but slaughter.

Kace dragged a hand down his face, letting out a grumble.

"You need another minute, Red?" Marshall asked, poking his head inside the room. He held a hoody in his hand, the garment new with the label still attached. It wasn't designer, or anything ostentatious that would likely be stolen. It was simply black, thick and warm.

"Marsh, do you still work at that dance place over on the West End?" The question came out without much thought, Eva still prominent on his mind.

"The Dollhouse?" Marshall responded with a frown. "Nah, left a while ago now to concentrate on here. Not that it's there anymore."

"What do you mean?"

"It went boom. Gas leak or something." Marshall gestured an explosion with his free hand. "Why? You thinking of a career change?"

"There was a performer there, Eva..." He didn't know her last name, and that realisation pissed him off. "Brunette, blue eyes and about five foot seven."

"Eva Morgan?"

Morgan, he repeated inside his head, committing her name to memory.

"Yeah I remember her, she could seriously dance." Marshall smiled before he frowned, striking Kace with a confused look. "It was a while ago, man. I think she went home one night and never returned. Her boyfriend came in a few weeks later and told everyone she had gotten another job and to not contact her."

Any tranquillity Kace had tried to hold was long gone. "And no one checked with her directly?"

"What was they supposed to do?" Marshall shrugged. "She's an adult."

Kace took a second to control his anger, ignoring his beast who clawed to be free. "I need you to track her down." *Before I do something I'll regret,* he mentally added.

Marshall tilted his head, lips pursed. After a moment of hesitation he nodded. "What details can you give me?"

It was exactly the reason he had asked Marshall for help. He didn't care why Kace had asked such a strange request about a woman he barely knew. Their relationship at The Vault was strictly professional, but after working with him for so long, Kace trusted him.

But honestly, what the fuck was wrong with him? Eva

was a woman he had met only a handful of times. A woman who tried her hardest to get under his skin, and had destroyed his control with barely a glance. A woman he had forced himself to stay away from, and in that time she had gone missing. Taken. Hurt.

His beast's growl vibrated inside his head, and at Marshall's sudden step back he realised it had come from deep within his own chest.

Fuck.

He knew he should just leave it with Titus and Xander, who were actively looking for her. But even with all their skills and technology they were struggling, as if she had disappeared without a trace.

Until five nights ago.

"I'll check the tapes of your fight and see if I can sort something," Marshall said after Kace explained everything he already knew. "Leave it with me."

Kace followed Marshall out into the main room, the kids busy amongst themselves. Some of the newer attendees ate from the selection of sandwiches and snacks they always provided, while the ones who had been coming for a while were chatting by the stacked benches. They never asked the newer kids to stop eating to prepare for training, not when they knew it could be the only time they had full stomachs.

If they wanted to just watch for a while, they could. They knew the deal when they joined, they were to be taught how to defend themselves, and how to deal with their own traumas. But if they needed a few weeks to adjust, then so be it.

Marshall handed the black hoody over to Bella, one of only two girls who had signed on. She was fifteen, the awkward age between a child and adult. Scars, both old and new covered her skin, her knuckles split and scabbed over. He never asked anyone their history, not wanting them to believe their past defined their future, but he couldn't help but drop his gaze to her tiny hands. There were scars there too.

Bella's face creased into a grin. "I did exactly what you taught me!" she said, showing Kace how to make a fist without breaking her thumb.

He nodded, unable to replicate her excitement when he felt like a block of cement had settled on his chest. He had taught her how to punch, and she had used it to defend herself. She shouldn't have had to defend herself. "I knew you could do it."

Bella blushed, dropping her gaze to the floor. "Thanks," she mumbled, all her confidence gone.

Fuck.

Kace kept his frustration to himself. Slowly, as not to startle her, he knelt down to her level. "You defended yourself amazingly Bella, you should be proud."

Her blush deepened, but a shadow of that smile returned as Marshall appeared beside them, a dramatic gasp bursting from his lips.

"Holy fuck, Bella. How bad does the other guy look?" He lifted his hand, and after Bella grimaced in the way teenagers sometimes did when something was uncool, she reached for the high-five. When she got close Marshall lifted his arm further, making her work for it with a giggle.

Kace was grateful that he had Marshall to help, his personality better suited to calm the kids compared to his own intensity. Hudson was only marginally better when he decided to join them, showing the kids defensive moves. But between them it seemed to work, the kids returning over and over.

"You done a check?" Kace asked Marshall who had returned a laughing Bella to the others, who were all ready and waiting for their lesson. Thirteen had turned up, but sometimes there was closer to twenty. No one was forced to be there, but if they signed up and didn't attend they liked to check in on them. Which meant once the session was over, Marsh would head to where some of the kids hung out, making sure they were okay.

And if they weren't okay... Well, Marshall got to work out his own frustrations.

Marshall's smile strained, but he nodded. "Hunter isn't here."

"What do you mean he isn't here?" Kace snapped, knowing Hunter always attended because he was one of the boys who stayed there. "Where the fuck is he?" Images of the large derelict house full of adults with needles sticking out their arms flashed through his mind. It was where they had found Hunter, beside his passed out mother.

It was Noemi who spoke up, her voice strong amongst the others. "I heard him say he went to fight." At twelve she was one of the youngest, but she always acted older despite her size. She tilted her chin up and met Kace's gaze, holding it even though he felt the tell-tale sign of his irises change. "He said he didn't want to be treated like a child anymore." Her bottom lip quivered.

Kace kept his voice soft. "It's okay, we won't be angry." Marshall shot him a frown, so he relaxed his face as much as he could. "Noemi, what did he say exactly?"

"He said you were bullshit, and that you didn't really care about us." Her eyes glistened, and she wrapped her thin arms around herself, as if she was about to break. "Why would he say such horrible things, Red?"

"Aw, you know what he's like Baby-cakes," Marshall said before Kace could reply. He stepped closer, always keeping a cushion of air between himself and the kids unless they invited the touch. It was always their choice. So when Noemi turned her body towards him he wrapped her in his arms, holding her as she began to cry.

Kace remained where he was, unable to offer comfort right when his beast was so present. Not that he permitted touch in general, but when he saw how some of the kids needed the connection he would force himself. It wasn't natural, unlike Marshall. No, he was brought up understanding touch and intimacy came with pain, so he tried to keep everyone at a distance. It was his brothers who understood it wasn't healthy, who had slowly worked with him to accept touch in the smallest amounts from those he trusted.

"Red, are you okay?"

It took a second to realise someone else had spoken, his body so tense it ached when he forced himself to relax. "Excuse me," he said, needing a moment to himself. "Everyone needs to start warming up, I'll be back in a second."

He didn't stay to check whether they had started their routine, knowing Marshall would supervise to make sure they wouldn't hurt themselves. His boots were silent as he stalked towards Hudson's office, not bothering to knock.

"When was the last time you saw Hunter?" he demanded as soon as he stepped inside.

Hudson raised a brow, looking up from the glow of his computer. "Hello to you too." The light dimmed, the monitor turning dark. "He's been gone a few days."

"And you didn't think to look for him?" Kace all but growled.

Hudson stood, hands planted on his desk. "Fuck off, you know I looked for him, but you know the rules. He doesn't have to stay, it was his choice. We can only give them what we can, they have to want to be here." His tone was harsh, but his eyes were tired.

Kace tried to swallow the lump in his throat. "Apparently he's gone to fight."

"I know," Hudson said with a nod. "I've called around and warned anyone who signs him on has *you* to deal with." His smile was hollow. "He hasn't been spotted at any of the other venues in the city, or surrounding areas. If he's fighting, he isn't doing cages."

Kace breathed heavily through his mouth, his stomach twisting into knots.

"We don't know he's there," Hudson said, reading his expression.

"We don't know he's not." Kace no longer cared that his beast could be heard through the timbre of his voice. "I'll fix this. I'll bring him home."

"Red, wait!"

Kace ignored his friend, ignored the kids who turned towards him as he stormed through the room towards the door. The coolness of outside did nothing to calm his panic, nor the gentle rain as he pressed his fist against a brick wall. Bile burning his throat he turned and sat back on his heels, his head low between his knees. He breathed in shallow breaths, the nausea rising with every beat from his aching chest.

A shadow, Marshall hovering by his side but not touching. He didn't offer any words of comfort, because he knew too that once you became a fighter for the Pits, you didn't come out.

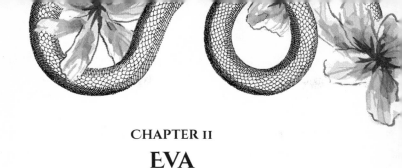

CHAPTER II

EVA

Augustine adjusted his cuffs, his black suit a stark contrast to the paleness of his skin. Not a surprise considering vampires slight sensitivity to sunlight. He had remained silent the whole drive, yet his eyes never left her once. His attention prickled across her face, lingering at her throat, moving down her arms before repeating over and over. It was only when the car slowed to a stop, and the privacy partition between the back and the driver opened that he even blinked, finally looking away.

It allowed her to swallow, to breathe a little easier even if it was for a few seconds.

The driver closed the partition immediately when Augustine nodded, and his attention returned to her. She couldn't stop her flinch when he finally spoke.

"Tell me, are you faster than a bullet?"

His eyes narrowed when she purposely took her time replying. "No."

"Good, then we're on the same wavelength." His smile was cruel as the door opened, Floyd his personal security waiting with his hand wrapped around a gun. Earth, timber and fur, that's what she remembered every time he was close, the taste on the back of her palette. The other meat-head, who she was never given the name of, had tasted of grass, citrus and what she assumed was parental disap-pointment.

Her scent had improved along with all her other senses, but not enough to gloat about. Being able to smell fish and salt despite not being able to see any body of water was more of an inconvenience than anything. They must be by the sea, or maybe further down The Thames, the seagulls above squawking high in the sky. It matched the time she counted on the drive, at least two hours out of the city.

Lifting her arm she studied her skin beneath the sun, frowning at how perfect it was. There were no spots or blemishes, nothing other than the small silver scar from when she was a child that was so faint compared to before that if you didn't know it was there you probably wouldn't see it. She didn't even burst into flames like the ridiculous rumours she had heard as a kid, despite it being common knowledge that vampires didn't, in fact, die at the sign of a little vitamin D. She grew up in a small town that had an even smaller Breed population, and out of three-hundred kids at her school only twenty hadn't been human. She had never met a vampire until she moved to London.

Glancing around Eva was faced with shipping contain-ers, the pinks, blues and greens rusty and stacked on top of one another between three to five high. They surrounded the large, derelict warehouse, blocking it mostly from view.

Five more metal containers were stacked in front on the left, hiding the smashed glass and graffiti that just peeked at the side. She squinted, her eyes more sensitive than she remembered. Three of the five were open, empty other than dust, grime and some thick ropes, the edges frayed.

"Are we ready?"

Floyd nodded, his irises brighter than they were, his

thick neck darkening as if fur pressed beneath his skin. "Dutch is inside making a mess," he said with a rumble.

"Dutch is supposed to be in a meeting, what do you mean he's making a mess?" Augustine frowned, storming through the heavy metal doors.

Inside was what she would expect from the outside, dilapidated and worn with a circular desk in the centre. Every window was covered, more containers blocking the sun, pressed as close as possible to the glass. It made the room dark enough Eva had to blink a few times for her sight to adjust. It took a second, but she realised she could clearly see the health and safety poster pinned on the opposite wall despite the lack of light.

Blood was a strong scent, the copper pleasant enough that her stomach tightened and her fangs descended a little.

It had only been a few hours since she had fed, and already she felt... better. Her senses heightened. Augustine had been right, when she ate from someone other than a vampire she noticed improvements. Even her throat had healed entirely, leaving only smooth skin.

Augustine's hand on her lower back, pushing her through a set of double doors. "What the fuck is this?" he growled at the half naked man in the centre.

A masculine voice chuckled in reply, loud enough it echoed around the room, open two stories with empty balconies overlooking scarred concrete. The windows had been blocked there too, making the room dark except for a few streams of sunlight caused by holes in the roof.

Dust glittered in the rays, and Eva couldn't seem to take her eyes off the particles, almost clear enough for her to count until the owner of the laugh stepped forward, acting as if it were his own personal spotlight.

"Hello there pretty lady. Have you come to watch the show?" Eva pulled her eyes from the surrounding dust to settle on him as he pressed a bloody palm across the large snake tattoo on his bare chest.

It took a second to realise what he had meant, her attention settling on the pool of blood by his feet. Eva blinked, watching it ripple before tracking the drops to where a man hung from a metal hook, impaled through the shoulder. He swung gently, eyes open and empty with his mouth taped shut. He made no noise, no groans or grumbles, nothing other than the delicate patter of his blood and the slight creak of the rope.

She shouldn't have been able to see how his hands were held at his chest, wrists attached together with metal manacles, not in the dark. Yet she could make out that the tips of his fingers were missing, every single one just a bloody stump. His feet were bare, only his big toes absent.

"First your mate, and now this," Augustine shot at the bare-chested man, who in return grinned. "What the fuck do you think you're doing, Dutch?"

"Just kill Hana, I'm bored of her anyway and I'll just find another bitch to fuck." Dutch shrugged before letting out a low whistle, eyes dipping to the brands on her arms. "She will do." Another laugh, the manic sound bouncing between the old rusty boats at the edge of the space.

"This one's *my* fledgling," Augustine said, anger curling his fingers.

"Oh really?" Dutch clicked his tongue, his hair the same dark shade as Augustine's, but longer, sweeping past his ears. "She must be something special then."

Augustine pursed his lips, gesturing to Floyd who positioned himself closer.

"Is there a reason you have a man hanging there? We're supposed to open in a week and you're out here torturing one of your toys. Where the fuck is Bishop?"

"Bishop couldn't make the meeting, which is fine

considering he's a *silent* partner. But he sent us this present." Dutch grinned, almost frantic in his expression. "I was going to put him with the others, but I just couldn't help myself."

"You wanted his investment and assured me he could be trusted."

"Patience, uncle. We have his money and we both know we don't need his opinion in the way we run things. It's perfect." He clapped, loud enough that Eva flinched.

Augustine cocked his head. "Why the man?"

"This is our gift from Bishop. He was caught stealing."

"Stealing?" Augustine turned to Eva, his eyes hard. "Isn't that what your boyfriend did?"

"Ex-boyfriend," Eva replied before snapping her mouth shut. Dutch watched her, his eyes black as he stroked his tongue down one fang. If Augustine made her feel uneasy, Dutch's attention felt like spiders crawling across her skin.

"At least now you will see exactly what will happen if you disappoint me."

Dutch clapped his hands together once again. "Well, how exciting. I'll make sure to be more creative for you, pretty lady." A wink before he reached for a lever, the man dropping until he barely hovered above the harsh concrete. The flesh in his shoulder squelched at the impact, the hook holding him steady. "Hello shit-bag, how's it hanging?" Dutch pulled the tape from his mouth.

The man spat, the blood congealed as it missed and landed by Dutch's feet.

"My uncle and I don't take too kindly to cunts who try and sell on our territory without permission. We take fifty per-cent of all profits, or we have a problem." Dutch's fist blurred, landing perfectly in the centre right thigh. Eva heard the snap, dropping her eyes to the floor when she saw the bone pierce through skin. "Which faction do you belong to?"

Hair pulled into a fist. "Watch." A demand as Augustine pressed himself closer, forcing her head up.

"You won't have the territory for long." The voice came out deeper than she expected. "*He* will take everything you own." His lips hadn't moved as he spoke, his blood-stained teeth clenched tightly.

Dutch clicked his tongue. "Oh yeah, we seem to have a ventriloquist."

Augustine tightened his grip in her hair, her scalp screaming. "He? Who the fuck is He?"

The man jerked his head to the side, the voice seemingly forced from his throat. "*He's* already here, watching, waiting for you to fall." His eyes brightened until they glowed as red as the blood that dripped.

Dutch let out a low whistle. "They're some pretty cool irises you have there, mate. If you're not careful, I may poke them out. Now, which faction do you belong to? Because surely you're not stupid enough to deal on our territory without the protection of a Lord?"

"This is a waste of time." Augustine paused, staring.

Dutch smiled, and then in one swift movement hit the left kneecap. It shattered, and yet the man barely flinched. "He hasn't given me anything interesting. Others cried when I cut their cock off, but this one has been a lot more fun to play with, even if he's worthless to us." Dutch swiped a finger through the blood, frowning as his tongue stuck out to lick. He spat a second later and hissed. "Tastes like shit too. I have no idea what the fuck he is, but he's not something I've seen before."

"What he is doesn't matter," Augustine said. "Human, shifter or fucking angel I don't care. We shouldn't be getting so many new dealers popping up on our territory."

"I've had one of those new angel people, and this ain't it," Dutch grunted. "It's like his blood has gone off."

The man twisted, the movement pulling at the wound in his own shoulder. "You're all going to die."

Augustine angled her head, lips brushing her ear. "Watch and learn. If you look away, even once, you will be the one strapped up on that hook." The grip on her hair was released, and Eva remained rooted to the floor.

Dutch bounced from one foot to the other, handing Augustine a single blade when he approached. She wasn't sure where it came from, and was too scared to take her eyes away to check.

"Are you watching?" Augustine looked back at her, mouth set in a tight line. "Good, now the carotid is the artery in the neck, one on each side." Augustine gently pressed the tip of the blade to the man's throat, first his left side, and then his right. "If you cut either open your victim will likely die within minutes, since it's under such high pressure. Now, beside them are the jugulars. These veins have a much lower blood pressure and spills rather than sprays, meaning you can keep your victim alive much longer." He turned back to face her for a brief second. "I personally prefer the inside thigh."

In one smooth movement the edge of the blade sliced across his throat, slashing through the skin with little resistance. Eva let out a gasp, trying to ignore the gurgling as the man's lifeblood pumped to the concrete. A cold sensation burned through her chest and failing to swallow the bile, she bent forward and emptied the contents of her stomach.

"Pathetic," Floyd muttered, but before she could snap back a snarky reply, she vomited again. There wasn't much as she hadn't eaten a physical meal in months, the bile an uncomfortable pink hue.

"Does that count as looking away?" Dutch's eyes glittered when she finally looked back up, her stomach twisted. "Can I punish her?"

Augustine waved his free hand. "Later. Why does everyone think they can fuck with us just before we reopen?"

"Boss," Floyd grumbled, "Your territory is in the largest of the Undercity, with direct connections to the troll market. It's not a surprise there are those seeking a vulnerability within your control while your attention is split."

Dutch grinned. "We need to remind the other Lords who we are."

Augustine stilled, so immobile it was unsettling, the knife seemingly forgotten in his hand as a smile spread across his face. "This is exactly why we need to push up our new event."

Tears burned down Eva's face, created from frustration and disgust because as she stared at the remains swinging gently from the rope she felt... nothing. The nausea had faded, leaving a hollow void where she should have felt anger. Anger at Augustine. Anger at her situation. Anger at herself. Instead she felt just as lifeless as the corpse.

"You'll get used to how I run things," Augustine commented when he turned to her. "It's important for a Lord to be feared in the Undercity."

"By killing everyone?" Eva whispered, jerking her arm free from Floyd as he began to guide her back into the first room.

Augustine's movements blurred, a dark smear across her vision before he stood only an inch from her nose. Blood splatter was blunt against his skin, a bright red that smeared when he swiped his cheek. "You need to remember you are no longer human." He brushed his thumb across her bottom lip, spreading the blood until she could taste the copper. "We are apex predators, literally created to kill and feed on those weaker than us. We are designed to be beautiful, tempting. Our skin, our voices, and even our scent is just something else we use to trick our pathetic prey." His lips descended on to hers, the kiss forceful as he sucked the blood from her skin.

Eva lurched backwards. "Touch me again and I'll kill you," she hissed, fist clenched and ready to strike before Augustine gripped her wrist.

"I think it's time to show you exactly what we do," he smirked, eyes brightening. "Dutch, shall we escort my fledgling downstairs?"

Dutch grinned, moving close enough she felt a burst of heat that bristled against her skin. "This is going to be fun." Blood flaked on his bare chest, and even dried it caught Eva's attention, her fangs descending a little. "After you, pretty lady." He bowed at the waist, lifting his arm towards the doors to the first room.

Floyd moved first, turning towards the circular desk in the centre of the room. The floor was marble, Eva realised when she stepped inside, high quality and clean compared to the cold and split concrete. The edge was lined with gold, the metal a slight lip that surrounded the desk in a complete circle. Floyd brushed dust off the wood, moving his fingers across the desk until he found a carving of a skull, inserting a key into the left eye socket.

Augustine pulled her towards his chest, an arm around her waist to keep her immobile while Dutch watched opposite, his attention unwavering. "Don't move," he whispered as the entire area surrounding the desk began to descend as Dutch hummed to himself.

Eva would have fought Augustine's hold, but her legs felt unsteady as the floor beneath her feet vibrated, gentle at first but then her muscles began to ache, the tremors rattling up her spine. Cracks opened up in the marble, a pale white light leaking through the gaps.

The lift continued to descend, the walls climbing until she was trapped on all sides, a coffin enclosing around her. The mechanism was silent as they finally stopped, the marble continuing down the corridor, pale cream with bursts of gold that glittered against the glowing light.

The cracks seemed to spread from the lift, connecting to white veins that pulsed brighter with every step, and then dimmed as they passed. They climbed along the walls, hypnotising as they walked, passing a few darkened corridors until they finally stopped before a door with a large metal snake coiled in the centre, surrounded by thick metal bars.

Dutch's humming became louder, clear enough she realised he was going through a children's nursey rhythm.

Floyd remained silent as he carefully unlocked the door using the same key as before. The snake in the centre creaked, the head moving until it slowly slithered along the indents towards the top left of the door. The bars slid back one by one, hunted by the snake in a clockwise circle. When the last bar slid away the snake returned to its original position in the centre.

"How many Units do we have?" Augustine asked as the door opened.

It was Dutch who answered. "Thirty-three fresh meat at last count."

"Yes, but we have enough cells for Fifty," Floyd added.

"Good, make sure you send more scouts. I would like us to reopen next week at full capacity. You know how quickly they die," Augustine sniggered, his footsteps silent as the marble changed to a cold, grey concrete and stone.

Eva remained silent, her heels tapping along the floor. The white veins continued their flow throughout, shooting off into multiple direction when the corridor opened up into a bright open space, the high ceiling replicating natural sunlight.

"Holy shit," she whispered beneath her breath, surprised to see the large arena deep beneath the city. The walkway wrapped around a centre circle, the half wall allowing her to clearly see the red stained sands below. There were three levels of tiered seating, with the ones closest to the sands protected by a reinforced metal lattice. The fourth level seemed to be split into individual rooms behind thickened glass, all with perfect view of the action.

"Welcome to the Pits."

She bent slightly over the wall, noticing the metal bars that circled the entire structure on the sand level. A walkway jutted out above, higher than the private boxes. "What is this place?" she asked, turning only for a hand to grip her throat.

"This is where the elite watch those who have been forgotten, just like you, fight to the death." Augustine's fingers tightened, pushing her until her back bowed, her body up to her waist hanging over open air.

Eva clawed at his arm, holding on as her stomach strained, clenching to stop her falling.

"I wonder how long you would survive down there."

She felt herself fall, her heart skipping a beat as his fingers loosened. She let go of his arm, nails scraping against the wall to stop her descent before he yanked her towards him, Dutch hysterically laughing behind.

"We've lost business to those fucking cages and professional fights, membership is already down twenty percent even before our reopening," he said, turning to face the others. "Even with someone as pretty as this fighting, it won't bring in the same numbers as before."

"Which is exactly the reason for the new event," Dutch said.

"We need to remind the other Lords who we are and why we're feared," Augustine continued. "What's the saying... Keep your friends close, but your enemies closer? If this *'He'* or another nameless fuck wants our territory, then they're going to have to come and take it." Augustine smirked, clasping his hands together. "So let's invite him, and everyone else who would see us dead. Let's invite them straight into the Vipers den."

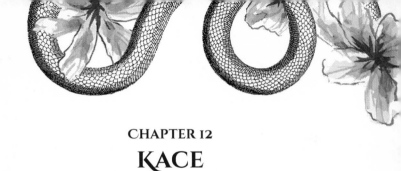

CHAPTER 12
KACE

He could feel them watching, their concerned stares little pinpricks across his skin, eating away at the stitches barely holding his shit together. But he wouldn't break, wouldn't give in to the desire to feel nothing but rage until it consumed him entirely.

"Hunter's description matches one of the new intakes," Sythe said carefully. "There's already a betting pool outside the entrance in The Market."

Kace's beast pressed at the confines of his mind, his anger so strong it blended with his own until they were both in agreement. He needed to remain the man, to have a voice before he finally gave into the monster he kept buried inside. Because he was a monster, someone who craved violence in the same way everyone needed oxygen. It was survival, something that kept him just on the edge of sanity.

His brothers all watched with a controlled patience as he paced back and forth. They thought he had lost it, finally broken. It was written all over the expressions they tried to hide, except he knew them all too well. It was only Riley, sat at the top of the table, who didn't have the same look of pity.

"I'm getting my kid back." Even his own voice sounded

different, strained as if was ready to combust. Which wasn't entirely inaccurate.

No one answered, not until Riley, the fucking leader of a bunch of messed up barbarians let out a heavy sigh. "You can't go back."

"Why? Do you think I would fuck it up?" The words snapped out like bullets.

Riley's fist cracked down against the heavy wooden table. "Don't even fucking try it, K. You know why you can't go back. You've never spoken about it, but we know what you've been though."

"You have no *fucking* idea what I went through. You could never imagine what I had to do to survive, and I'm not leaving Hunter *there*." He made sure he met every single fucking pair of eyes of his brothers.

They were all thrown together against their will as children, and bonded over a shared trauma that made them brothers. They were the only people he trusted with his life, but he didn't trust them with this.

"I'm no longer a defenceless child." He allowed his beast to deepen his tone, his words more of a growl.

"Sythe can go," Xander added, nodding across the table. "He doesn't have the same history. He can bring your boy home."

The roar that echoed from his throat rattled the walls. "Fucking try it!"

Chairs toppled, his brothers all ready to fight if he were to shift and attack. What shamed him even more was the fact they had done it before, but this time he kept himself in control, barely. His lungs were constricted, making it harder to breath as he concentrated on every breathe, on calming his racing pulse.

"He's my kid." Kace quietened his tone, even as his knuckles ached, the need to hit something growing. "I'm the only one amongst us who has ever fought in the Pits. I would never want any of you..." He couldn't finish his sentence, emotion constricting his voice.

Titus was the first to re-take his seat, resting his arms on the table as he slouched back, ankles crossed beneath the table. "There's no official opening date yet, but if there's already a betting pool it's probably within the next week or two."

Kace took a second to check his brother, relaxing just a little at the healed flesh of his chest. "Then we have to move fast." He swallowed through the panic that was creeping, memories teasing at his mind. The fighters were property, stolen outright or bought and forced to fight dirty. You either survived, or you didn't. Kace hadn't been scared of death, not even as an eight-year-old who had stood on the scratchy claret sands for the first time. Because sometimes there were things worse than death.

"We will find a way in," Riley said, meeting his gaze. "A way that doesn't risk you."

"I'll..."

"You're not fucking expendable," Riley snarled, interrupting. "Do you not think we see it? I will not allow this guilt you carry to consume you. You take risks Kace, risks that will get you killed. You're more than your past, and we will get Hunter back, but not by sacrificing you."

Chest tightening, Kace turned on his heel before he said something he would regret. He moved in quick strides, not paying attention to where he was going. All he could see was blood, the faces of the men and women he had been forced to murder for his survival. Most had been adults, but some had been other kids even younger than himself, and each had fallen beneath his hands. He always embraced the memories, never wanting to forget each and every soul. They haunted him, deservedly so.

"Kace?" A soft hand brushed along his arm.

He moved without thought, a feminine cry searing through his consciousness. Kace blinked, and found Kyra pressing herself against the wall, her mouth open in surprise. He staggered back, flinching as she held her hand out as if to touch him again.

Alice stepped between them. Her eyes were hard, fractured irises glowing as she pulled on her chi, arcane teasing her fingertips. She was a warrior as much as they were, and while it took a while to understand why Riley had chosen her as his mate, Kace finally understood. Alice suffered from just as dark memories, but unlike him she didn't let them weaken her.

Kyra tried to move closer, features set in a resolute expression. "Kace, you'll be..."

He aimed his words at Alice. "Keep her away from me. I just... I can't." Why did she want to save him? Some people were beyond help.

"Kace!" Kyra called after him. "Wait!"

It was Alice who stopped her from chasing after him. "Let him go."

Kace knew he was running, but he didn't stop until darkness wrapped around him like a comforting blanket, the high moon casting barely a glow through the clouds. The wind was quiet, almost silent as he finally paused a few meters from the trees edge.

"What's got your knickers in a twist?"

Kace didn't need to turn to know who it was, Lucy's chi dark enough against his senses that he would never have trouble identifying him. "You weren't at the meeting."

"Of course fucking not," Lucy sneered, stepping forward until the moon light settled gently across half of his face, softening his scowl. "I'm never invited anywhere."

Kace rolled his shoulders, his hands trembling. He

needed to fight, to feel a little pain before he fucked every-thing up.

Fuck! Fuck! Fuck!

He needed a release. One that made him bleed.

"Batboy, hit me."

Lucy's eyes narrowed, his lip lifting into a snarl. "What the fuck is wrong with you? Other than the obvious."

Kace didn't bother asking again, instead his fist smacked against Lucy's jaw. Bone crunched, the sound satisfying amongst the silence of the surrounding grove. It was the rush, the adrenaline as Kace stood and accepted Lucifer's hit, savouring the quick shock of pain that burst in his nose.

"Your face is like a fucking stone wall, you psycho bastard," Lucy groaned, flexing his fingers. "At least take me to dinner first. Wine and dine me before you try and fuck me."

Kace touched his nose, the cartilage broken. He care-fully moved it back into place, knowing it would be fully healed by tomorrow. "Sorry, you're not my type."

"I don't know why the fuck I stay," Lucy grunted, yanking off his t-shirt to swipe the blood from his lip. "You're all arseholes."

"We don't keep you here, you can leave."

Lucy's head snapped to the side, his red eyes glowing. "And go where?"

It was the first time Kace had noticed Lucy's façade slip. The Daemon was powerful, but right then he looked almost vulnerable. Lucifer was a friend, or at least slightly more than an acquaintance. The only Daemon Kace didn't want to rip the head off, well, most of the time anyway. He had chosen to help them rather than his own kind, and while he was freed from the chains that kept him below in The Nether, he seemed lost up on the surface.

He no longer looked like a Daemon, other than his eyes

which he preferred to keep for the shock factor. He looked just as they did, his skin no longer grey but a warm brown that only complimented the black of his hair. His horns and wings were hidden, only appearing when he was provoked. Even his tattoos, runes that they all bore were so similar to the Guardians despite being hundreds of years old, if not older. He was covered, the sharp lines and curves of the markings a reflection of his lifetime as a druid, before he changed into the Breed the Guardians were created to destroy.

"You're so bloody impulsive," he said with a click of his tongue.

Kace couldn't argue with that. Lucy's presence infuriated his beast, and before he would have shifted and gone for the kill. The fact he hadn't while rage burned through his veins like fire proved he had the control, and he could save Hunter from the same horrors he had suffered as a child.

A curse cut through the silence, grass crushed beneath heavy boots. Titus pulled at his hair, yanking strands away from his face. "You guys cool?" he asked, snaking his attention between them both.

Kace wanted to bite back, to act like the arsehole they expected when he was in a mood. Except he didn't, instead clinging onto the pain from his broken nose. It allowed him to breathe, to think clearly. He was so fucking damaged he wanted to laugh.

"Of course, we're cool," Lucy said, picking at his brightly painted nails with a bored expression. "Psycho here was just showing me the size of his fist. It's impressive by the way, eight out of ten for the knuckles. One out of ten for the bloody warning."

Titus's lips tightened, eyes narrowed when they met Kace's. "You good?"

Lucy appeared at his side, leaving a cushion of air between them. "Of course he's good, look at him. I just punched him in the face without getting eaten, now that's progress."

Kace met the red of Lucy's irises, brow raised. His beast roared at the Daemon being so close, but not as loud as it was before. "I'm good."

Titus patted his chest, right above where he had been sliced almost in half. "Good, now you set up a needle and fix the glyphs that have healed weird, and I'll tell you everything I've discovered about those snakes that run the Pits."

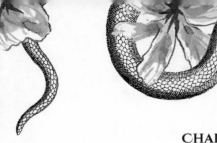

CHAPTER 13
EVA

E va tried to ignore the lecherous gaze of the man sat on the other side of the small table. She seemed to have finally mastered the statue stillness of other vampires, every muscle in her body solid.

"Tell me more about this special event," he asked, his eyes dipping to her breasts. She would have crossed her arms, but she didn't want to direct any more attention back to her. In the three meetings Augustine had had, this was the first he made her join him on the leather sofas. Before then she had been dancing in the corner of the office, a free-standing pole set up beside his desk. At first she was disgusted, but after a while she lost herself in the familiar movements.

"You've been a loyal spectator for a long time, Mac. I thought maybe you would want to have a more personal stake in my games, a fighter that stands just for you," Augustine said, sipping the whisky from his glass. "These games are only for the most generous of clients, and will have three rounds over three days, as well as the usual shows you have come to love. We predict this to be a success, and that it'll become an annual event."

The man known as Mac licked at his lips, his fangs prominent before finally looking over to meet Augustine's smile. "You have my attention. What's the buy in to become a sponsor?"

"One-hundred thousand." When Mac began to laugh Augustine added, "per fighter. We want to make this exclusive. We're a reputable business, after all."

"That will definitely make it fucking exclusive," Mac said at the end of his chuckle.

"We don't want to invite just anyone to join us," Dutch said as the door to the office opened. "I'm sorry I was late, I had... business to attend to." He winked at Eva as he took the space beside her, sandwiched between the two. He wore a suit, identical to Augustine's except it looked like a costume, a wolf in sheep's clothing.

Mac laughed, sipping from his own drink before returning it to the small table. "So, you're telling me for one-hundred I can enter a fighter into these games? Why exactly should I spend that sort of money when I can just spectate and bet like before?"

"Because the games are different, more difficult. We expect our sponsors to enter only the strongest warriors who will really make a show." Augustine raised a brow, his spare hand brushing down over her collarbone until it rested on the top curve of her breast. "And the winning sponsor gets ten million cash, plus free entry to the following games."

Mac wheezed out a breath as his eyes tracked Augustine's fingers. "Ten mil?"

Augustine's hand moved down, drifting over her stomach and then lower until it met her thigh, his fingers digging in hard enough she couldn't stop her cry. She was stronger now, able to withstand more damage, but she still felt her flesh give way to the pressure. Eva kicked out, forcing him away before he slapped her across the face. The sting was sharp, her own blood vile on her tongue.

Mac didn't even flinch as he continued the conversation, as if violence was a daily occurrence. "You having auctions like last time?" His heated eyes prickled her exposed skin. "You know how I like them broken afterwards."

It was Augustine who laughed this time, the sound seemingly forced. He pulled her across his lap, his breath foul against her face as he settled his empty glass on the table. "Mac likes to purchase the fighters when they lose," he explained to her, the wound on her leg already beginning to knit back together, the surrounding skin slick with red. "He likes to fuck them while they're ruined," he continued, ignoring her struggle. "He was one of my biggest customers until we took a break."

"You were shut down by The Council," Mac said, his voice deepening as his attention remained on Eva. "Caused a huge fucking ripple amongst the Undercity."

"The Pits have been refurbished with the highest of security." Dutch chuckled, reaching for the decanter and an empty crystal glass. "Our new partner has assured us The Council will not be a problem."

Augustine tensed for the briefest of seconds. "Don't worry Mac, the Pits will always be the Pits and that includes the auctions. We just wanted something special, something unique for the grand re-opening. Something for even the darkest of tastes."

"Hmmm." Mac leaned forward, mouth twisted into a smirk. "And what does this pretty thing think of these new games?"

"My fledgling doesn't speak," Augustine said before she could respond. "Not unless I give her permission."

Dutch laughed, his eyes sparkling with challenge. "Or unless she wants to be punished."

Mac cocked his head. "Is she registered with The Elder? Or can I buy her from you?"

Eva froze beneath his scrutiny, Augustine pulling her tighter against his chest. "My fledgling's not for sale."

"That didn't answer the question." Mac's smile was sleazy. "She's young, not strong enough to be classed as her own master and if she isn't registered, I'm entitled to make a bid for her."

"She's been officially registered with The Elder, don't worry, my friend." Augustine's smile wasn't friendly. "Which means she's mine, and must do everything I say as her master." Augustine dropped her onto the carpet, her arms landing on the table in the centre with a thwack. "Get on your knees." His hand moved to the fly of his trousers.

"Come near me and I'll bite it off," she growled in return.

His hand was suddenly wrapped in her hair, yanking her forward while Mac laughed hysterically at her back. Augustine's fangs pierced into her skin, lower than she expected, at the hollow where her throat met her shoulder. It was painful, not even his venom easing the shooting pains as he sucked hard enough to mark. She pushed at him, his grip tightening before he pulled back slightly, his lips brushing the shell of her ear.

"Scream more, It's how Mac likes it," he whispered, his breath a foul caress. The hold on her hair squeezed, his free hand cupping her jaw as he turned her to face him. His kiss hurt, her head immobilised as he swept his tongue against her closed lips, trying to enter, pushing and nipping with his teeth. With a cry of frustration she opened, only to immediately bite down.

The next hit darkened her vision, her arm bent, but not

broken beneath her as she fell. Dutch grinned at the wooden table which had splintered into pieces, glass shattering as alcohol splashed across her skin.

Eva coughed, her chest tight. "Touch me again, and I'll kill you," she managed a whisper.

Augustine stood, and Eva couldn't stop the flinch. "Bend over."

She squeezed her eyes shut, dread settling in the pit of her stomach. If he touched her again, she would fight until there wasn't any breath left in her lungs.

"Your struggle makes it so much more fun," Augustine said from only inches away, pushing her onto all fours. "It makes it even more amazing when you finally submit yourself to me." A finger brushed against her spine, gentle, a caress as he pushed her dress up over her hips. She almost puked.

"Fuck you." She opened her eyes to slits, reaching forward and curling her hand around a chunk of sharp wood, hiding it beneath her arm.

"A woman shouldn't curse." The finger drifted lower, dipping beneath her underwear.

Her arm tensed, the wood splintered as she swung, aiming for the man who kept her imprisoned. A movement at the corner of her eye, her body instinctively twisting towards the bigger threat as Dutch tackled her to the ground. She landed with a grunt, the sharp tip of the stake slicing across his cheek before it was yanked forcefully from her grasp.

A single second passed, long enough to realise she had seen Dutch move, his actions no longer a blur. Eva's excitement was short lived when she noticed Augustine's expression.

Shit.

"Dutch, I think you should keep her outside until the

meeting is over," he said with an eerie calmness as he took a seat once more. "I won't be long."

Eva tried to think past the roar inside her ears as she was yanked to her feet. He continued to grin, the slice on his cheek already stopped bleeding as he pushed her through the door.

"Come on," Dutch said, seeming to follow one of the reactive veins of light into another corridor, the glow brightening as they walked, and then dimming as they passed. They must have had at least thirty to forty people working for them, and not one cared as she screamed and fought.

"Get off me!" she cried, her voice strained. She wasn't stupid, she knew Augustine would use her for more than her blood, just as Lucas had. But she wouldn't lie down and take it. She'd probably die, but she would make sure they all burned in hell along with her.

"Do you know how territorial we are as a Breed?" Dutch asked, spinning to press her against the wall, her skin coming into contact with one of the light veins. "Augustine claimed you as his fledgling, which makes you his property."

"I'm not property," she hissed, ignoring the shock of pain as the vein vibrated. It was like a pulse, the painful beat increasing every few seconds until she had to clench her teeth from crying out.

Dutch smirked, his fangs bright compared to his lips. "Tell me, has he ever called you by your name? Any name, in fact?" A flash of wood, the tip of the spike he had removed from her only moments earlier piercing into her shoulder.

Eva let out a squeal, the point where she was impaled burning.

"You're nothing." He pressed himself closer, the spike pushing further into muscle until she was caged against the wall, the light vein now a constant sensation. "Poor little

Eva Morgan," he purred at her. "You have no living family, your boyfriend left you to us as a gift, and your friends have all forgotten you even existed."

Eva sucked in a breath, the burning pain from the wood radiating across her shoulder and down her arm like flames eating away at her flesh. "Please," she begged. Her back hurt from the light, but the stake was like nothing she had ever felt before.

Workers moved behind them, but she was invisible.

"You're no one." His tongue brushed the side of her cheek, moving down to touch the bite that had almost healed. "Despite your scene back there, Augustine tells me you have a talented mouth."

Eva froze, the burning moving across her chest until every breath was agony.

"You see, my uncle enjoys the fear, that's why he's done everything but fuck you. He thrives on you not knowing when. Just that it will happen. Maybe today." Dutch pulled the stake from her shoulder, and Eva let out a small scream. "Maybe tomorrow."

The burning stopped immediately, the respite only lasting a second before Dutch pressed a finger inside the wound.

"I think I should fuck you first, break you in for him." He nibbled at her neck, curling his finger inside her shoulder until it came out with a pop.

"I'm *his* property, remember?" Eva said through clenched teeth. "Not yours."

"I would rather beg for forgiveness, than ask for permission." He pushed away just as Augustine turned the corner, Mac smiling beside him.

"I look forward to seeing your entry," Augustine said before he barked at a man who was passing. "Richard, please escort our newest member back to the top." He didn't wait for a response before turning to Dutch. "I need you to go hunt down Mr Whitlock."

Eva's ears perked at the mention of her ex-boyfriend's name.

"It seems he's failed to meet his payments, and the coward has gone into hiding."

"Excellent," Dutch said with a smirk. "Looks like we get to kill him after all."

"Go. Find him." Augustine's features tightened when he turned to Eva, his pupils dilating. "Now tell me, how do you think I should punish you?" He stepped forward, but she remained where she was, swallowing the panic. "Beating you doesn't seem to be working. Maybe a little public humiliation? You didn't seem to appreciate Mac watching, and usually I wouldn't either. But he's a notorious gossip, and getting him excited for our little opening next week will be perfect for business."

Eva clenched her fist to stop the trembling. "Fuck. You."

Augustine stilled, pupils returning to their natural size. "The day you realise there's no hope, is the day you truly understand your role in my world."

"What? That I'm nothing but a toy."

"See, you're learning." he said, never taking his eyes off hers. "But just so you understand, if anyone touches you, I'll rip out their heart."

Eva had no time to process that comment before he nodded.

"Now come, I have something to show you." Augustine didn't wait for her to acknowledge him before moving in the opposite direction as Dutch had gone. When she remained exactly where she was, he stopped, not bothering to face her. "You can run, but there's no way out, only a harsher punishment."

Eva bit her lip, but began walking. She tried to memorise the twists and turns, counting the doors they passed through and the stairs they descended. It was the first time she had seen his men other than the handful of security back at the penthouse, forgetting that he, along with Dutch, ran a business, if that was what she could call it. The men didn't acknowledge her existence, their eyes skittering past her as if worried their attention had lingered too long.

The light veins were harsher in the lower levels, pulsating violently as they ran along the floors and walls, reacting when they stepped closer. It gave an indication of someone walking in the opposite direction, the wall or floor brightening before she the person came into view.

Eva reached over, snapping her hand back as the intense vibrations stung her fingertips.

"They're designed to weaken you," Augustine said as he stopped at a thick metal door, slowly unlocking the deadbolt. "Wild magic that can take your strength away, remove the ability to shift as well as strangle your chi, if you were a magic bearer. Perfect for what we need, but like many Fae stuff it interferes with modern equipment and electricity. Good thing I came from a time where we didn't have those luxuries." A smirk. "Through here."

The room Augustine stepped into was in complete darkness, large if she guessed by how the sounds of crying echoed, Eva's eyes taking a second to adjust as random bursts of light brightened in the corners. It distorted her vision, her ability to see somewhat in the pitch black flickering every time there was a new random glow.

It was only when she stepped further inside that she stopped, able to make out the cells that surrounded the entire room. Men and women stood behind thickened bars, floor to ceiling that criss-crossed. The light veins tracked beneath the bars, forcing whoever was inside to carefully move in the tight space. Most were dark, but some brightened when the occupants moved closer to the door.

"What is this?" she asked.

The prisoners' cries and angry screams became louder. She couldn't distinguish their words, their voices a confusing muddle. Augustine's hand snaked around her wrist, yanking her further inside, closer to the bars.

"These are my Units. Each one will fight for their survival on the sands, and if they outlive one-hundred fights they can negotiate their freedom." He shoved her forward, straight into the bars. "Not that many of them will survive that long." The prisoners shrunk back, further away.

Eva tried to pull back, but he held her there. "Please!"

"Look at them," he whispered. "Look at the faces that are about to die a painful death for mine and my clients enjoyment." Augustine stepped behind her, pressing her further into the bars, his body flush against hers. "My patience is wearing thin, if you embarrass me in public, or try to escape I'll put you in there. Because even if you do escape, you'll be returned to me where I'll make you fight on the sands, and then be auctioned off afterwards when you lose. You won't die, because I won't allow it. But make no mistake, you'll beg for death that will never happen."

CHAPTER 14

KACE

Kace recognised the decrepit townhouse despite the garden having overgrown to the point the rose bush partially concealed the broken front door. It had been condemned, which wasn't all that surprising considering the damage he had witnessed the last time he was there. The official sign had been repurposed, blocking a window either from the sun or the cold, nails haphazardly secured into the thickened cardboard. Smashed glass and hypodermics crushed beneath his boots as he ascended the steps, having to step over someone passed out in the doorway.

"Hey, you can't just come in here," a man growled from the corner, a rucksack open beside him full of various powders and pills in neat little plastic bags. "You gotta..."

The dealer shut up as soon as Kace turned his head, the blade that flashed hidden quickly beneath a sleeve. "Miss Smith, she here?" he asked in an irate tone.

"Upstairs," the dealer replied quickly. "Think she's servicing."

Kace couldn't stop his growl, fists clenched as he found the stairs at the back of the house. Each room was full of dirty mattresses and blankets with used food cans laying forgotten bar the flies, mould and shit a heavy odour.

Fake cries of pleasure echoed down the upstairs hall, and Kace didn't bother to knock as he searched each individual room. There were no locks, nothing to stop his kick as the final door on the hall opened to reveal a naked couple.

"Fuck off, would ya?" the man snapped, not stopping the pumping of his hips. "I paid for an hour."

The man yelped when Kace yanked him by his hair, slamming the door shut when he shoved him out into the hall cursing. The woman barely let out a cry, trying to hide herself with a sheet, the material hardly covering the track marks that decorated her arms like a red siren. Hunter's mother was slimmer than before, more bone than flesh.

"When was the last time you saw your son?"

Miss Smith frowned, reaching over for a cigarette that was balanced in an ashtray. She flicked the lighter three times, Kace's patience wearing thin before it finally brightened with a flame and she took a deep drag.

"I don't care what he's done, it's not my problem," she said with a splutter. "That's exactly what I told the other prick who came looking for him a few days ago too."

"Answer the question."

Her eyes narrowed, lip tipping into a smirk. "If you want to talk, you gotta pay."

Kace threw some cash on the bed, careful not to get too close as she shuffled forward to count it, the sheet long forgotten. If she was beautiful, she wasn't now, her skin shrunken and scarred from abuse. There were fresh bruises across her shoulders, deep bites that looked infected on her throat. It took serious effort to look like that when a shifter.

"Hunter was around here a few days ago," she said, licking her lips. "Was all upset about something, said he knew a way to get some quick cash. He was meeting with someone that night."

"Do you know where he went or who he met?"

"Look, I've already told the other guy this shit," she said with a huff, her eyes slightly glazed. "I don't know, and I don't care. I've told him to stay away, I don't want him here after what he's done."

Kace breathed through his anger, knowing how fine an edge he walked. The woman naked on the bed should never have been made a mother, not when she would rather hand off her child to known abusers rather than skip a high. It was Hunter who reached out to the Vaults once the dealers turned their eyes to his younger sister. And it was Hunter who was blamed when his sister was beaten to death by the same people his mother fucked for money.

"Do you know how to contact The Vault if he comes back?"

She took her time replying, the orange tip of her cigarette only highlighting the gauntness of her face. "Sure."

Confirming Hunter hadn't gone home only tightened the ache in his chest. He knew Marshall and Hud had looked for him, but he needed to see for himself, had hoped they were wrong.

"Fuck!" Kace snarled when he stepped outside, ignoring the scared glances of a few walkers crossing the road. "Fuck! Fuck! Fuck!"

"I take it he wasn't there?" a familiar voice commented.

Kace growled at Axel, who leaned casually against his SUV. "What the fuck are you doing here?"

Axel's eyes flicked to the house before quickly returning. "Looking for you."

"Yeah, sure you were." Kace swung his arm out in the direction of the house. "It's all yours. Careful though, you don't want to share fucking needles."

Axel pushed off the car, standing boot to boot as he snarled. "Don't be a fucking arsehole K, I came to apologise."

"Not interested." Kace passed his brother, needing the walk. He had parked his motorbike a few miles away, knowing it wouldn't be safe if left alone anywhere in The Bricks.

"It's not an addiction," Axel said, stopping Kace dead in his tracks. "I'm nothing like them." He gestured in the vague direction of the house.

Kace paused. "I'm sure that's what every addict says."

"Fuck you," he growled. "It's the only thing that helps the noise." Axel tapped his head. "I thought you would understand better than anyone."

Pain wrapped about Kace's chest. "How often are you on something, Axel?" When his brother didn't reply he stepped forward. "Are you on something right now?"

"Fuck you," Axel said instead, his eyes darkening with impatience. "Now shut the fuck up and come home, we have an update on the Pits. They've announced a special games, and I'm betting Riley can get an invite."

CHAPTER 15

EVA

Augustine's hand tightened in her hair, tilting her head at a painful angle. "Look at yourself," he whispered intimately against her ear, his fangs scratching her skin. "I said look at yourself!" His voice had sharpened to a bark, forcing her to face the mirrored surface of the lift.

Eva stared at the woman that she didn't recognise. Her eyes were once again black, empty bottomless pits pinched with anger. Music played from the speaker as they ascended, an obnoxious orchestra that was far too upbeat for the chaos that surrounded her.

His smirk was cold in the reflection, his eyes void of anything but disdain. "I told you to wear the red," he said as his free hand came up to swipe at her painted lips. His fingers gently brushed down until he gripped her chin, keeping her still as his fangs continued their path across her skin, scratching hard enough blood began to trickle. It was becoming a habit, his mark almost permanently evident somewhere on her body.

Her lips. Her throat. Her thighs.

It was as much a brand as the vipers.

Augustine's smirk deepened, turning into a grin when he finally looked up. "I can feel your hunger. I wonder how long you'll starve yourself before you beg me for it?" His tongue licked across the mark he had made, sealing the wound before he repeated once again with his fangs, but this time deeper.

Eva tried to swallow the needles that stabbed down her throat, ignoring the intense burn as Augustine's fangs sliced through muscle. "I'll never beg you." Augustine had forbidden her to feed from anyone but him, knowing that she wouldn't gain as much strength than from someone not a vampire. She refused, the final rebellion before he took the last piece of her.

"Oh," he said, lifting his head. "But you will, because if you don't..."

He let the warning hang in the air, licking the blood that dripped too close to the fabric of her dress. She expected him to heal the fresh wounds, but instead he left them as they were, her blood a bright contrast compared to the black of her ballgown. Not that it really mattered, because all anyone noticed were the tattoos that curled around her arms, ignoring the bruises, welts and tears that streaked down her face. She was property, for him to do with as he wished, and no one would interfere.

Fuck vampires, she cursed inside her head. *Fuck everyone.*

"You're my fledgling, therefore an extension of my dominance," Augustine said, his tone matter of fact. "As I've mentioned before, if you run, you will be simply returned to me kicking and screaming. Under vampire law you are nothing, and a fledgling without a master will be disposed of by The Elders. So disobey tonight and you will suffer for it. Understand?"

At her silence his smile deepened, and Eva fought the

cry as his arm whipped up to pin her painfully against the cool surface of the lift.

"Do you really wish to test me on such an important night?" He pressed closer. "You've already seen where I'll put you if you don't be my pretty little bauble, to be seen and not heard. Do. You. Understand?"

"Yes," she whispered, his finger brushing along her jaw. "I understand."

"Good." He stepped back, tugging his tuxedo jacket to cover his somehow still pristine white shirt. "Look how beautiful you look in red," he said, gesturing to the blood that was still wet across her skin. "If you had obeyed me, I wouldn't have had to punish you, would I?"

"My Lord." Floyd met her gaze for a brief second in the mirror before turning to Augustine. "We're here."

"Good." Augustine rotated to face the doors. "Let us greet our guests."

Panic tightened her muscles, but she turned just as the lift reached the seventy-fifth floor. Eva had always wanted to visit Revelations, the expensive restaurant reserved for the rich and famous. It was bitter that she was finally visiting as Augustine's pet.

She had seen the place featured enough in magazines, but it still took her breath away when she stepped onto the plush carpet. Three of the four walls were made entirely of glass, giving the most astounding view of the city she adored. The bar was the showpiece in the large room, selkie mixologists creating artistic cocktails while an oversized crystal chandelier hung just above, glittering against the spotlights. The usual dining experience had been removed, leaving only poseur tables strategically placed around.

She was grateful when Augustine's booming voice greeted everyone, distracting the curious glances she was trying to ignore. He demanded the room's attention, his strides long as he made his way towards the furthest wall. Eva kept back, blending herself into the background, Floyd keeping close.

"My fellow Lords, how great of you all to attend the opening ceremony of the first of what I hope to be many special events. You are here because you have been invited, or because you have enough money." He paused until the light laughter stopped, expertly responding to the audience. "In a few days the Pits, the most profitable gladiator fights on Earth Side will open once again. We will all put our differences aside, and enjoy one of the realm's oldest entertainments, fought by only the fiercest of fighters. And don't worry, there will be a few surprises thrown in there too."

Eva tried to filter out the sounds of everyone in the room, heartbeats, shuffling of fabrics and tapping of fingers all blurring together as one white noise. It was hard to concentrate, the applause not helping her hear Augustine's speech. Not that she cared what he had to say, not when all she needed to know was the location of the exits.

It took a few seconds, but she was finally able to filter out the sounds and focus on the palpable tension, thick enough to cut. Designer suits and thickly muscled men stood off in distinctive groups, flicking hostile glares between one another like disgruntled schoolchildren. There were very few women, the ones that did attend wore similar gowns to her own. Their faces were perfectly painted, smiles fake as they hung off the men wearing suits more expensive than her rent. There was only one woman Eva could see who didn't seem to wear a gown, instead opting for tight jeans and a black t-shirt that showed off thickly muscles arms despite her slim frame. Her face seemed to be marked with a permanent scowl, eyes darkening when they scanned around and noticed her appraisal.

"Some of the most dangerous businessmen are in attendance tonight," Floyd said to her quietly, his hand relaxed by his side, close to the gun she saw him place earlier. "I would watch your behaviour, you wouldn't want to embarrass our Lord now, would you?" Floyd wore his sunglasses, despite it being night and the room being comfortably lit.

"I should say the same to you," Eva replied just as quietly, conscious of who could overhear their conversation considering she still had no idea how to tell the difference between Breed. "Wouldn't want Augustine's authority to be questioned when his fledgling is being ordered by a simple lackey now, would we?"

Floyd stilled beside her, a distinctive rattle vibrating up his chest. It should of scared her, but right then she was beyond rational thought.

"What animal are you?" She knew it was rude to ask of a shifter, but found herself asking anyway.

She felt his hot gaze through his sunglasses. "Bear."

That explained his size, she thought. "And why is a bear working for a vampire?"

"Because I get to eat disobedient little girls."

"That's a weird thing to say to *your* Lord's fledgling." Eva stepped to the side.

"Where do you think you're going?"

"I'm going to go get a drink from the bar, and if you don't want me to scream, I expect you to back off and go hover somewhere else. Trust me, I'll do it. I'll scream so loud the entire party will turn this way."

Floyd's hand snaked out to grab her wrist, a sharp nail pressing against her pulse. "No one here will help you. Not only because of those brands, but because vampiric law means he fucking owns you. There is nothing you or anyone else can do."

Eva tilted her head, looking him dead in the eye without flinching. "I just want a drink, alone without a shadow stalking my every move. Like you've said, no one will help me." She pulled once more, and was pleasantly surprised when he released her without breaking skin.

"Be good, I'll be watching."

His glare pricked along her bare back as she walked across the room with purpose, hiding the storm of panic tightening her chest. She met every single pair of eyes who looked her way, realising Floyd was right. They all saw the blood on her throat, the vipers on her wrists and quickly turned away in disgust. The ones who didn't turn away smiled, but it wasn't friendly.

Grabbing a flute of champagne from a passing waiter Eva strolled straight past the bar, searching the room for Augustine. She found him in the corner beside Dutch, their attention contained by the slim man with not one, but two women clinging to his arms. Another man stood just off to the side, the suit he wore ill-fitted and his expression uncomfortable.

A fighter, Eva thought, realising that in every group there was one person who distinctively looked different. Dangerous. It was in the way they held themselves, their eyes constantly scanning the crowd for threats.

Lifting the champagne to her lips she sipped at the gold liquid, savouring the slight burn as she stepped closer towards the kitchen, only stopping when she noticed a guard standing before the door.

Fuck!

He looked up to meet her glare, brow raised as he purposely moved his hand towards his hip. He wore a suit, one that looked just as expensive as all the other rich bastards who enjoyed blood sport, except he also had an earpiece. His gaze flared in challenge as he shifted his weight more evenly on his legs.

131

What did he expect, for her to tackle him in front of everyone?

Eva pursed her lips, recognising him from one of the security back at the penthouse, Mr grass, citrus and parental disappointment.

"There are men at every exit, and we've been given permission to stop you by any means necessary."

Of course he fucking did, she thought before she said aloud in her most innocent voice, "I was just looking for the bathroom." When he frowned she continued. "You know, I was told that this would stop when you transitioned, but no, I pee just as much as I did before." Which was actually quite annoying, but not really surprising considering her diet was almost entirely liquid. She hadn't had to experience eating solid food for a while so wasn't sure whether *that* still worked. "Well?" she prompted with an impatient stamp of her foot.

His nostrils flared, and she was sure she would pay for it later. Her mother had always complained when she was awkwardly inappropriate in tense situations, but she couldn't seem to help herself.

Eva clenched her fist, ignoring the crack in her champagne glass. If they were alone she would have tried to get past him, hoping she reacted just as fast as she had before. She wasn't an idiot, and even with her supposed vampire strength he was twice her size. So she needed to be faster, fight dirtier. Except Augustine had stopped her feeding.

She wasn't sure what Breed Mr Parental Disappointment was, but she was sure he wasn't a vampire. In fact, other than Augustine, Dutch and Floyd, none of the security or workers were anything but human.

"Well this was a riveting conversation, I appreciate it," she said as she drank the rest of her champagne, turning away from his audible grunt.

Broken glass in hand she walked towards the bar, carefully placing it onto the wood.

"What can I get for you?" the bartender asked politely, her pale blue irises seeming to swirl like the ocean. She grabbed the champagne flute, not commenting on the state as she carefully hid it from sight.

"An emergency exit."

Her professionalism slipped for the briefest of seconds. "I'm sorry..." She began with a strained smile.

Eva didn't bother waiting for the rest of her apology. "Vodka then, please. Straight." If she was going to be stuck there against her will, she could at least have a few drinks before she returned to his bed.

Fuck everyone in this room.

Fuck Floyd and his warnings.

And fuck Augustine.

The woman nodded once, producing her drink quickly, the glass cool to the touch with a slight salty taste. As soon as Eva had swallowed the first another appeared, and she drank that one down too.

"I hope you realise it'll take a lot more than a few shots of vodka to get a vampire hammered," a voice chuckled from beside her.

Eva ignored the man, tapping the bar for another. He was right, and that pissed her off even more. When she was human a couple of shots would have definitely affected her, even if it was a slight buzz to calm her nerves. But now there was nothing other than a biting chill in her stomach.

"Another, please," she said after her third.

"You seem stressed," the man beside her continued, sliding closer until he pressed her arm. "Maybe I can help with that?"

Eva was ready to snap a sharp reply when she noticed the gold coin he held out in his palm. It glowed beneath the lights, the centre burning bright. She finally looked up, noting his hair was as bright as the coin, his beard a few shades darker orange.

"Cool tattoos," he continued, gesturing to her arms. "They mean anythin'?"

Eva took a second to reply. "No." If he didn't recognise the brand, then he may not know who Augustine was. "How can you help with my stress?" She licked the vodka from her bottom lip.

The man didn't seem to have the same reservation, his gaze tracking her tongue.

Fae, that would be her guess. His skin was a shade lighter than hers and seemed almost pearlescent beneath the lights. His body was strong, lean beneath his tighter than necessary suit and his eyes were orange, the same as the centre of the coin. He smelt of copper, coins rather than blood and she wondered if he would taste the same.

"Three wishes, that's what I can offer you."

Eva blinked, realising her attention had drifted to his pulse. "Wishes?"

Shit. Shit. Shit. What type of Fae offered wishes?

"Leprechaun wishes are superior, and never fail," he said with a grin. "It's how I made my fortune."

Eva stepped back, looking him purposely up and down. He didn't look like a leprechaun, considering the only fact she knew about them were their shorter stature, but then again who was she to judge someone on their appearance when she was a vampire who bruised.

"What could I wish for?" she asked quietly, remembering from childhood cartoons that there were always rules and restrictions when it came to wish magic. Not that she should base her limited knowledge of magic on silly animations. But it showed her inadequate education growing up regarding Breed in general, and if she ever had a child, she would make sure they grew up knowing as much as possible.

She was in a game of chess where they thought she was the pawn, when she was actually the mother fucking queen.

"You can wish for anything," he said, sliding closer until his chest almost touched hers. "Wealth. Health. Freedom..." He moved his palm closer, and her eyes flicked up to meet his. Guess he did know what her tattoos meant.

"And what would you want in return?" Her hand itched to take the coin, repercussion be damned. Her life couldn't possibly get worse, could it?

His grin spread across his face, the fingers on his spare hand reaching up to brush across her skin. "I heard you were a Venus Dark..."

Eva wrapped her smaller hand around his wrist, feeling his bones creak beneath his skin. "Don't touch me."

Hot breath against the side of her neck. "You should never accept anything from the Fae," a deep, familiar baritone growled.

CHAPTER 16

KACE

K ace's mind went blank when he spotted Eva across the room, her eyes darkened in such hunger that his beast responded with an equally ravenous snarl.

What the fuck was she doing here?

He hadn't realised he had spread it along the mental connection until he noticed Riley turn his head, his body freezing when he spotted her too.

It was Sythe who responded, which meant Kace really was distracted. *'Well, isn't this interesting,'* his brother said, serving drinks at the same time as a waiter. *'Looks like Kyra's bestie is part of the Vipers. The little Valkyrie kept that a secret, didn't she.'*

Kace clenched his fists, his arms folded across his chest as he leant back against the coolness of the glass. Rage burned, hot enough that Riley cut him a sharp glare.

'Remember why you're here,' he said telepathically inside Kace's head. *'We'll deal with her.'*

Kace kept his attention on Eva, unable to look away as he slowly traced every inch of the black glittery dress. The fabric hugged her in all the right places, cut high on her

136

chest to only hint at the soft curves beneath. Her hair had been messily twisted on her head, with a few strands framing her face and leaving her back entirely exposed, the skin there as perfect as silk.

He was going to cut every fucking male's eyes out in the room. Starting with whoever left the bite mark on her throat.

"Kace?"

He had heard Riley's warning, but he still felt himself pulled across the room. His anger bubbled in his bloodstream, harshing his steps as people wisely moved out of his path. She couldn't be there, not when he needed to stay focused. He was there to find Hunter, that was his only priority which meant the woman who had wormed her way into his head needed to get the fuck out of his way.

"Three wishes, that's what I can offer you."

Kace heard the faerie from across the room, his intentions towards her clear. Which meant he was either stupid, or had a death wish. The Vipers were notoriously barbaric. Kace knew that well, considering they had controlled the Pits since before he was even conscripted. And Eva was marked with their fucking calling card.

Violence thickened the air when he lifted a hand towards her, but before Kace could intervene Eva had almost broken the fucker's hand. He didn't bother stopping his beast's urge to bare his teeth over her shoulder, stepping close enough to cast a shadow.

"You should never accept anything from the Fae," he growled, leaning close enough the hairs on the back of her neck responded. "Especially not wishes. You wish to run fast? You'll run until your legs are nothing but bloody stumps, and then you'll keep going."

Eva's shoulders tightened, but she didn't turn as she released her grip on the Fae.

"Fuck off," Kace said to him before he could respond, "or would you rather offer me your fraudulent wishes?"

The faerie snarled just as a larger man stepped up behind him. "Do you know who I am?" he said, angling his body to emphasise the sheer size of his friend. It made him look weak, nothing but a rich twat playing a hardman in a room full of lions.

Definitely stupid.

"No." Kace met the glare of the new guy, recognising the similarities. Related, possibly even brothers. One was family money, and the other was soon to be dead. Because that was how everything on the sands worked. "Now fuck off."

The Fae turned several shades of red before he stepped away, taking his brother with him.

"I didn't need any help," Eva said in her naturally husky voice, finally turning to face him. Her lips were painted a dark purple, which only emphasised the darkness of her eyes, the blue of her irises teasing the edges. He knew little of vampires except their pupils, which could widen to encompass the entirety of their eye, improving their sight. They were perfectly devised predators, designed to kill.

"Clearly." Kace crossed his arms, stopping himself from brushing the skin of her cheek, wondering if it was as smooth as it looked. He had touched her before, knew what she felt like beneath his palms but that was before. Now she was different. "What the fuck are you doing here, Eva?"

Hostility narrowed her eyes. "I could ask you the same thing," she said, replicating his tone perfectly.

"Do you have any idea what you've gotten yourself into?"

He could have sworn tears wet her eyes, but she blinked and they were gone.

"You seem to think I have a choice." Her voice was quiet, but no less severe.

Everything stilled, blood roaring in his ears as his beast tore to the surface. Claws prickled at his fingertips, so sharp he could almost feel nails splitting while fur pressed against the inside of his skin. Riley and Sythe were in his head, their voices nothing but a hiss.

'Breathe!' Riley's voice finally broke through, quickly followed by Sythe.

'Calm your fucking balls, dude!'

He was so close, the edge of oblivion but a step away. So he focused on Eva, her lips opening on a gentle exhale to reveal the shiny tips of her new fangs.

"Kace?" She reached forward, her hand brushing gently across his arm. "Are you..." Her eyes widened, hand snapping back as if burned.

"Well, if it isn't the notorious Red. I've seen you've met my fledgling." Augustine appeared beside them, his smile tight. "Go play elsewhere," he said, directing the words at her.

Eva stood exactly where she was, spine straight before Augustine nudged her away. Fire burned through his chest, but he remained still as he fought for control.

"Go." A final warning.

Eva blinked, a slight tremble in her jaw as she stepped away, and it took everything for Kace not to pull her back.

"What a pleasant surprise you're here," Augustine continued. "I was told you only participate in the cages."

Kace couldn't speak, his vocals strangled as kept his gaze on Augustine, his muscles bound so taut he was sure they would snap.

"Lord Augustine," Riley said as he appeared, his hand landing on his shoulder, fingers pressing hard as Alice, his mate stepped up to his other side.

Kace anchored himself with the pain, using it to calm his beast while pulling from Riley's strength.

"Lord Storm, always a pleasure," Augustine lied smoothly, ignoring Alice completely. "I'm sorry to hear about the death of your father, he was a great man."

"I don't go by Lord." Riley smiled, and it wasn't friendly. He oozed power and dominance, and even in his tuxedo he looked closer to the fighters than one of the rich elite. Except Riley was brought up in that world, was able to manoeuvre through the subtle politics and bullshit with ease. "I decided not to inherit that title from my father."

"No, only his legacy then. Which I've been told you've also decided not to carry on. Shame." Augustine smirked, returning his attention to Kace. "I look forward to watching you work, Red. Until then."

Kace waited a breath before rolling his shoulder, dislodging Riley's grip when they were alone.

"Can someone explain to me what just happened?" Alice asked.

Riley gently tugged Alice towards him, his hand in hers. "K, if you can't keep it together..."

"I'm fine," Kace interrupted, scanning the crowd for Eva.

Riley frowned. "Remember why you're here."

Kace snapped his head back, a dark current rippling beneath his tone. "As if I could forget." Hunter wasn't at the opening ceremony, but that wasn't completely unexpected. It just meant Kace had to go further inside the place he had sworn he would burn to the ground.

"I'm not joking, K. No distractions."

Kace's nostrils flared. "Where's Eva?"

"Sythe followed her into the bathroom. Wait, we will deal with..."

Kace didn't bother waiting for him to finish, turning

towards the bathrooms at the other side of the restaurant. He bypassed the small groups, each not wanting to mix without risking the carefully constructed truce of the event.

The Undercity was full of deception and corruption, the Lords making money from those weaker than them. Slavery, fights, drugs and sex work, it didn't matter what it was or whether it was legal, if it made money the Lords controlled it.

Kace ignored the glares from the other fighters, some he recognised and others he didn't. There was a reason he went by a different name in the cages, separating his life from the dregs of the Undercity. Not that he had much of a life outside of it, the Guardians working more in the shadows. Except Riley, who through his father was familiar to the Lords. Mason Storm had once owned and ran half of the city, only to be just as crooked as everyone else in the room.

He had bought Kace from the Pits when he was eleven, and including his son had cursed seven children to a fallen angel. Mason may have pulled him from the Pits, but he hadn't saved him.

If Riley hadn't already killed his Father, Kace would have.

A man stood outside the bathroom, as tall as Kace with thick arms and even thicker legs. He frowned as Kace approached, eyes glowing over the sunglasses he had perched on his nose.

The door to the bathrooms swung open with no resistance, whispers drifting from the women's at the end of the hall.

Sythe stood beside Eva, her shoulders hunched forward as she pressed her palms down onto the wide central marble sink. His brother turned, lips pressed together.

"Get the fuck out." Kace kicked the closest cubicle, the

door swinging open to reveal no one inside. "Sythe, I said get out."

"There's no one here, arsehole," Sythe snarled. "What the fuck do you think you're doing?"

Kace kicked the second cubicle, and then the third until he was happy they were alone. The room was larger than he expected, with three toilets and three sinks overlooked by huge gold edged mirrors. A chaise lounge sat in the corner beside a short wooden table, a crystal vase full of flowers and a box of tissues positioned on top.

"I'm not leaving you in here with her when you're like..."

"It's okay," Eva whispered, her hand reaching up to touch Sythe. "Please."

Sythe looked between them, a frown pinching his brows. "Just shout if you need help." He shot Kace a dark look as he grabbed the metal tray that still held several glasses of champagne, the door swinging closed behind him.

Kace fought the urge to beat the shit out of his own brother, and the thought cooled his anger to a simmer.

What the fuck was wrong with him?

Sending a quick mental command for Sythe to block the door and to distract the guard he turned to the woman who had the ability to ruin everything.

"You can't be here," he said, jaw rigid. "Why the fuck are you here?"

Eva hadn't moved from the sink, her eyes tracking him in the mirror's reflection.

"Is it true that if I was claimed as a fledgling, that I have no control over my life? That if I run, legally I would be taken straight back to him?"

"Did Augustine change you?" Kace was proud his words didn't come out an unintelligible snarl. Point to him.

Eva's shoulders tightened. "No."

142

Kace stepped closer, meeting her eyes in the mirror. "Then what the fuck happened?"

"What happened is I have shit taste in men." Before he could reply she spun, pressing her back against the sharp marble edge of the sink. "So you're a fighter?" She chuckled, the sound hollow as her eyes flicked up. "A fighter called Red, how original."

"I wasn't nicknamed Red because of my hair," he growled. "It's because I make my opponents bleed."

Her lip twisted. "You're just like them."

He placed his palms beside her hips, crowding her without touching. It forced her to lean back, back arched. "I'm nothing like them."

"Says the man who entered an arena where death is the only reward. Tell me, *Red,* why are *you* here?"

"I need to find a kid who's been tricked by the fucking Vipers," he snapped back. "And you have no idea what I'll risk to save him," he said, voice dropping to a whisper, his lips moving closer to her ear. "Or what I'll do."

Eva's breath hitched, pupils widening until her entire whites were obsidian. Kace waited to see a blush darken her skin, was disappointed when her complexion remained the same.

"When did you last feed?"

Vampires were almost immortals, designed to be the perfect predator to humans. They wore their humanity like a mask, a fine line between the person they were before, and the enhanced hunter they had become.

"You have a bite," he continued when she just stared. "You should have healed this almost instantly. Which means you're not feeding properly." Kace reached for one of the hand towels, wetting it beneath the faucet and stroking it along her skin.

"You know about vampires?" she asked quietly, tilting her head for better access.

"Only their weaknesses."

She froze beneath him, even her breathing slowing to an almost stop. "Tell me again why you're not like them?"

Kace took his time cleaning, only stopping when nothing but the initial holes and scrapes remained. "Who hurt you?" Whoever had bitten her had intentionally done it for the pain, so he would make sure when he found them, he would make them suffer even worse.

"Where do I start?" she said with a forced laugh.

Kace waited a breath, conscious of his anger. "What did Sythe say before?" The towel made an audible thwack when he threw it into the furthest sink, splattering pink-tinged water across the mirrors.

Eva pursed her lips, and he fought against the urge to brush his thumb along the velvety skin. He hated to be touched, and yet he craved her physical connection.

"He said that he could get me out now, but I would never live my life as my own, forever looking over my shoulder because vampire laws are fucking barbaric."

Kace suppressed his growl.

"That if it was true and I was officially Augustine's fledgling, then only an Elder would be able to dissolve the relationship without risking a feud. I don't even know what a fucking Elder is! I don't know anything about being a vampire."

Her scowl deepened, wrinkling her nose and he could have sworn her fangs appeared longer, pressing against her bottom lip.

Why the fuck did that turn him on?

Kace pushed away from the sink, putting distance between them. "Vampires have to follow certain rules because they are dangerous and feared amongst most Breed, as well as humans. An Elder is the head of a certain territory, and it's their job to make sure the vampires that settle there don't go into bloodlust rampages."

"Do you have an Elder?"

Kace shook his head. "No, as a druid we would usually have someone called a Vector, which I guess would be the same. Or the Archdruid himself."

"I don't understand what any of this means," she said, letting out a little growl. "I'm my own person, not some bloody toy for an arsehole with a superiority complex."

"I'll get you out." It was a promise to them both. He knew there was The Council, but the government that represented all Breed was just as corrupt, if not more so. If it didn't benefit them, they didn't care.

Eva closed her eyes, hair brushing forward as she let out an exhale. "He will kill you if you try."

Kace remained rigid, keeping himself from touching her. "You can walk out right now with me. Augustine isn't going to make a scene in front of all these Lords, it would make him seem weak."

"You really think he would let his property walk out of here without him?" Her eyes opened, and this time there were tears. "He'll kill you. If not now, then later for even trying. And what if I did go with you? It still won't be freedom, because legally I'm *his*."

"Eva," he growled. "We will..."

"You're here for a reason. Don't let me distract you from what you have to do, finding your kid." Eva turned her head, looking away. "I've already lost everything, don't let that happen to him."

Lightning beneath his skin, the realisation he would have risked his only chance at finding Hunter. Grabbing her arm, he pulled her until her palms slapped against his chest. "You need to feed."

"Kace!"

He stepped them both back until he found the chaise lounge, dragging her over his lap. Her eyes narrowed, and he was sure she let out a little hiss as she moved her legs to better straddle his leather clad thighs, her dress split at the sides.

"I said feed." Kace moved his hand up her back, dragging his fingertips across her spine until they reached her neck. He wasn't sure what the fuck he was doing, his beast just as puzzled as he pulled her even closer. He could have offered her a wrist, and yet he found himself tilting his head, exposing his throat.

"What are you doing?" Eva tried to wiggle free, but his grip tightened. "I can't, he will find out and I'll be punished." Her words strangled, the tears finally spilling. "I'm so angry that he's made me this weak."

"You're not weak." He pulled her down, her lips brushing his skin. "I can feel your hunger Eva. Take from me. Use me."

Eva let out a strangled moan, her breasts pressed against his chest. Her fangs struck, the pain lasting only a second before warmth spread, a euphoric sensation that hardened his cock like granite. It was the sweet spot between pleasure and pain, and rather than feel overwhelmed with the full body contact, he wanted more. Needed more.

Kace released her neck, one hand clutching at her soft thighs as she rocked against his erection, while the other circled around her back, pressing her impossibly closer. He found himself moving along with her, his body on fire as he reacted to her little moans that tingled along his exposed throat.

Her fangs released, her body trembling as she pressed against his chest.

"Shit, my venom..."

Kace swallowed the rest of her words, his lips crushing as his tongue swept inside her mouth. Her venom mixed with the copper of his blood made her kiss the sweetest poison.

The bite ached, and all he wanted was for her to sink her fangs into him at the same time he buried his cock into her. The image flashed behind his eyes, and he let out a groan as Eva reached up to tug his hair, her tongue fighting for dominance in a battle she had no hope of winning. It was almost violent, a clashing of tongue, lips and teeth while his fingers brushed higher on her thighs until he found the damp heat of her pussy. Her dress shifted, the slits high enough to allow him easy access.

"Kace!" Eva broke free from his grip, his blood in her system the only reason she was able to do so, and he wanted to roar in fucking victory. Because it was *his* blood that gave her strength. "It's not real, my venom is making you..."

She moaned, his fingers brushing between her legs.

"Your venom isn't the reason your cunt's wet for me, Eva." As soon as he said her name, his finger passed the lace to spear through her slick folds, thumb moving to flick her clit in the way he had before, all those months ago. He's dreamed about her moans, remembered how fucking delicious her pussy was against his tongue.

How fucking dare she invade his thoughts, his cock aching for so long just for her. And there she was, drenching his fucking lap while being the pretty pet of his enemy.

Her mouth opened, her pale fangs tipped in red, and Kace almost embarrassed himself right then and there like some pathetic teenager. He may not have had much experience with physical sex, or with pleasuring a woman, but right then he was glad his brothers were so vocal with their exploits. He could watch her pant with desire for hours, learning what she liked through every cry and moan.

"Why the fuck can't I get you out of my head?" he growled, inserting a second finger while his thumb moved in slow circles. He curled them, finding exactly the right spot that had her gasping, riding his hand.

"That seems like a *you* problem." This time she pulled him down with a sharp tug of his hair, her kiss desperate. He stilled beneath her, shoving past the nightmare before it took root. It was only for a second, a single breath but it was enough for her to notice.

Eva hesitated as she pulled back, and before any negative thought could ruin the moment he pressed harder against her clit, her eyes glazing over as he concentrated on that little bundle of nerves. Until his moment of weakness was long forgotten.

He watched her get to the very edge, the lips he had dreamt about opening as her head tilted back to reveal the elegant slope of her neck. She looked so fucking beautiful, and he couldn't stop himself from leaning forward, capturing her pulse in his mouth and sucking, marking. Her scent, her whimpers and even her weight, which would usually have caused him to panic gave him something to hold on to reality, chasing the darker memories away.

Her hand reached down, tugging at the fastening until he gripped her wrist.

"Remember where we are." His cock strained against its leather prison, so hard it was painful. "This isn't the time or place." He wanted to pleasure her, watch her break apart into a million pieces because of him. Eva's pleasure was his, and his alone.

She let out a frustrated cry. "Look, I know we don't like each other, but let me have this, let me have this one thing that's been my choice." Her voice was deliciously husky, her face finally flushed with desire thanks to the blood he fed her.

He didn't really care for sex, not wanting the vulnerability to be with another person in such an intimate way. It was only when his beast pressed him for a release other than violence did he seek out women, and then it wasn't much more than a quick joining with as little contact as possible. He needed to remain in control, a hand wrapped around their throat. Despite not giving a fuck about the women, they always came back wanting more.

"Kace!" she growled as she clenched around his fingers.

A better man would have stopped, would have given her the distraction she craved and then left. Good thing Kace wasn't a better man.

She was a disruption he didn't need, and this was one way to get her out of his system.

He slipped his fingers from within her warmth, much to her frustration.

"Kace!"

She was pure fucking attitude, a cyclone of sunshine that he wanted to punish.

Punish her for being in his way.

Punish her for making him want her despite it.

Lifting her by the thighs he walked them both to the sinks, placing her down roughly. "Turn around," he growled, moving her until she had placed her palms on the cool marble, facing the mirror. "Don't take your eyes off me."

He needed a little more control, his beast pressing, pushing until he was ready to unravel in the sweet scent of her.

Eva's eyes widened in the reflection, but she kept her gaze on him.

"That's it," he murmured, lifting the rough glittery fabric of her dress. It came up easily, exposing her bare skin inch by inch until he got the view he would forever imprint in his mind. He pressed just above her voluptuous curves, fingers brushing the soft skin. "Bend."

Her shoulders tightened at the brooding command in his tone, but she didn't argue, not when he moved his hand to stroke across her hip until his fingers found her hot pussy once more. He teased her entrance from behind, never giving her the pressure she needed.

A low rumble came from her throat. "Kace, do it or I'll find someone else."

Kace continued his tease, letting a finger slip inside to the first knuckle, and then the second. It was supposed to be her punishment, but right then he felt like it was his, his cock ready to combust unless he felt her tight heat wrapped around him. "Find someone else," he whispered, leaning forward until his head was beside hers. "And I'll kill them."

Her eyes glittered, and before she had the time to shoot him a sarcastic comeback he ripped her underwear, the fabric falling away to expose her folds, slick and swollen. He smiled at her in the reflection, and it wasn't friendly as he finally released himself, pressing the tip of his cock at her entrance.

"Keep quiet."

Her eyes closed, a groan vibrating down her until he felt it along his cock.

"Eva," he growled, hands moving down to grip her hips. "Eyes on me, now."

Her eyes snapped open, and in one thrust he was inside her, and he never wanted to leave.

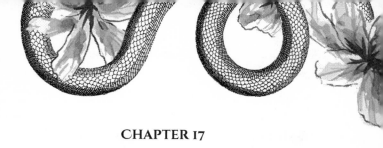

CHAPTER 17
EVA

Eva had never felt herself stretched to the absolute limit, and Kace didn't give her any time to adjust to his size before he moved in such powerful thrusts, she had to steady herself with the sink.

He fucked as if he hated her, rough and without restraint. It was exactly what she wanted, what she needed, as he reached places inside that she never knew existed. Everything was more intense, the eye contact heightening the experience until she felt every inch of him going in, every hot breath against her back and every stroke of his fingers along her sensitive skin.

It was too much, the pleasure, the dominance as he watched her with green eyes hiding something dark, something mysterious that had fascinated her in the first place. Her orgasm was close, lower stomach tingling as her thighs trembled. Without thought her eyelids fluttered closed, and Kace stopped completely, just holding himself inside as she begged for her release.

"Eva," he growled, and if she hadn't been so turned on, she would have called him an arsehole, or worse. The man infuriated her, but right then she didn't care, not when he made her feel so alive. She was stretched almost to the edge of pain, his grip on her hips bruising, and she loved it.

Licking her lips she smirked, keeping her eyes closed for just a few seconds more, wanting to see if he reacted.

He pulled out fully, leaving her achingly empty.

Letting out a cry she finally opened, watching him through lowered lashes in the reflection. His gaze was even more intense, his irises seeming to glow a slight silver rather than his usual green. She would have thought more on it if she wasn't so distracted by his lips. He had such luscious lips for a man, soft compared to the sharp angles of his face. She wanted to bite them, to mark them.

"Last warning." His hand released her hip to move around the front to circle her clit.

With a moan she finally lifted her eyes to meet his, and he pushed inside in one thrust, his thumb pressing her little bundle of nerves at the exact same time. Her orgasm was forced from her, so powerful it stole her breath, her body convulsing as Kace kept moving his hips. Eva collapsed on the sink, her legs weak as she rode the aftershocks, able to feel every ripple as his cock pulled more pleasure from her.

A hand wrapped in her hair, pulling her back up to face their joint reflection. She had nowhere else to go, unable to look away from Kace even if she had wanted to. His expression should have scared her, but instead she clenched around him, enjoying his groan as he pumped his hips even faster. His cheeks were flushed, delicious lips parted slightly and his eyes were now entirely silver, almost liquid.

Another orgasm tore through her, and just as it peaked, Kace stiffened with a groan. She couldn't control her cry, nerve endings on fire as he pulled her until her back touched his chest, another hand pressing against her lips, keeping her quiet.

So she bit him, drawing enough blood that she licked

across his palm and felt him jerk inside her, still heavy despite the wetness that was leaking from between her thighs. She should have felt embarrassment, but instead she felt relieved. For a man who was so cold, his touch burned.

His dark red hair was deliciously tousled as they both stood fully dressed, her dress still in one peace because of the high splits. Eva couldn't stop her smile, and then her grin. She must have looked mad when laughter bubbled, the idea that she was thankful for the dress Augustine had picked out so she could have sex with a man who she didn't even like. Kace didn't seem to understand her sudden eruption of giggles, and she couldn't really blame him.

He pulled his hand away, and Eva tried to hide her disappointment.

"Well that was... nice," she said, before laughter exploded once more.

Nice? she thought. It was the best sex she'd ever had, and it was in the bathroom of an expensive restaurant where only a short distance away her 'Master' was entertaining.

"Nice?" Kace's lip lifted as he stepped back, fastening his trousers. Her eyes dipped, only just realising he wore fighting clothes, the leathers a second skin that emphasised the sheer size of his thighs. She should have really noticed considering she was straddling them only moments before.

"You have a habit of ripping my underwear."

"I don't like obstacles."

Another laugh, which was the most she'd laughed in months. She was happy for the first time in as long as she could remember, or she's totally lost it. Likely the latter option.

"Eva, you can't..." His words were cut short as he pulled her behind him, hiding her as the bathroom door opened. "Alice, what are you doing?"

A woman stood in the doorway, quickly stepping inside and closing it behind her. "I could say the same for you. Fuck's sake Kace, this is the women's bathroom," she quipped with a roll of her eyes. "Riley needs to talk to you, and we only have a few minutes before they find Eva."

Eva stepped from behind Kace at the mention of her name, ignoring Kace tensing as if to stop her. She didn't recognise the blonde who wore a simple black dress with a similar design to her own. She met Eva's gaze without hesitation, with no hostility or pity.

"You need to trust me," she said, her words for Kace when he remained exactly where he was. "Think of Hunter."

A low growl. A warning. "Alice..."

"Go, before Augustine suspects anything," Eva said, gently placing a palm on his upper arm. He pushed into her touch, and Alice's attention dropped to the connection. "I'll be fine."

Kace looked as if he was ready to argue, but he finally left without another word.

"Okay, we don't have long." Alice hiked up her dress, revealing a dagger attached to her thigh.

"You have weapons?"

"What? You don't?" With a quick tug she released the strap, holding it out. "I want this back, by the way. Kace gave me the blade as a gift, it's perfectly balanced for throwing."

Eva was surprised at the sudden jealously that knotted her stomach. Why would Kace give this woman a knife? "I don't know you."

Alice let out a frustrated huff. "No, but you trust Kace?"

"Yes." Eva was surprised by her own quick response. Since when did she trust Mr tall, dark and brooding? She was clearly desperate.

"Then take this and hide it beneath your dress. You'll have to be careful with your slits, but it's something until we figure out how to get you out of here without compromising Hunter." When Eva hesitated Alice dropped everything beside the sink. "Look, why do vampires not have any friends?"

"What?"

"It's because you're all a pain in the neck!"

Eva was unable to stop the smile that curved her lips. "So you're *that* Alice. You're exactly how Kyra described you."

Alice narrowed her eyes. "I'm going to take that as a compliment because you're in a very stressful situation right now."

Eva ignored the garter, instead turning to the mirror. Her makeup wasn't as bad as she expected, her lipstick only slightly smeared considering her kiss with Kace was more of a violent clashing of lips than a gentle caress. Blood flaked on her jaw while her eyes had returned back to their natural blue. It had been so long since she had seen her own eyes, so long since she hadn't been starved or in pain. It had made her forget, if only for a few seconds everything that had happened. But then she remembered she was there against her will, that she had been turned into a vampire, beaten and assaulted for months.

Shit.

"What's the date?"

Eva's stomach sunk as she counted in her head.

"It's the twenty-first of April."

"I haven't had a period in three months." Panic spiked her voice. "What if..."

"Eva," Alice interrupted, stepping forward slowly. "You can't have periods anymore."

Eva froze, blinking at herself in the mirror. "No periods? That would mean..."

"I'm sorry," Alice said carefully. "But vampires can't have children."

Eva swallowed past the lump in her throat. "Of course they can't, I just..." The words caught, and Alice wrapped her arms around her as Eva broke. Rather than recoil at the embrace Eva pushed into it, needing the soft comfort.

Vampires were always unable to have children, but for some reason she hadn't connected the information. She was only twenty-five and had wanted to live her life before she settled down, but she had always known children was something she desired. To become a mother. And now it was just something else that was taken from her.

"I'm so sorry," Alice whispered.

Eva pulled back, wiping the tears from her cheeks. "I can't take the knife, if I was caught with it, they will know someone is helping me. I've already put Kace at risk and he needs to concentrate on that kid."

"Kace will find Hunter, but you need to take the blade." Alice reached for the garter, handing it over once more. "Stab with the pointy end and then run like hell."

"I'm sure I know how to stab someone." Eva folded her arms. "But I really can't take it." When Alice began to protest Eva growled. "Look, I'm stripped every night. I can't risk it being found, not right now." Not when she knew she was about to be punished. At least this time she would recover faster.

Alice's eyes darkened.

"He hasn't... It hasn't gone that far. Not with him." The word *yet* echoed inside her mind, leaving a sour taste on her tongue.

She had forgotten in the moment that her inside thighs also had bites, cuts and bruises. As Kace hadn't reacted, she hoped his blood had healed them before his fingers brushed across her skin.

"I will be fine, I have super strength now." The joke fell flat, but it was enough for Alice to relax just a little.

"I'm supposed to warn you to stay away from Kace."

Eva blinked, surprised at the change in tone. "Really? That's what you're changing the subject to?"

"He's unpredictable, dangerous. You should stay away from him." She held out the towel. "But he let you touch him. He doesn't let anyone but his brothers touch him."

"I don't know what you're trying to say. Kace is... Kace. I don't really know him." He was a man as moody as the moon, but also one who kissed her as if she mattered.

"What I'm saying is that blood on your face isn't yours, and I'm sure Kace had a mighty love bite on his neck." Alice gestured to the towel in her hand. "He fights his own nightmares, but maybe you can save him."

"Save him?" Eva felt like a confused parrot.

Alice smiled, but it was sad. "Save him from himself."

The room was a chorus of noise, an irritating buzz before Eva concentrated on ignoring the multiple conversations. She had waited a while longer in the bathroom, needing time to conceal her emotions as well as clean. No one deserved to see her sorrow, not when she needed to wrap herself in anger, to survive long enough to destroy everyone who had hurt her.

Alice and Kace were nowhere in sight when Eva moved to stand beside one of the glass walls, pressing her back against the cool surface. Sythe, one of the men who had guarded Kyra's place all that time ago was still dressed as a waiter, smiling politely as he took orders. His eyes swept to her, but she refused to meet his gaze, not when she still felt so raw.

"Ah, there you are," a feminine voice purred. "I've been looking for you. How have you been wandering around without an escort?" Hana appeared at her side. She hadn't been there at the beginning, because Eva sure would have noticed someone dressed in a luminous red dress amongst the various shades of black and grey.

"You look like a blood stain."

Hana pursed her lips, hand snapping out to grab Eva's wrist as something tingled her nose. A shot of pain, the lines of her tattoos throbbing.

"I see he's showing off your brand. Just think, those tattoos will never fade. Your skin will never wither or age. Well," she chuckled. "Unless you die." Her eyes glinted, a cruel smile teasing her lips. "They will grow bored of you, you know. You're too... ordinary for their tastes." Hana released her arm, turning to smile as one the guests wandered past.

Eva stopped herself from rubbing the skin on her arms. Her tattoos looked exactly the same, and yet the pain she felt was real. "You're delusional if you believe you're not as expendable as I am."

"You should have taken the wishes."

Eva frowned. "How did..." That Fae had known she was a Venus Darkling.

"Your Master is coming," Hana said before Eva could comment, her voice edged with a slight challenge.

A heavy grip on her upper arm, a body pressed against her side. "Now why does it look like my fledgling has fed without permission?" Augustine growled, tugging her closer. "It's time to go." He didn't release his grip as he stormed out of the restaurant, Floyd, Dutch and Hana joining them. Dutch kissed along Hana's throat as they descended, but his dark eyes were on hers.

Hana moaned, her lips opening on a sensual gasp.

The limo was waiting at the curb, and Eva found herself thrown inside as everyone else took their seats around her. She remained on the floor as the car rocked into motion.

"Crawl to me."

Eva dug her nails into the carpet, shoulders rigid.

"I. Said. Crawl to me."

She looked up through her hair, the strands loose around her face. Very slowly she crawled forward, conscious with how her dress moved. When she arrived at Augustine's knees he lay a hand on the top of her head, gentler than she expected.

"Good. Now, who was it?" It was almost a whisper, his fingers moving down to grip her jaw. "Who did you feed from?"

"I don't know who it was."

"Liar!" Hana cackled, her eyes were bright, excited as she leaned closer. "You picked a little blood whore there, Augustine."

Augustine raised a single brow, and then Eva heard a harsh slap, followed Hana's pained cry. "Let me repeat the question," he said directly to her. "Who was it?"

"I don't know," she repeated as she tried to pull back, but his grip tightened until her head was immobile. "I didn't ask for a name."

"But you fed from them anyway." Augustine's smile was dark, his fangs descending as he opened his lips. "When I find out who it was, I will make sure everyone is witness to what I will do to them. Nobody touches what's mine." He released her so suddenly, Eva flinched, but remained unmoving.

Dutch's laugh filled the cabin. "Didn't think you would have such defiance with a fledgling, did you Uncle?"

"Defiance is something that can be beaten out of them, it makes their submission all that much sweeter." His hand settled on the top of her head, gently stroking the strands of her hair. "Despite her little rebellion, tonight was a success, it's making me feel almost generous, maybe I'll only strike you over my knee."

Eva breathed through the anxiety.

"But she disobeyed you?" Hana whined before Dutch wrapped his hand around the back of her neck.

"Shhh, little faerie," he whispered against her cheek. "The big boys are talking."

Hana's fingertips sparked, but she smiled when Dutch brushed his hand beneath her dress. Eva watched from the corner of her eye, noticing how Floyd kept his gaze squarely on her, his thick brows lowered in barely contained anger.

She could make out the animal behind his irises, a large predator hidden behind the face of a man.

Augustine tugged on her hair, forcing her attention back to him. "In a few days we will be celebrating, my little fledgling, and the Vipers will rule the Undercity once more."

Eva nodded as much as she could.

He smiled, his irises expanding to the point they encompassed the whole eye. "You should be on your knees more, it's how to correctly present yourself to your Master."

Eva bit back her reply, not wanting to aggravate him when she seemed to have gotten off so lightly. Instead she read his hunger, tilting her head to give him access to her throat. She braced for his fangs, closing her eyes as he took great pulls. She wouldn't fight, not this time because she was no longer lost. People knew where she was, that she was alive.

She just had to survive a while longer.

CHAPTER 18
KACE

"There's better ways to kill yourself, you know?" Lucy mumbled as he leaned on one of the mirrors in their underground gym, Poe wrapping himself around his feet. "Working out for several days straight seems pretty stupid when you can go out in style."

Kace ignored the annoying Daemon, and the cat as he continued with his very precise crunches. His stomach killed, the ache a distraction as his beast rocked at the edges of his mind. He couldn't use the cages, not when he was so close to getting on to the sands. He needed another way to control his violent urges, especially considering he had already worked himself through everyone except Lucy.

"Like lighting a firework up your arse. That's a pretty funny way to die." He reached down to Poe, his multi-coloured eyes looking up at the Daemon with a meow.

Kace growled, trying to remember why he decided not to fight Lucy again.

Oh yeah, he thought as he exhaled past the intense burn of his muscles. *Because in this mood I'll probably fucking kill him.* He had too much pent-up frustration, his beast raring to tear and shred. He knew he would never go too far with his brothers, because his beast saw them as brothers too. But with Lucy it was different. Kace was built to destroy his kind, and right then he wasn't sure if he would be able to stop.

"You sound like one of those dogs, the ones with the flat faces, but with asthma."

"Fuck off," Kace warned, frustration deepening his tone.

There was a reason he was distracting himself, stopping his anger from festering into something heinous he could no longer control. He needed that control, and with Hunter he knew he would be on the sands, fighting. Eva, on the other hand, was a complete clusterfuck.

She was The Viper's property, and according to some primeval vampiric law Augustine owned her. He legally could do anything he wished to her, and there was no repercussions, not until she was strong enough to become her own master. According to his research it was created as a power structure to help the weaker Vamps from killing innocents, which was apparently an issue for several millennia.

It also meant there was nothing Kace could do, not without killing every fucker who tried to stop him. Which was exactly what he planned to do.

"What about drowning in beer? I bet If I called a brewery we could get one of those massive barrels. Just say the word and I'll hold your head under," Lucy continued without a care.

"Lucifer," Kace growled. "Why are you even here?"

He just wanted a little reprieve from his beast before he entered the Pits. But nothing was working, not since he tasted real serenity. Kace always chased the tranquillity of exhaustion, and he had never felt so... calm. Until *her*.

He had expected a rough fuck, a quick release of pleasure for them both, but her sharp tongue ignited something inside him that should have been dangerous to any other woman. Yet rather than violence he found himself craving her attention, her eye contact a brand that had seared beneath his skin.

Fucking Eva was like a catharsis, her cries of pleasure purging him of every guilt, bad memory and nightmare until there was nothing left but her. Her scent. Her skin. Her moans.

And he wanted to do it again.

Fuck.

Lucifer let out a low whistle. "Okay, stay with me on this one. What about getting crushed beneath the entire national rugby team?"

Kace stopped his crunches, his breathing heavy as laid flat on the mat.

"I'm pretty confident one of them is an elephant shifter, now that would be interesting to see in a scrum." Lucifer clicked his tongue, eyes narrowed. "Hey, are you even listening to me?"

If Kace tasted serenity, it was short lived. His beast was riding him hard, harder than he ever had before and if he didn't concentrate, he would lose. Eva had been a high, but right then he was freefalling into oblivion.

Mine. A growl through his mind, one that he ignored.

"No, I'm not listening," Kace said through clenched teeth. "I wanted to be alone."

Lucifer tutted. "Okay, no need to be rude."

Kace dragged a hand down his face, focused on his breathing. In. Out. In. Out. Maybe he would beat the shit out of Lucy after all. Chase that much needed exhaustion. The thought made him laugh, which caused Lucifer to glance over with a confused expression. In all his years he had never reached peace, and now he had found it in the warmth of a woman. A man who hated touch.

Eva was definitely a disruption he didn't need, and it was clear that once was never going to be enough.

Mine.

Fuck.

CHAPTER 19

EVA

Darkness was comforting, calling her into its depths as Eva raised an arm, watching as her skin became wrapped in the shadows. It took concentration, the swirling gloom like a blanket that started at her fingertips before moving up her hand to her arm.

"Neat trick," a low, raspy voice said. "I see you've been practicing, now let's go."

Eva released the shadows, stepping back to stare at the security guard, the one who had been with her for the last several days. He was punishment for her feeding, she was sure of it. He was the first to watch her so openly, the others never looking at her directly when she was undressed, too afraid of Augustine. Except this one didn't skirt his gaze away, his attention remaining on her until it was like barbs beneath her skin.

It made her nervous, that he either didn't know that she was Augustine's fledgling, or that he didn't care. There was something about him, something wrong that kept her on edge. He watched her as she bathed, and even when she slept. Not that she really slept, especially since she had been moved into Augustine's room inside the tunnels of the

Pits. The first night she had remained rigid the whole night, waiting for him to come through the door and get in the bed. She flinched at every creak, knock or groan of the door.

The nameless security tilted his head with a poisonous smile. He wasn't a vampire, she was sure of it, yet his pulse was slow, sometimes even slower than her own.

He was her chains, and she couldn't wait for him to be replaced.

"I don't need an escort, I know the way," she said when he walked too close.

His reply was a snarl, his hand reaching up to grip her upper arm as he moved her faster down the corridor. "Get in the fucking office."

Eva pulled to a halt. "Do. Not. Touch. Me." She held no guilt, not when he worked for an organisation who literally forced people to fight for their survival. "Let me go, or I'll tell Augustine."

"Tell Lord what, exactly?" he seethed, fingers digging in. "How you're a little whore who can't follow orders?"

"That you offered your throat."

His jaw was rigid as he forced her through the door into the office. "Threaten me again and see what happens."

Eva put on her most seductive smile. "You don't know who I am, do you?" She stepped closer, hoping her nervousness wasn't reflected in her movements. She only had one shot. She had run out of time, having never been left alone in the tunnels. She would never have gotten away with it if it were Floyd, or even Mr Parental Disappointment, but over the last few days everyone had been busy, including Augustine.

It was now or never.

She just really hoped he was human, or something weaker than herself otherwise it would be a huge mistake. Not that it could get much worse than it already was. She still had some of her strength, Kace's blood more potent than anything she had been given before.

You've got this, kid.

It was always her father's voice she heard when she needed a pep talk. Although, she doubted he expected what she'd planned. Or maybe he did, considering he was the one who taught her how to punch in the first place.

The nameless security snarled. "Like I give a shit who you..."

His words were cut off when her fist connected with his nose. There was an audible crack, and more blood than she anticipated. She had put all her weight behind it, but he didn't go down.

Shit!

His angered cry echoed, but before he could react, she hit him again, trying to blur her movements just as she had seen Dutch do before. His head snapped back as he finally fell to his knees, slumping forward onto the wooden floor.

Eva grinned, barely stopping herself from pumping her fist in the air with victory. Quickly, before anyone peaked inside she dragged him further in to Augustine's office, pushing him behind one of the leather sofas. Blood was smeared on the wood, a lot of it.

Well, he definitely wasn't a vampire.

Ignoring the puddle forming she slipped out of the office, closing the door behind her. No one other than Augustine or Dutch would enter when it was closed, and she hoped that gave her enough time. She was alone in the corridor, her eyes adjusting to the restricted light until she moved away from the wall, the veins brightening.

Trying to wrap the shadows more tightly around her she walked down familiar twists and turns, the workers who she passed not giving her a second glance. When she felt the shadows fade, the light too strong, she made sure her body language was convincing, that she was allowed out on her own, and hadn't in fact knocked her security out and left him bleeding profusely.

When she found the stairs she needed she descended quickly, running to the deadbolt and pulling it open with a creak.

The room beyond was just as she remembered, the cries and whimpers quieter than before, almost hesitant when she stepped inside. At first it was pitch black, but the veins inside the separate cells quickly reacted as people stepped forward.

There were a few cells open, the contents empty. Eva rushed over, careful not to step on any of the veins that pulsated. Each cell was marked with harsh lines, some gouged out of the rock while others were painted. Food, basic and beige lay half-eaten on the floor, the toilets dirty at the back. The cell hadn't been vacant long.

"Hunter?" Eva whispered, turning to check that the main door was still dark. "Hunter?" She stepped closer to the next cell, the occupants scattering back as if scared. There was a man and a woman, both filthy with the same tray of food left uneaten. The woman's face was swollen, her left eye shut completely while her right was black and blue. The man didn't look much better, a large gash across his bare chest.

The cell door was simple, the lock needing a key that she didn't have. Other than the veins there was no added security, no runes or markings that she could see that would indicate any other type of magic. She reached for one of the thick metal bars that criss-crossed, unsurprised when even with her added strength she was unable to dent the metal.

Of course you can't break it! she cursed herself. *Honestly, Eva!*

"Hunter?" she whispered again, panic spiking her voice.

She could hear every movement of the prisoners, every shuffle of fabric and drip of a broken faucet. The veils that were bright let out a gentle buzz, hurting her ears if she concentrated on it too much.

A vampire was in the next cell, his eyes pure midnight as he glared at her approach, fangs long past his bottom lip. He was alone, the lines carved on the wall twice that of the others. "Fuck off you bitch, you're marked as theirs."

Eva didn't have time to correct him, scanning each cell quickly before she was caught. "Please, I'm looking for a kid, his name is..."

"What do you want?" a voice whispered from the other side of the room.

Eva turned, tuning out all the other sounds until she spotted him, his hands wrapped around the bars as he peeked through the small gaps. "Hunter?"

The young boy blinked, his eyes glowing a bright green, his pupils thinning to slits. "Who the fuck wants to know?"

He stepped back when she approached, his face all high cheekbones and a sharp jaw. His features were closer to a man than a child, but his age was obvious in the way he held himself. His clothes were torn, his hands scabbed over and his face was covered in a fine layer of grime. Evidence of tears left a slightly cleaner streak down his cheeks, which he reached up to rub across with his thumb.

Eva gripped the bars. "I need to..." She turned at the first crunch of stone, but was too slow as an arm wrapped around her waist, pulled back against a masculine chest.

"Ah, there you are."

Augustine's hold was like iron as she tried to twist out of his grip in a panic.

"Fight harder," he whispered as he shoved her hard into the bars, pinning her to the cold metal. "You know how I like it." His hands reached beneath her skirt, lifting the fabric until her skin was bared to the air. "What is my fledgling doing roaming the lower tunnels alone?"

Eva tried to settle her dread, licking at her dry lips as Hunter scrambled back. "I don't need an escort," she said, trying to conceal the slight tremor in her voice. "I just wanted a... better look."

Augustine chuckled against her shoulder, his fangs stroking across her skin without piercing. "Was the dead security guard a present for me?" he asked.

Dead? Oh shit.

"I don't need an escort," she just repeated. "Don't treat me like a child who needs to be constantly watched."

"Oh, you're definitely not a child." Her skirt lifted higher. "Did you feed from him first?" His fangs pressed down, the pain quickly dulling as his venom tricked her brain into thinking it was pleasure. She stayed as still as she could, knowing if she moved it could rip her skin further. His fangs finally released, her blood hot as it dripped freely down her back. "You know you're not allowed to feed from anyone but me."

Eva tried to nod, her head heavy. "I know. I'm... yours." The lie caught on her tongue.

"I think I'm going to fuck you right here, right now with everyone watching. Give them all a little show before they fall to the sands."

Eva froze at his words, all the fake confidence she had before disintegrating as his fingers teased her bare thighs. "Don't." The repudiation came out a whisper.

"Get off her!" Hunter shouted, struggling to reach through the bars. His nails had turned into claws, but they were useless, unable to reach.

"Have you been anxiously waiting? Knowing that I'm coming, but not sure when I finally decide to claim what's mine?" Augustine continued, his tongue wet against the

170

skin of her shoulder, lapping up her blood. "I can almost taste your fear. It's going to make it so much better when I take you screaming beneath me."

It brought her out of her stupor, the panic jack-knifing into pure anger. She fought dirty, knocking back, twisting and turning until he had no option but to loosen his hold. Eva dropped to her knees, falling forward onto her palms.

"You've shown me that you truly are a Viper, and it's a shame we haven't got the time right now." Augustine's chuckle echoed, morose against the cries of his prisoners. "Now get up, the first round is about to begin."

CHAPTER 20

KACE

K ace tried to not recall his memories at the Pits, but being back at the same place that broke him was a test of perseverance. Everything was bigger, newer, shinier. It wasn't the same, but then again, he was no longer a small child.

He was ready, calm as he leaned back against a wall with his arms crossed. He didn't bother looking at the other fighters, fifteen including himself. Most stood alone, waiting for the gate to the sands to open and for the first round to begin, everyone's sponsors already in their cushioned seats.

"Let's do this!" one of the fighters barked, clapping his hands together while his friend hopped from one foot to the other. They whooped and hollered, spurring each other on while everyone else remained composed, their voices more subdued as the tension thickened with every passing second.

They had all been asked to wait in what was supposed to be a locker room. Benches lined two of the four walls, an alcove above with hangers and shelves. In the centre were some weights, an empty bath, a freestanding metal cabinet full of medical supplies and a chair. It was basic, but more than he expected.

"We're going to win that prize money," the other man chuckled, ruffling through his coat. "No one will stand in our way."

Kace finally looked up, noticing the two who stood together while everyone else kept to themselves. The left was around six foot with bleach blonde hair while the other was an inch or so taller and dark. Other than that, they looked identical. Their eyes were both brown, slightly wild and even their noses were matching, crooked. They noticed him assessing, their similarly thin lips twisting into a snarl before footsteps echoed, and everyone turned towards the sound.

Kace braced himself, eyes drawn immediately to Eva who stepped into the room. She kept her gaze purposely away, and even the sight of her stilled his beast, until he noticed the blood dried at her throat. She stood behind Augustine, the vampire the same man who had first thrown him onto the sands almost two decades ago. It was a face he could never forget, that and his partner, a Viper even more dangerous than the suit. Dutch was a notorious killer, taking out their competition until even the Lords of the Undercity knew not to mess with the Vipers.

Kace couldn't wait to cut off the heads of the snakes.

"Everyone, can I have your attention," Augustine said, raising his voice. "Today marks the first of what we hope to be annual games. Before we begin, I must remind you of the three rules. One; you must enter the sands when asked, any hesitation and you will be disqualified."

Slight grumbles between the fighters, uncertainty as Augustine continued.

"Rule two; you must enter unarmed, and you must return unarmed. There will be no souvenirs allowed."

He paused to sweep his gaze across the fighters, and Kace shifted his attention to meet his eyes.

"Rule three; survive."

Nervous laughter, which showed there were rookies amongst them. Fighters who didn't have the experience of what they were about to suffer.

Augustine's smile was predatory, the double door unlocking behind him with a loud click. It swept open with a dramatic creak, the arena grounds just behind. There was no roar of the crowd, no cheering or applause as the fifteen of them stepped onto the sands, the grains stained red. Their audience wasn't the same as the cages, or any other fights Kace had fought. They were reserved, the tiered seating separating the simply wealthy from the ludicrously rich.

It wasn't what he remembered, the thunder of the crowd another sense that overstimulated a child. Eyes prickled his skin, their appraisals unapologetic as people sat open in the stalls, protected by a metal mesh. Higher above were the separate executive suites, the privacy glass protecting those hidden inside. He found Riley and Xander quickly, their glass remaining transparent as they both sat in expensive suits with a glass of amber liquid set on the table between them.

'You look good in a monkey suit,' Kace shot to Xee, unable to control his smirk.

Xander's expression remained the same, but his voice was grumpy when he replied. *'Fuck off and concentrate on the fight.'*

'Pull on my power if you need to balance your beast.' Riley's upper lip quipped, which meant Xander had added him to their mental connection. *'Stick to the plan.'*

'Which means don't die,' Xander added. *'For some*

reason Kyra has a soft spot for you and your death would really put a downer on my sex life.'

Kace didn't bother with a snarky reply, needing to concentrate on his opponents. Augustine's voice rumbled around the arena, his words similar to the opening ceremony. It wasn't until there were a few gasps that he finally listened.

"Fifteen fighters, and only ten will walk out alive. Let round one of the games begin!"

The fighters looked between one another, naturally separating into their own spaces as two beeps blurted above them all, distinctive and spaced a few seconds apart.

The ground rumbled beneath their feet, the sands jumping from the intense vibration as the grains began to split. Kace counted two podiums raising from the floor, ascending at different speeds as the fighters scrambled to get there first. One of the podiums shot up, revealing a long sword, the pommel a bold gold. The lone woman won, surprisingly fast as she wrapped her hand around the blade and pointed it towards her closest opponent.

"Back off!" she growled, shuffling until her back almost pressed against the metal mesh that surrounded them. A spark as her skin connected, her hand opening to release the sword which was quickly grabbed by someone else.

Kace remained where he was, watching the chaos around him as the fighters panicked. Both podiums began to descend as one, opening up the arena once more with no obstructions.

"No one explained this was to the death!" a voice screeched beside him. Kace turned to find a man, young, crouching in the corner. His chest was bare, body rippling with muscles too big for his frame. Scales covered the left side, blue and green pearlescent that glittered beneath the lights. He hadn't had scales earlier, which meant magic and glamour was being absorbed, or at least muted.

Kace tried to call to his arcane, his chi strangled as he failed to even light a spark with his fingers. It wasn't surprising, and nothing to worry about just yet. He never used his magic in the cages, and only barely when fighting Shadow-Veyn. He had always preferred the physical rather than the arcane that was amplified through the glyphs tattooed across his body. Glyphs he hoped were still working, otherwise everything was about to get a lot more interesting.

A flash of steel, the Fae with the scales screeching as a blade soared across the arena to slice into his chest. The momentum knocked him off his feet, his back connecting with the mesh. Electricity immediately stiffened his body, and Kace said nothing as the man who had killed him reached for the blade, grinning. The electricity shot into his palm before he even touched the metal, causing a high-pitched squeak to escape as he jumped back.

It left only one weapon at play, and four more deaths to go.

Two beeps, again the same distinctive sound that was high-pitched enough he felt it in his back teeth. This time he was ready for it, the ground rumbling as two more podiums began to rise, different from the ones before.

Kace shot off towards the closest, skidding to the edge just as a short dagger appeared inside.

"That's mine," a voice growled, a heavy body barrelling into his side with enough force to knock him away, allowing someone else to swipe the dagger from the podium. Kace turned, shoving the man to the sands as he jumped back up, barely missing the sharp edge of a blade. One of the benefits of already having fought in the Pits was Kace knew how to steady himself in sand, spreading his legs to better take his weight. His body was prepared, muscles reacting instinctively to keep him steady.

Many of the fighters didn't have the stability, their swings missing as they struggled with each individual grain moving beneath their feet. It gave him a little advantage, but not for long.

Kace dodged the fist that appeared, reaching up to grab the extended arm and pulling the fighter with their own momentum. It caused them to stumble, barrelling into someone else who was sneaking up behind.

Three more high-pitched beeps.

Three more podiums began to rise, their weapons quickly snapped up.

Blood soaked into the sands, and Kace wasn't sure how many had fallen. He took a second to sweep his gaze across the arena, blocking out the audience. Excluding the knife stuck in the barrier there were six weapons, and twelve fighters left.

If there was hesitation about the games before, they were long gone. Not when survival was the most basic instinct.

Kace spotted the lone woman fighter in the corner, a headless body at her feet. She had managed to obtain another sword, using it to keep everyone back while two others approached her with malevolent grins. It was the bleach blond and matching dark, their brown eyes now circled in red, and Kace's beast roused enough inside his mind to growl. He knew they weren't Daemons, his beast unable to sense anything from them before, but now they were something other. Something he couldn't identify.

A sharp pain across his chest. The leather he wore parting with ease along with his own flesh. He had been distracted, slower to react and it had cost him.

"Imagine Cillian killing the infamous Red," a man

snarled, slicing out with his sword once more. "Cillian would be the winner."

Kace bent back, the blade barely missing the edge of his nose before he was already moving, his arm coming out to knock against the flat of the blade. It placed him close enough he could grip his opponent's wrist, twisting hard enough to break.

The larger man hissed out a breath, his bone snapping with a crunch as his fingers loosened around the pummel enough for Kace to grab it. He recognised the bright orange hair and matching irises. He had never seen such a tall leprechaun, taller than even himself. He would have guessed it was a glamour, but every other magic in the arena was being restricted.

Pain seared down his chest, the wound that sliced from one pec down across his stomach bleeding profusely. It wouldn't kill him, but it also confirmed that not even his tattooed glyphs were working while he was in the arena.

Kace began to chuckle, the sound dark.

Definitely makes it much more interesting, he mused to himself.

"Fucking cunt!" the tall leprechaun screamed, cradling his wrist to his chest. It left him vulnerable, and Kace couldn't have cared less. "You hurt Cillian!"

"You're lucky," Kace rasped, remembering how his friend had reached for Eva. "If you were the other faerie, I would have cut off your fucking hand."

The leprechaun's eyes widened, mouth opening with a reply, but Kace was already moving, sprinting across the arena with the sword clutched tightly in his palm.

EVA

Eva couldn't tear her eyes away from the arena, the clash of flesh and steel sickening along with the lingering scent of copper. She knew it wasn't from the sands below, but from the security she had accidently killed. His body had been removed, and despite there being no evidence, his blood was still there in the grains of the wooden floor. It made the aggression from the fighters that more real, as if they cared so little about another's life.

"Beautiful, isn't it." Augustine stood behind his desk, the entire wall made from glass. Eva hadn't noticed it before, not until he clicked a button and the wall shimmered, turning transparent. "The power to end someone so easily. I'm sure you understand, considering."

Eva swallowed the bile that burned up her throat. She hadn't felt powerful, the exact opposite in fact. She had felt so small, so weak that she was forced to hurt someone for just a little control over herself. What was worse was there was no guilt, nothing for her to seek penance for taking a life. "Yes," she said, the lie easy. "I've never felt anything like it."

She wasn't any better than those who fought with little hesitation on the sands.

"It's addictive, that feeling. You'll start to crave it, and then with age you'll understand that it's nothing but your nature." Augustine took the seat beside her, his hand reaching out to grab her wrist. "Our kind is told to suppress our instincts, but you'll soon learn that we should embrace it."

Eva nodded, knowing he faced her rather than the fighting below. She tried to keep her eyes off Kace, finding herself clenching her fists so tightly her knuckles cracked when she saw his blood tip the end of a sword. She forced herself to relax, to look elsewhere but always found her attention drift back to him. He moved like liquid, each twist and parry as elegant as any dancer.

"It's exciting you, isn't it?" A brush of his thumb along her jaw. "Watching them fight. Watching them die."

She knew if she were human her pulse would have given her away, and it was the first time she was grateful for the vampiric stillness. On the outside she was perfectly calm, but inside she was a storm.

"Do we stay here the whole time?" she asked, hoping he heard interest in her voice.

His thumb drifted down the side of her throat. "You will stay wherever I am, and at the moment I will be staying on site until we are back to full operation. These games are a new concept to help get us back to where we were, before we were shut down by The Council."

"Why were you shut down before?" *Despite the fucking obvious.*

"It doesn't matter because it won't happen again. The Council will no longer be an issue." Augustine's attention burned the side of her face, his thumb pressing. "If the games are a success, we should be back to full capacity within the week. Betting is where the real money is made, and before the arena would carry around five hundred people. Each would bet, and most would lose."

"And then you would auction off the losers," Eva added quietly.

"Only if they survived. Which most don't." A chuckle. "You learn about people here, secrets even the rich and powerful can't hide. Being able to watch, bet and sometimes participate brings out the most primal of personalities. It brings out their most basic desires. We allow people to be who they truly are, and it's why the Pits are the most successful fighting arena in the world."

Eva clenched her fist in her lap as Kace dodged another

swipe of a sword. If she wasn't careful Augustine would see. "They're able to participate?" She finally turned, his face closer than expected.

"Of course. With enough money they can take one of the reserved Units into our private room."

"And they fight?"

"Sometimes, and sometimes it's just about pain."

Sometimes it's just about pain. Eva tried to conceal the dread that gripped her chest. She had already been hurt beyond what she thought survivable, but being surrounded by such glorified violence was somehow worse.

His smile was cruel, as if he could see through her guise. "Watch the fight."

The demand in his tone set her on edge, but she followed it anyway, finding Kace quickly on the sands. He was across the arena, a sword gripped in his fist as he fought two men at once. Heart in her throat, Eva watched as blood coated the entirety of his chest, his face carefully controlled. The swords clashed, the clang echoing as he defended each swipe without making any advances of his own.

What was he doing?

It was hard to keep composed, to not react as the blades got precariously close to Kace's throat, his opponents movements frenzied. He had plenty of opportunities to make the final strike, but he always pulled back at the last moment. They needed one more death to end the round, and Eva spotted a third fighter sneaking up behind him, a dagger gripped firmly in his fist.

Eva shot to her feet, her palm pressed to the window as the third fighter made his move. Kace pivoted at the last second, the dagger missing his back only to land in the chest of another.

Augustine had remained seated. "Perfect."

Eva couldn't hear anything past the roar inside her

head. Her fangs throbbed, her stomach tightened. The lights around her began to brighten, her eyesight sharpening as one by one the podiums ascended, a light beacon that seemed to pulsate until a weapon was placed inside. As soon as the podium was full, it immediately dropped to the floor, so fast the fighters had to jump back or risk losing their toes.

She waited a few seconds, watching as the survivors were beckoned back through the oversized double doors before she returned to Augustine.

"Perfect," he repeated, his eyes swelling until black. She suspected her eyes were the same. "You're overexcited, which can cause bloodlust. It makes you dangerous, your desire for blood and death overwhelming until your thirst has been sated. Don't worry, the urge will lessen as you age. Sometimes."

He was right, she craved blood to the point she imagined tearing his throat out with her fangs. Imagined sinking her face into the gaping hole she had caused and drinking her fill. Her sight had heightened even further, along with her sense of smell which meant the lingering blood of the security only made the thirst worse. She could make out the slight bumps beneath his skin where his veins were, and count every slow beat of his pulse. It was a siren's call, and it excited her.

It scared her.

"Now I will feed you before you kill another one of my security." He shrugged out of his jacket before rolling up the sleeve of his left arm, holding his wrist up to her.

Eva stiffened, forcing herself to not grab it.

Augustine's smile was harsh. "Your control is impressive, I forget sometimes that you're still so young. Now, come here." It was a demand.

Eva reached for his wrist, but he pulled it back to his chest as soon as she was close.

"On your knees." He sat back in his chair, legs slightly spread with his wrist resting in between. "Now." He faced the glass, still transparent. She had no idea whether anyone else could see inside, could see her humiliation.

Eva closed her eyes as she sank to her knees, only opening them when she was sure she had calmed down. She needed to remain composed, otherwise she risked everything.

His blood tasted vile on her tongue, especially now she had others to compare it to. He tasted of death, rot and smoke, his blood lacking energy as she sucked in long drags.

She heard the door click open to the office, and rather than pull back Augustine held her down by his wrist.

"Hey there, pretty lady."

"Dutch," Augustine greeted. "How much?"

"One million was bet, with six-hundred thousand kept by the house. It seems your favourite really made a statement considering he didn't kill anyone."

Eva forced herself to slow her swallowing.

"We made money either way," Augustine said, his grip tight in her hair. "And six on opening night is more than we could have ever hoped. I assume our classic performance has started?"

Eva recoiled as something brushed against her back, but she was unable to see anything but Augustine.

"You were right, everyone seems to be staying for the classic, and I've just heard that we're already at capacity through the Troll Market entrance. Membership is up fifty percent. I've just heard from Bishop, and he's impressed."

"Did you ever really doubt me?" Augustine finally released her head, and Eva shot back on her heels. "We have any issues?"

"No, but I found something interesting in the locker room." Dutch grinned, which brought her attention to his mouth and jaw which were stained red. "It seems the fighters wanted a little party before the big fight." He pulled out three silver canisters, his thumb brushing over the engraving of a skull with horns, a black 'X' crossed through the image.

Augustine caught one when Dutch tossed it to him, dismissing it almost immediately. "It will make them more aggressive, which can only be a good thing. You figured out where they're coming from yet?"

"Working on it." Dutch lifted one of the cannisters to his nostril, his nail piercing the metal. The cannister wheezed as he inhaled the entire thing. "This stuff is fucking good." He dropped his gaze to Eva, and the look in his eyes wasn't friendly.

She climbed to her feet, trying to ignore the new cries and screams through the glass. Curiosity got the better of her when she looked back out over the arena, the crowd having almost tripled in the stalls. They roared and cheered, almost drowning out the sounds from the two who fought below.

One was Hunter.

Eva couldn't stop her own cry as she turned to Augustine. "He's a child!"

Augustine slowly lowered his sleeve, buttoning his cufflink before reaching for his jacket. "A child who wanted to fight, and now he is." He stepped up beside her, watching as Hunter scrambled to get away from the man twice his size. "Did you really think I wouldn't notice he was the one I found you in front of downstairs?"

"Compassion is a weakness," Dutch added, the edge of his irises already teasing red. "We cannot have any weaknesses in the Vipers."

"I'm not a Viper," she snapped, realising what she said a second too late.

Augustine cocked his head, and when he smiled she knew there was nothing she could do as she watched Hunter fight to survive on the sands.

CHAPTER 21
KACE

K ace immediately moved to the medical cabinet, conscious of the other fighters close behind his heels. It was every man for themselves, which meant he had to watch his back at all times.

"You're going to need stitches," someone said, but Kace ignored them as he searched through the drawers until he found something to wipe the blood from his chest. It had finally stopped bleeding, the blood itchy as it flaked with every movement. He still couldn't feel his chi entirely, which meant whatever was blocking the magic wasn't localised to the arena floor. It also meant the cut that started on his right pec and sliced down his stomach wouldn't heal by the next round.

He could still feel his beast though, the fucker forever present in his mind.

"What the fuck just happened?" the only woman barked, pacing from one side of the locker room to the other. She had caught a fist to the face, her left eye socket broken and bruised. "I didn't sign up for this shit." She looked at her hand, frowning at her palm.

"As if you didn't know," someone replied, a man with

darkened scars crisscrossing his shoulders in such a way they looked decorative rather than accidental. "It's what the Pits are famous for."

"Cillian didn't expect that," the bright haired leprechaun said, holding his arm against his chest carefully. He shot Kace a scowl, placing himself in the corner of the room. "Cillian was told only to fight, not to kill."

"You sure as hell didn't hesitate," the first fighter said. "But it looks like we're all stuck in this fucking situation so we may as well get familiar before we slit each other's throats. My name's Gus." He pressed his palm to his chest, his ring finger missing.

"You shouldn't joke about getting your throat slit," Kace grumbled. "It isn't fun." He looked up with a straight face. "I would know."

Gus wasn't sure whether he was joking or not, his dark eyes narrowing slightly as his upper lift lifted to show his fangs. "What about you?" he grunted at the woman.

"Mikayla." The woman clicked her fingers, still frowning. "Fuck," she whispered to herself, and Kace suspected a witch, or at least a mage. She couldn't call her magic, which would put her at a large disadvantage.

"Cillian doesn't give a fuck about your names," the leprechaun growled.

"Says the guy who speaks in third person," rumbled the guy with the slight Daemonic aura. The red around his irises had faded almost entirely as he scrubbed a hand down his face. He was the bleach blonde, while his dark-haired friend stood to the side, equally as tired. His eyes were still red, but the sense of 'other' his beast had detected had disappeared from them both. "We're not here to make friends."

"No shit." Mikayla chuckled darkly. "What about you?" she asked the man with scars on his shoulders.

"None of your fucking business," he growled. Possible shifter, but in reality it was difficult to recognise a Breed without a blatant tell.

There were three more fighters who were yet to speak, with two sitting on the benches by their belongings. One leaned back as he watched everyone calmly, someone who clearly wasn't deterred by the death. His face and chest were splattered with red, his eyes hard when they met Kace's.

The other man who sat a few seats away was muttering to himself, touching the deep slice across his cheek. Grabbing a spare pack of antiseptic wipes Kace threw it, the pack landing by his feet.

"Thanks," he grunted, not offering up his name as he hissed at the first stroke of the wipe.

The last man was as pale as snow, eyes wide as he nervously licked his lips. "I don't know about any of you, but I'm out of here."

Kace moved himself closer to the exit, placing his back against the wall.

"I don't think that's an option," Scar-man grunted.

"They can't stop me!"

"Actually, we can," one of the security who had first taken them to the locker room said as he stepped inside. "Congratulations to the winners of the first round, I'm sure you're all exhausted and wish to clean yourselves up in the connected washroom. I will also be escorting you to your accommodation for the entirety of the games."

"I don't give a flying fuck about any accommodation. I want out!" The last man stepped closer to the security guard, who quickly whipped out a gun.

"Number Five, once you enter the games, there is only one way out. It had already been agreed with your sponsors when they paid the buy in."

"Who the fuck is Number Five? Fuck you! Get out of my way!"

More security entered, a wall of authority with guns.

"Number Five, I must ask you to step back."

"I said get out my fucking way!" the man screamed, claws piercing through his clenched fists as he jumped at the closest security. They all scrambled to subdue him, not one actually using their weapons.

Kace slipped out the door, quickly moving down the corridor while everyone remained distracted. He was sure he would be disciplined for moving out of the dedicated quarters, but then again there wasn't a rule strictly forbidding him from exploring.

Riley had been uncomfortable agreeing for him to stay on site for the duration of the games, but Kace had assured him it was for the best. It would give him three full days inside the Pits, and he knew he wouldn't get another opportunity to infiltrate the place that ruined his mind, body and soul.

The corridors were dark, and it wasn't long until he found the arena, the thunder of the crowd pulling him towards the light. He knew nothing of the layout, Titus unable to find anything on the new structure.

The audience had tripled, screaming and cheering as they watched and bet on the hand-to-hand fight. The slap of flesh on flesh was so familiar it put his beast at ease, but from his vantage point he couldn't make out who was on the sands. Not when his eyes were immediately drawn to Eva on the highest floor opposite, her hand pressed to the glass as she watched with such focus.

A frustrated growl from his beast, and Kace quickly snarled back, trying to suppress the fucker to the back of his mind.

'Calm down.' Riley's voice was crystal clear, calming

the beast's spike in temper to a subtler simmer. *'I can feel your beast pressing for release.'*

'It seems our curse isn't affected by the magical block,' Kace shot back the same way. He moved away from the edge, dragging his eyes away from Eva to find both Xander and Riley on the floor below. *'Did you guys find out anything while I was on the sands?'*

It was Xander who answered. *'You're all numbered from one to fifteen. You're Number Thirteen.'*

Good thing Kace didn't believe in bad luck.

'You all came out from a different entrance to the Units,' Xander continued. *'There's five scheduled fights for today with eight more planned tomorrow after your event.'*

Even through the mental connection Kace could hear the concern in his voice. *'You're not telling me something.'*

Silence as he ascended the closest stairs, climbing the floors until he reached the correct floor. It brought him back out towards the arena, each exclusive room closed as Kace walked behind them in a circle, stopping once he counted the right one.

"What the fuck is going on?" he growled as he stepped inside, closing the door quickly behind him. The room was small, dark with only two high-backed leather chairs.

Riley quickly stood, mouth set in a grim line when he turned. "We didn't expect them to call him out yet, he wasn't on the schedule."

Kace took a step forward, looking through the glass. "What are you..." He found Hunter on his knees, panting as the assistant dragged away his unconscious opponent. Rage immediately burned, and not even Riley could calm him down.

"We've already put an offer in to buy him, we're just waiting on a response."

"He fought great, you've taught him well," Xander added. "We'll get him out."

Kace was rigid as blood rushed in his ears, his beast pressing against his mind. He was scratching to be released, to destroy everything in his path until his fur was slick with blood, and death was the only fragrance.

He would not allow Hunter to suffer as he did. To carry the deaths and guilt of those killed. Murdered.

Red at the edge of his vision, the handle breaking in his palm, the metal bending as if it were made from soft plastic while his brothers voices buzzed inside his head, louder, but no less incoherent.

'That's enough!' Riley's voice finally broke through, his own beast pressing until Kace felt the heaviness of its dominance. They weren't shifters, and didn't have a typical hierarchy system like those that shared their bodies with animals. But they did have an alpha, Riley who was the first of them to be cursed with his beast. He was stronger, bigger and more in sync with the man.

Normally it would have made Kace hesitate, Riley's words alone able to bring him back from the edge. But it seemed he was beyond reason.

Or maybe he was just as fucked up as his beast.

The door cracked when he pulled it open, his muscles rigid as he stepped out... only to come toe-to-toe with Eva. And just like that his black rage quietened.

Mine.

Fuck.

"Red, I didn't realise you would be here." Augustine stood to the side, along with a large security guard. "Fighters are supposed to remain in their quarters until the next game," he said, failing to hide his annoyance with a slight pinch of his eyebrows.

Kace blinked, forcing himself back into the room, his

muscles rigid as he fought the urge to kill. His beast tore and shredded inside his mind as Eva disappeared out of view, immediately calming once she moved into the room too.

With her there it gave him time to breathe, time to think.

"Mr Storm," Augustine said with a professional smile, dismissing Kace. "I thought I would personally congratulate you on your win."

Riley returned the professional smile, his mind still connected to Kace's. Soothing, or at least trying to. "Always bet on your own," he said with a grin, and only those who knew him well could hear the stress in his tone. *'We will save him, K. But if you react with violence right now, you will kill him,'* he added telepathically.

Riley was right, but Kace was beyond words, only managing a jagged nod.

Augustine's smile tightened. "Unfortunately, despite your generous offer, I must tell you your bid to buy Unit 4576 has been denied."

Xander flicked his gaze to Kace, but he remained exactly where he was.

"I'll double the offer," Riley said.

"He's not for sale," Augustine replied smoothly. "You are unable to buy the winning Units. When he loses, you'll be able to make your offer then."

Riley reached for his glass, seemingly relaxed despite the underlying tension. "I've bought a winner before."

"Exceptional circumstances, and we both know I was not present the last time you graced my establishment with your presence. Now, I'm happy to discuss this further over a drink, and maybe we can discuss your fighter in a little bit more detail?"

Riley sipped the edge of his glass. "Sure, I could use the company. Let's hope the next couple fights last longer." He clicked at Xander, who took his position up as Riley's security. It was all a con, giving the illusion Augustine expected. In reality Riley could easily defend himself, being one of the most dangerous men in the city.

Augustine smiled, sitting in Xander's vacant leather chair. "Floyd," he said, lounging back. "Escort my fledgling back to our bedroom and get us a bottle of whisky. We may be here a while."

Eva stiffened, and only because Kace was staring did he notice the slight tremble in her lip. "I know my way back," she said, her tone strained. "I don't need an escort."

Augustine gave her a pointed glare. "We all know what happened to your last escort." When she remained where she was Augustine chuckled. "Fine, we shall see if you can be trusted. Go, before I change my mind."

Eva dropped her gaze to the floor. "Master," she said as Kace let out a growl, unable to stop the sound.

Mine.

CHAPTER 22

EVA

Eva had waited. Five minutes. Fifteen. At thirty she couldn't wait any longer, walking the tunnels until she descended to the fighters' quarters. She knew Kace had left the executive suite not long after her, but he hadn't found her like she had anticipated.

This is bullshit, she thought. *I don't chase after fucking boys.*

She hadn't expected to see him so soon after the first game, his face creased with such rage that she almost didn't recognise him. His attention had been intense, his eyes burning along her skin as she checked out the wounds on his chest, the slices deep and raw.

He was more hurt than she initially thought.

Anxiety wrapped its icy fingers around her throat, turning her lungs to cement. She stopped just as she pushed open the door to the locker room, hesitating. He probably didn't want to see her.

Shit.

Well, she *needed* to see him. He was the only chance she had to escape, so he needed to suck it up.

Please, please, please be alone, she prayed to herself,

hoping the other fighters had already moved on. *Please, to whoever created this shit-show that's my life, let me have this one thing.*

Relaxing her shoulders she stepped into the locker room, which was thankfully empty. *Oh, thank God.* She wasn't sure what she would have done if the other fighters were still hanging around, she didn't have a plan B. Not that she really had a plan A, either.

Eva hadn't had a chance to look around, but she knew it consisted of the locker room, an attached shower room and a separate sleeping area where the security usually slept when on site.

She could hear water through the wall, walking past the little cubicles full of bags, coats and other random stuff to the door that led into the showers. Knowing she didn't have long she stepped inside, the room warm and misty as she searched the open space.

His silhouette was at the back, head resting forward with both hands pressed against the tile as water cascaded over his very much naked skin.

Fuck. Me.

Eva knew she should look away, but she couldn't help but stare, his body built with such defined muscles he looked like an artist's depiction of the perfect man. Intricate black and red markings patterned down the entirety of his left side, tattoos she itched to explore in detail if he wasn't such a moody arsehole.

She hadn't seen his body before, and she definitely felt cheated of the experience. Her eyes drifted up his strong back, over his wide shoulders to where his red hair plastered to his head, the strands darkening to almost black.

It took her longer to realise that blood stained the water by his legs, and she realised the wounds on his chest had opened and were bleeding freely against the strength of the spray.

Cold coiled itself around her stomach when she looked up, only to be met with narrowed green eyes.

"You're hurting yourself," she said, gesturing to the water. It was the one time she wished she hadn't had fed, the blood she took from Augustine earlier only highlighting her embarrassment at being caught gawking at him like some sex crazed weirdo. Just because he had given her the best orgasm of her life did not mean she wanted to do it again.

She didn't. Probably.

Stop it Eva!

He turned the water off, and she made sure she concentrated on his face when he turned and not on what hung below. He was a mountain as he stalked closer, his feet somehow silent on the slick tiles. She braced for him, but instead of stopping he slipped past, moving into the locker room and leaving a smear of red in his wake.

"Honestly, you're insufferable," she muttered as she followed, almost running into his back when he suddenly stopped and reached for a towel, wrapping it around his hips as he turned to face her.

"What are you doing?" he growled. "Do you know what you've risked by coming here?"

Eva blinked, dumfounded at his tone. "Who do you think you're talking to?" she shot back. "I came because you were hurt and we need to discuss Hunter."

"I'm fine, and he will be fine when I get him out of here." His words came out cold. "Go back to your *Master*."

Tears burned her eyes, and it infuriated her more that her body's natural response with anger was to cry. "Fuck you!" She went to shove his chest, pulling back at the last minute before her palms could connect. "Fuck you! Fuck you! Fuck you!"

"Quiet." Kace reached forward and gripped her wrists, yanking her closer until she almost touched his raw skin anyway. "Eva, you need to leave. Don't push me right now, I'm so fucking close to losing it," he said as he released her, his next words closer to a whisper. "I'm trying not to hurt you."

Eva licked across her lips. "You wouldn't hurt me." She was sure of it, despite the rage that still carved vicious lines into his face. "Why didn't you kill those other fighters?"

Kace frowned, lashes dropping to hide the expression in his eyes. She wasn't sure whether he would answer, but after a heartbeat he seemed to just let out a breath, leaning down to rest his face in her hair. Eva froze, unsure what to do as he gradually relaxed, his muscles not as stiff.

"You shouldn't have come here," he said, softer his time.

"You had a sword, yet you pulled every strike. Why?"

"Because there's such a fine line, and I would rather not tempt fate."

Kace finally shifted back, and just like that she immediately wanted to close the gap up again, missing his warmth that was a blanket along her skin.

"Sit down," she said in what she hoped was an equally soft one, despite the butterflies. She wasn't sure how she felt about his answer, but she still couldn't watch him standing there hurting.

Kace crossed his arms, pressing the wounds on his chest. "It's fine, I don't need help."

"Look, I know we don't exactly like each other, but stop being a baby and let me at least clean it up." She reached forward, intending to pull his arm away when the tattoos on his skin began to glow. Eva snapped her hand back, and when she looked up Kace just stared, his face composed into a careful mask.

He didn't say anything as she slowly moved closer, and once again the tattoos closest to her fingertips brightened.

"Eva," he warned, his voice strained.

He had stilled beneath her palm, a warm statue that was strung so taut. Eva couldn't help herself as she traced the intricate designs down his left arm, tugging at his wrist to reveal the wounds that sliced across his chest. "You need stitches," she said quietly, as if she had any medical experience. "It could get infected or..."

"They will heal on their own," he said, his deep, rich voice a low grumble that was pure temptation. "I've survived worse."

Eva looked up, and beneath those forest green eyes she glimpsed something else, something filled with such predatory force it pinned her to the spot. And then he blinked, and the green swirled into a liquid silver that only heightened the tension between them.

It wasn't Kace who looked back at her, not completely.

She swallowed, and his eyes dipped to follow the movement of her throat.

"Eva..." It was a final warning, her name an echo of dark threats, and even darker promises.

It was less than a heartbeat before he decided for her, his lips crashing down to shape them perfectly to hers, his tongue sweeping in with force as his hands wrapped painfully in her hair. He was ruthless, taking from her with a intensified violence that she welcomed like a woman starved. It was a clashing of teeth, of tongue and souls as her fang accidently nipped his lip. His moan vibrated into her mouth as he angled her specifically so she would cut him again, his blood ambrosia compared to everything else.

Steel. Rain. Ember.

That's what she tasted with Kace.

He was pure, unapologetic power that washed away her sins, and gave her the strength that was stolen. Kace kissed as if he could consume her, as if nothing mattered but his lips on hers and she wanted to drown in him until she forgot everything else. But she couldn't forget, not when a child's life was at risk. Not when Kace's life was at risk.

Eva slowed the kiss, savouring the connection until she stopped entirely. Kace pulled back, only to rest his forehead against hers. It was too much, too intimate for two people who were thrown together by some fucked up fate.

"That wasn't supposed to happen," she said, her voice humiliatingly hoarse as she squeezed her eyes shut. "I've got to get back."

Kace wasn't listening, his little impatient growl causing her to melt when he kissed her again, his fingers tightening in her hair as if he was scared she would run.

Eva enjoyed it for the barest of seconds before cupping his jaw, knowing her next sentence would ruin everything. "I have to get back to Augustine's bed."

He tensed beneath her touch, his hands releasing the strands of her hair until she missed the slight pain. She opened her eyes just as he drew up to his full height, his face carved from stone. His irises were the same startling shade of silver they were before, only there was no heat left in his gaze, only anger.

Of course he's angry, she thought. *I'm in the bed of his enemy.*

"Hunter is being kept two floors below this one." The words came out in a rush, panic tightening her chest as she nervously stroked down the vipers on her arms. "There's stairs leading down in the southern tunnel, but the cells are reinforced, and I haven't found the key."

Kace remained silent, and before she humiliated herself

further by crying, she turned towards the door, needing to get away before the panic and disappointment consumed her entirely.

———————

Eva had managed to compose herself by the time she made it back to the bedroom, Augustine nowhere in sight as she rushed to the en-suite. She had never suffered a panic attack before, and wasn't even sure if it were possible as a vampire. But she had felt panicked, her breathing coming in such spasmodic exhales that as a human she would have surely passed out.

Get it together, woman!

She had been through too much shit to allow anyone the satisfaction of seeing her so distressed. She glared at herself in the bathroom mirror, frowning at the loose strands of hair around her face. Her skin was unblemished, a pale colour that was only emphasised by the natural pink of her lips. There was no swelling, no evidence of Kace's kiss.

The door to the bedroom opened with a click, and Eva swallowed the sudden dread. Reaching over she turned on the shower, stepping in fully dressed. The water was freezing, cold enough it bit at her skin in sharp little nips. She waited for the shivers that never came, her new body dealing with the cold easily, as she waited for the water to wash away any evidence left on her clothes.

A few seconds passed, her eyes holding the open space between the bathroom and bedroom until a dark figure appeared, followed by another. Eva flicked her attention between The two Vipers, continuing to stand beneath the heavy spray.

Dutch grinned, while Augustine's eyes turned dark with impatience.

"Why is Dutch here?" she asked, remaining in the shower as if the water was a protective barrier. "I thought you didn't share."

Shut up, Eva! she scolded herself, immediately regretting the words. She knew she was about to be forced into something that could destroy her completely, and it looked like her natural reaction was defiance. There were worse ways to respond to the fight or flight response, she supposed. At least when he took her she would be as cold as the dead. Which was exactly what she felt inside.

I hope you get frostbite on your dick! The image softened her panic, her breathing back under control.

Augustine blurred as he pulled her from the shower, ripping her dress down the middle with one tug. Eva held back her flinch as the sodden fabric fell to her feet, leaving her in matching black lace underwear with gold snake detailing. His hand cupped around her throat, his thumb pressing the centre until it crushed her vocal cord.

"You should respect the clothes I provide you," Augustine said, his voice edged with irritation. "The water has ruined it."

Eva was unable to respond, her nails searing down his arm as she tried to break free. They broke skin, but still Augustine didn't budge.

"If you treat everything with such disregard then maybe I will make you wear nothing at all."

Eva stopped struggling, dropping her arms as he pulled her into the bedroom, his hand remaining tight until he pushed her to sit on the edge of the bed.

"She's losing her fight," Dutch said from the doorway. "Disappointing."

"Fuck you," she rasped, unable to stop the curse.

Augustine stared, his eyes sweeping across her exposed skin. It was foul, his attention like hornets crawling. His hand was deceivingly soft when he brushed it along her shoulder, finger teasing the strap of her bra as she fought the urge to react with violence.

"Will you scream for me?" he whispered, fingers continuing their journey down.

Eva froze, panic swelling low in her stomach once more. "No," she said between gritted teeth.

His eyes shot up, the inky depths showing her fate.

But she had already decided she would fight fate every step of the way.

Her body tensed, hands curling into fists as her fangs pierced into her bottom lip. She knew she had little chance of winning, but she could still make him hurt.

Dutch cocked his head as if he could read her mind, his smile spreading as he chuckled in a manic way. He stepped closer as if to join before a bang rattled the floor. Augustine whipped around, barking orders at Dutch who had already moved towards the noise.

"Stay here," he demanded her, disappearing after his nephew.

Eva sagged against the bedsheets, arms shaking as she covered her face.

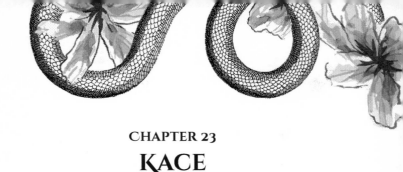

CHAPTER 23
KACE

J ust like the first round, the audience were morosely calm as they waited for the remaining fighters to step on to their designated 'X's' on the edge of the arena. Curiosity of the game's event quieting the fighters too.

'I have to get back to Augustine's bed.' Eva's words had caught him off-guard, and even his beast was outraged into silence. Crimson had teased his vision, and he had almost lost it entirely, the edge of sanity calling him into its dark depths. He jerked himself back from the oblivion, the crimson gradually residing until he could think of anything other than death and destruction, but by then she was gone. His beast hadn't understood why he didn't allow them to fall, not realising he would risk not only Eva in his actions, but Hunter too.

There had been no delay to the day's show, not that he expected there would be considering the bomb he had set off created only minor damage. It was shockingly easy to make something go pop with little supplies, especially considering he had smuggled in a few temperamental crystals. What many people didn't realise was that red tiger eyes were highly reactive under the right circumstances. Kace had forced his aura into the small stones, more than they could handle. When met with a catalyst such as a flame they burst, and the concentrated arcane he had forced them to hold escaped with a satisfying bang. Not that he allowed himself to express himself in bombs very often. At least nothing more than a small, inconvenient pop.

There was something so satisfying in watching things explode, and sometimes it was enough to keep his beast at bay when there was a break in physical fights.

'Looks like an obstacle course,' Riley's voice drifted into his mind, acknowledging the structure that had been added to the arena overnight. *'There are lower platforms that you may not see from your position, open beneath the construction. Some pits with spikes.'*

'Noted,' Kace replied the same way, spreading the telepathic connection as he looked up expecting to see his brothers, but instead was met with reflective glass. *'Tell me Sythe is already inside. We need to push up the plan.'*

'What happened?' It was Xander who replied, his tone sharp. *'Eva isn't with Augustine, which messes up the fucking plan.'*

'Sythe has been and gone,' Riley added. *'Three implanted and charged.'*

Kace let out a steady breath, thankful that his brother was able to sneak into the most secure areas unnoticed. A fucking ninja. *'And the others?'*

'Everyone is placed at the exits, ready to assist with the evacuation.'

'Good. You have until the end of this round, make it count.' Kace felt his eyes shift to those of his beast, and he decided to leave them as they were. Mikayla frowned when she looked his way, sparks brightened her fingertips.

Rolling his shoulders he called on his chi, the arcane burning in his palm. He had full access to his magic, which meant they had lifted the ban. At least temporarily. Cillian realised at the same time, smile widening as his wild magic tickled Kace's nose.

'K, we need to discuss...'

'You guys grab Eva, I doubt she's far from Augustine.' Kace interrupted just as Augustine began his opening speech over the tannoy. *'I'll find Hunter.'*

"And we have come to the second round of our new annual games," Augustine said, his presence presented in the only transparent window. "This one is simple, the first five to reach the top wins, and the others will fall to the traps below." At his words the ground rumbled, the sand separating as the platform began to rise up in a spiral. The arena opened up the basement, making the entire five-floor course over forty meters tall.

"What the fuck is this?" Scarface whispered to himself, his foot slipping off his dedicated 'X.'

A loud beep, followed by a sharp whoosh of air.

Scarface grunted, a sharp wooden stake impaled through his thigh.

"Someone's eager," Augustine chuckled. "The obstacle course is covered in booby traps, just like the one Number Eight set off. Each floor has been magically enhanced, which means there will be no advantages. Everyone is equal, and only the most ambitious will survive."

All the fighters stilled, making sure they were all within their spaces while Scarface touched the edge of the stake still protruding from his leg.

"Leave it or you'll bleed out well before you reach the top," Kace said without taking his eyes off the obstacle course. He was trying to memorise every jump and trap, but even as he watched the course was shifting, always changing.

For fuck's sake.

"No shit," Scar-face grunted, his skin slick with a slight sheen.

Two beeps blurted above them all, distinctive and spaced a few seconds apart. Kace braced, ready to jump to the first floor.

"Ten fighters, and only five will walk out alive," Augustine finished. "Let round two of the games begin."

EVA

Eva remained quiet as Dutch lead her further into the tunnels, descending the levels rather than ascending to the office. Augustine hadn't made it back to the bedroom the night before, but she hadn't allowed herself to relax, even for a moment. Not when she was so unsettled, the inevitable its own torture, worse than any of the physical beatings she had endured so far.

Dutch had explained Augustine preferred the fear, of her waiting, not knowing when he would complete his promise. It was only now that dread coated her tongue like a vile fur that she understood what he had meant. Anxiety chipped away, taking a piece of her each passing hour she waited, not knowing until there would be nothing left for him to take.

"Your master has set up a little surprise for you," Dutch said, turning his head so she caught his grin. "You should enjoy it, and if not... well. I don't care." He pushed open a door, an ouroboros carved into the heavy metal.

Inside was a highbacked metal chair, thick straps open

on both the arms and legs. The wall beside it displayed bright silver instruments, each hung neatly and in perfect symmetry. Drills, saws, knives and some things that looked closer to horror movie props than equipment, Dutch reaching over to click a circular blade that opened up to reveal several more blades inside, each spinning at a different speed.

"No!" Eva recoiled before Dutch pulled her inside.

"You're going to have a little fun," he said as weak growls filled the tunnel. He pinned her with a stare, Eva backing herself into the corner as heels tapped, click, click, click that was white noise to the increasing panicked cries.

Eva's head jerked up just in time to see a flash of dark hair holding a long metal pole, Hunter sluggishly fighting the attachment around his throat. Hana shoved him into the chair, her fingertips glowing as he stiffened beneath her touch. She made quick work of the straps, and only when she stepped back, releasing the pole did he sag in the bonds, jaw resting against his chest.

Thump. Thump. Thump. Hunter's heartbeat was slow and lethargic compared to Hana's increased, excited rhythm.

Dutch pressed himself closer, breath cold against her ear. "You hold your humanity too closely. You can never truly embrace your new life when you're still clinging to mercy."

Eva jolted forward, her reflexes naturally twisting herself around Dutch before he could grab her. She pressed herself to the other wall, a stack of metal drawers displaying a row of sharp, pointy things separating them.

"Don't do anything you'll regret," Hana added with a laugh. "Everything is metal, which is ineffective against my mate."

"But not against you." Eva mumbled without thought.

She saw the palm before it made contact, able to grab Hana's wrist with little effort. Hana gasped, and Eva realised she had been able to blur her movements.

A sharp pain along her arm, but rather than release her grip she squeezed tighter, feeling the bones beneath Hana's skin groan.

"You little bitch!" Hana screeched, the lines of her tattoos burning, the pain increasing with every passing second.

Dutch cocked his head. "Only wood can truly damage one of our Breed, it creates a reaction to our blood similar to how shifters react to silver and Fae to iron. We believe it's because wood is able to absorb natural magic from the earth. I'm sure you remember the pain of the stake from last time? That's the magic that the wood absorbed when alive attacking the virus within your cells. It's excruciating."

Dutch grinned, and Hana chuckled.

"No steel, glass or compound can harm us for long. But wood, wood takes us a while to heal. There's a reason we're known as almost immortals."

Emphasis on the 'almost,' Eva thought, wondering what other ways she could kill him. Not many things could live without a head.

She finally released Hana, who immediately snarled, holding her wrist to her chest. "You'll regret that," she hissed, and the pain along Eva's tattoos doubled.

Eva let out a shriek, rubbing down her arms as if she could remove the tattoos by force, but nothing stopped the agonising ache as if serrated, rusty blades were being sliced over and over along her skin.

"Hana!" Dutch growled, and the pain stopped immediately.

"When do I get a little fun?" she purred, strutting over

until she could stroke her hand down his chest, her fingers dancing along his belt. "Will you play with me?"

Dutch leaned down to kiss her viciously, his fangs tearing across her lips as she moaned, pressing herself closer. When he pulled away he licked across her face, collecting the blood that had pooled along her jaw.

"Show Augustine's fledgling how it's done, or you'll be the one in the chair."

Hana pursed her lips, the small cuts still bleeding. "You promise?" After one more kiss Dutch left, locking the thick door behind him.

Hunter groaned, his head rolling on his shoulders.

"Looks like it's time to start," Hana said in her ridiculously high voice. She brushed her hand along the instruments on the wall, almost caressing the shiny metal until she stopped at a small scalpel. "Shall I carve some pretty lines? I know he's a shifter, so if we add salt after I'm done, he will permanently scar." Her eyes brightened with excitement. "What do you think?"

"You're not touching him," Eva hissed.

Hana smiled as she raised her hand, and something tickled Eva's nose before pain so strong it forced her to her knees with a gasp.

"Did you really think those runes I tattooed meant nothing?" she giggled, gripping the scalpel in her other hand. "They give me complete control over you."

Eva cried out as the pain changed, twisting and turning beneath her skin. It started in her arms, slowly sweeping across her body until everything hurt. And just as suddenly as it started, the pain stopped.

Eva collapsed, body trembling as she recovered.

"Please, no!" Hunter's scream echoed around her, the scent of his blood piercing the air as Hana sliced a deep, thin line down his thigh.

"Your turn," Hana said, arrogance frosting her words. "Or not, either way I get to do this."

The pain renewed, lasting only a second, but it was enough to tear a screech from Eva's throat.

"You really should have taken those wishes, because now I'm going to have to show Augustine how truly weak you are." Hana's heels tapped as she approached, her long black hair sweeping over her shoulder as she kneeled. "And once he sees, I'm going to watch him break you apart, piece by piece."

Eva arched her back off the floor, arms no longer trembling at her weight. "How long have you wanted Augustine?" she whispered, her voice throaty from the screaming. "And how long has he not wanted you?"

Hana's mouth twisted, violet eyes flashing before Eva felt the pain shoot through her body once more, muscles rigid as if they were forced to hold an electrical charge. This time there was no relief, the pain seeming endless as it almost pushed her into oblivion. There were no more screams, her vocals shredded as the pain finally receded. Eva kept her eyes closed, her chest barely moving for a breath as she sensed Hana stand.

"Pathetic."

Eva counted in her head, her loss of sight allowing her to concentrate on her other senses. She could sense the blood thickening, the sound of each individual drop hitting the floor. Hunter's heartbeat gave away his pain, despite not one sound leaving his lips. His breathing was staggered, and Eva wasn't surprised to see his face scrunched up tight when she finally opened her eyes to slits. Tears wet his face, taking every slice of Hana's scalpel in silence.

His hands had partially shifted, his claws useless as they tore more at his own skin than the straps and metal that kept him contained.

"Do you know," Hana began as she sliced, her back arched over his thigh as she slowly and carefully cut. "There's a spell that can stop you from shifting ever again. I wonder how quickly you'll lose your mind? Your animal forever trapped inside the body of a boy."

Eva slowly climbed to her feet, knowing it was her only chance. She needed Hana to lift the blade, to get away from Hunter. "Hey, Hana!"

Hana turned, hand held out as the beats of a drum pounded in the distance.

Eva launched forward with all her strength, tackling Hana to the hard concrete. The scalpel stabbed into her side, but the pain was an insect bite compared to before. With little effort she broke the faerie's neck, her strength pulling a little too hard as the skin began to rip, and then her head separated entirely.

Her fangs punched down, the urge to continue to tear and shred until there was nothing but an indistinguishable mess of red an instinct she couldn't ignore. She would have been lost in her rage if bile hadn't burned, forcing her back to reality. Swallowing it down she threw Hana's head so hard it clattered into the instruments displayed on the wall, impaling itself on one of the horror movie props.

A low moan, Hunter convulsing violently.

"Hold on, hold on," Eva chanted, panic dimming the anger in her chest. "Let me just..." She released the straps, catching Hunter as he sagged off the chair. He jerked in her grip, back bowing as he finally let out a cry. Eva heard every bone break, his body twisting as he slowly transformed into his alternative shape. Skin ripped, exposed muscle rippling before fur forced its way through to cover him entirely.

She had never witnessed a shifter change before, it was violent and graphic.

His cries turned into snarls, his sharp fangs dripping

saliva as he shook his head, paws releasing long claws that scratched along the concrete. When he looked up, Eva finally realised she was locked inside a room with a large, angry cat.

Oh shit.

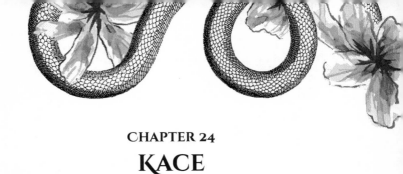

CHAPTER 24

KACE

or fuck's sake. Kace dodged the large spike that appeared from a small hole on the side of the platform, deciding to take the blunt hit of a swinging panel instead. He had braced for the impact, but the wood smashed him with more weight than he had expected. A grunt, the force dragging the breath from his lungs while the shock spread across his abdomen, reopening the wound on his chest. It pushed him to the edge, a dark pit beckoning death below.

He took a second sweep of the platform for traps. He had figured pretty quickly that there were pressure sensors that set off certain events, but they were well disguised amongst the constantly changing course. It was pure luck he hadn't accidently set one off, and even after four platforms he was conscious of every step. It slowed him down dramatically, and patience wasn't one of his virtues.

Click.

"Fuck!" The screech drew his attention further up the platform, Number Five impaled on a long metal spear that protruded through his foot. He tried to pull himself off before another one shot through his other foot, setting off a series of spikes that randomly pierced through the floor in an unpredictable pattern.

"Bloody hell," Mikayla cursed, stepping up beside him. There was a gap between the platforms, an easy enough jump with a slight run up. Except the rolling spikes caused an issue on the other side. "You got a plan?" she asked, her breathing laboured. A line of red wet her arm, and a bruise was already blossoming on her cheek.

"Do you have access to your magic?" he asked, feeling his chi. He had called his arcane to his palms, but as soon as his fingertips sparked pain had shot in his chest, his heart skipping a beat. It was an interesting repellent, one he hadn't come across before.

Mikayla nodded her head. "They need magic to control this shit-show, so they can't strangle it completely like last time. But whatever they're using is powerful, I've never been quite so controlled," she chuckled, the sound hollow. "I felt it activate as soon as the first charm rang. I'm pretty sure it can kill us."

Click.

Kace turned as he heard the whoosh, ducking just in time as a large log swung. It knocked Mikayla in the back, and she fell towards the open gap to the platform below. She scrambled on the edge, fingers clinging to anything she could hold.

Kace dropped to his knees, catching her outstretched arm just as she slipped.

Boots appeared in his peripheral. "You know this is a competition, right?" Gus grunted. "Only the strong survive."

Teeth bared, his beast tearing at his mind Kace pulled Mikayla up and back on to the platform just as Gus jumped, rolling and missing the spikes.

"You fucking..." Number Five screeched as Gus

knocked him to the side, dislodging the spears that had him pinned, only for him to slip straight down. He had finally moved off the pressure trap, deactivating the rolling spikes but not in time to stop one from impaling him through the chest.

Two distinctive beeps, signalling the end of an opponent.

Kace had lost count of how many beeps that had rung, so he had no idea who had died, and who had survived.

Mikayla coughed, her mouth spluttering red. "Fuck," she croaked as she collapsed under her own weight.

Kace could hear the rattle in her breathing, the log having done some serious damage. Witches had the same physiology as humans, which made them physically weak. Nothing but meat sacks held up by a brittle skeleton. Druids too, except he wasn't exactly a 'normal' druid.

"Just wait, and we'll get you out of here," he said, dropping his voice to a whisper. "Trust me."

Mikayla started to laugh, the sound pained. "I don't have much of a choice." She sucked in a wet breath, her front soaked in crimson. She reached for the front of his shirt, her fingertips sparking against his skin with a sting. "Make sure they fucking pay."

With a nod Kace eased her down, her breathing worsening as she whispered something beneath her breath. The arcane on her hands increased, the physical manifestation of her chi flickering. With a flash it launched across the space, exploding when it hit the other side. The trap triggered, splintering as the arcane ate away until the structure groaned, and an opening to the fifth level dropped.

Kace jumped the gap, landing in a crouch. Gus was right, it was a competition, but he still turned back towards Mikayla, who lay on her back, head fallen to the side.

Two distinctive beeps.

Rage burned hot through his veins, but he didn't have time as he climbed through the new opening, finding himself faced with two walls and a floor of spinning blades.

Two distinctive beeps.

Fuck.

Kace paused, ignoring the crowd who were starting to liven up. The obstacle course was designed to give a three-sixty view, everything slowly turning as if on wheels, allowing the audience to observe from the safety of their seats. They could follow each layer, watch everyone fight their way through hurdles and traps until they advanced to the next platform, where they started again. The first three levels had been simple enough, and it was only from the fourth that Kace had found a little more difficult, with the walls more enclosing. It would have been hard for the audience to get a good look at the people they were betting on dying, except for the windows, and glass was fucking impossible to grip.

There was no glass this time though, the walls too tall to comfortably climb with the ceiling open air, allowing only the super-rich and powerful to watch. Kace felt like a rat trapped in a maze, attention a prickling weight on his shoulders as they waited for him to make a mistake. To slip and fall.

Two walls, a floor and a fuck load of spinning blades.

Fan-fucking-tastic.

Five seconds left. Ten seconds right. Twelve seconds down. Kace counted each spin of the blade on both the walls and floor. Five. Ten. Twelve. He knew he could move faster than that, so without hesitation he ran, timing his first step perfectly as the spinning blade kissed his ankle. Kace twisted on the tenth second, and then immediately jumped on the twelfth. He made it to the end, skidding to a stop when he found the space in front suspiciously void of anything except Gus. He lay face down on the floor, his body sliced into pieces. Yet there was nothing to indicate what could have ended him.

Just like before, the walls were too tall to comfortably climb, the ceiling enclosed this time, but made entirely of glass.

Kace pulled his shirt over his head, bundling it into a ball before he threw into the open space. Another set of spinning blades immediately appeared through the floor from discreet slices. It lasted only a second, but it was long enough as the fabric disintegrated, and what already remained of Gus was essential minced.

His shirt had weighed next to nothing, which meant it was likely motion activated rather than weight. It also meant he couldn't go anywhere near the floor, and with nothing to grip on the walls he was essentially fucked, unless he figured out a way to climb.

Voices cursed just behind.

"Hey," Kace called to the two men who stood at the beginning of the first set of spinning blades, their auras were no longer tainted. "You need to grab some of those stakes, ideally metal but wood will do."

It was the bleach blonde that answered, his words more of a growl. "Why would we help you?"

The dark haired one leaned forward, his slim shoulders shifting beneath his shirt. "Why do you want them?"

"Because I doubt any of us will be able to get to the end without them," Kace grunted, frustration rumbling his beast. "So unless you want to die in here, I need you to grab some fucking stakes."

Blondey gave a tiny shake of his head, jaw rigid as he whispered to his friend. After a taut pause he turned back in the direction he came, returning after a few minutes with what Kace needed.

217

They crossed the obstacle quickly, the way they moved reminding him of a feline.

Definitely cats, he thought. Which wasn't a surprise in a city that was heavy in predators. Wolves ruled London, but that didn't mean there weren't other predatory animals.

"Well, what's the plan then?" Blondey asked, swallowing a gulp when he found Gus in pieces. "What's with the stakes?"

Kace didn't bother with a reply, grabbing the first stake and weighing it in his palm. It was reasonably heavy, and thick enough for his plan. Pressing his back against one wall he relaxed his shoulders, mentally marking the opposite wall. On his next exhale he threw, and the stake hummed through the air before it struck, imbedding itself deep. He didn't need to reach for the next stake, because Blondey was beside him with the rest. It took a few minutes, but in the end there were eight stakes sticking out the wall, each different in size and weight.

"You've created a path with the stakes," Blondey said with a grin. "That was fucking genius."

Kace looked up through the glass ceiling to glare at the spectators. "The stakes further along the wall are at a dangerous angle," he said, turning back to the two shifters. "So don't stay on them too long."

The dark-haired cat crossed his arms. "Who's going first?"

It was Blondey who raised his arm, not waiting for a contest before he climbed on to the first stake. It groaned at his weight, but kept steady as he hopped to the next. The roar of the crowd was growing, and Kace tuned them out as he pulled himself up on the first one. He felt the wood beneath his feet begin to weaken and splinter, so he repositioned himself as close to the wall as possible before he jumped to the next. He heard the snap, the space between the sudden inhale and the wet sound of the blades lasting an eternity. There was a deathly silence between the break and the fall, so still that he felt the pressure in his chest. But Kace kept moving, only a step behind Blondey who reached the end of the obstacle first, turning around to punch the air in victory. His happiness was short lived as Kace landed beside him, a cry of anguish ripping from his throat as he dropped to his knees, facing the remains of his friend.

Beep. Beep.

Those two distinctive beeps would fucking haunt him.

The pressure in his chest grew, consuming until he pulled the strength from his beast. Exhilaration pumped, his senses more acute he prepared from what was next.

A growl rattled from his chest, and as he took the few steps up to the podium he turned until he found Augustine high up in his office. Kace's smile was cruel, and as he flipped his middle finger he felt the rumble as the first of the bombs exploded.

EVA

The door was locked, her fists unable to make a dent.

"What is this thing made of?" she screeched, slapping her palm against the snake emblem on the door. "Also that was rhetorical, I know it's metal."

Hunter growled behind her, the sound pained. Eva felt the hair on the back of her neck raise, and as she slowly turned to meet the eyes of a seriously pissed off cat.

"Don't you dare eat me," she said, hoping her tone was light and non-threatening. "I will not go through all this and then be eaten by you. I just won't, could you imagine the humiliation when I tell all the other ghosts?"

Eva knew she was rambling, but the word vomit wouldn't stop as she moved slowly, grabbing one of the slimmer knives on the wall.

"I'm going to try and pick the lock," she explained, hoping Hunter understood. "Not that I've ever picked a lock before, but it can't be too hard. Can it?" She even looked at Hunter, waiting for him to reply.

He gave her a slow blink, which seemed like the only response she was going to receive.

"You're a great listener," she continued, hoping her talking was enough to stop him from wanting to use her as a scratching post. "Do you..."

The ground quaked, so violent the entire room rattled. A large crack appeared beneath their feet, splitting the hard concrete into a spiderweb. The fractures continued to move, breaking off and moving up the walls until it splintered around the door.

Hunter let out a hiss, scrambling back. His paw had caught a sharp piece of concrete, the pads sliced and bleeding.

Reaching for one of the thicker knives she shoved it into the crack beside the door, using all her strength and weight to force it open a little more. Fur brushed along her side, Hunter adding pressure against the wall as the cracks opened up further, wide enough she could just make out the corridor.

The knife snapped halfway up the blade, wedged in the concrete.

"This isn't work..." Eva couldn't get her next words out before another blast rocked through the room, and this time she threw herself over Hunter, protecting his back as a large chunk of the ceiling came crashing down, along with dust.

"What the fuck have you done?"

Eva froze at the voice, a hand snaking around her ankle

before she screamed, pulled across the floor and debris. Dutch sneered, face twisted so viciously he looked like a monster, eyes flicking to Hana who lay forgotten.

"What the fuck have you done?" he asked again, free hand circling around her throat.

Hunter roared, his large paw swiping at Dutch hard enough it loosened his hold. It allowed Eva to turn onto her stomach, reach for one of the weapons that had fallen off the display. Her fingers brushed metal, jumping to her feet just as Dutch threw Hunter across the room. He crashed against the chair in the centre, causing it to creak as it collapsed at the weight.

Eva let out a hiss, fangs lengthening. "Don't touch him."

Dutch stood covered in dust, his smile on the wrong side of sanity. Four cuts sliced along his face, including over his left eye. "You killed her, pretty lady," he said. "Which means you'll have to replace her."

"I'm not your toy," Eva snapped, gripping the broken knife tightly behind her back. "Or Augustine's."

He took a measured step forward, head cocked as his smile turned into a grin that creased his cheeks so far it pulled at his wounds. "This is going to hurt."

Eva blinked, and Dutch had already moved. He was a dark smear in her peripheral, and the shift of air gave her a millisecond warning before his fist brushed across her cheek. She twisted, her legs moving as she tried to blur her own movements. The initial contact with his fist had been a shock, but the pain was already forgotten as she danced back out the way, trusting herself not to fall over the debris on the floor.

She fucking specialised in movement, and in that instant she thanked her mum for forcing her to take dance lessons as a young kid. Because while she may not have even been able to match Dutch's fighting skills, she could move, maybe even faster than him.

Hunter groaned, pulling her attention away for the smallest second. It was enough, and before she knew it she was airborne, followed by a pain radiated down her spine and the back of her head. Warmth spread through her hair, her eyes darkening at the corners.

Dutch crouched before her, his face hazy as he reached down to grip her chin. Her arms felt weighted as she pushed his hold, blood roaring in her ears. She couldn't make out his words, his lips moving but no sound coming out.

Her strength seemed zapped as something was pressing into her hand, her fangs pulsating along with the headache forming behind her eyes.

Fuck. Did he have wood?

She couldn't die, not when she had to protect Hunter. He was just a kid.

Eva felt the broken blade hidden in her hand. What was once an impressive length was now barely the size of her palm, but it would be enough. It had to be.

"Fuck you," she wheezed out, using the last of her strength to thrust. The broken knife entered at an angle in Dutch's face just below his eye, and from his sudden inhale of air she knew it had hurt. She watched the pain ripple across his features, morphing into fury as the darkness pulled her into its welcoming depths.

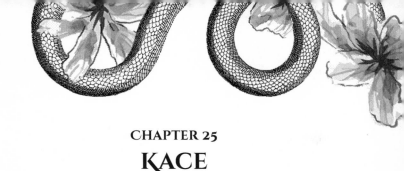

CHAPTER 25
KACE

The punch landed with a satisfying crunch, and Kace felt bones break beneath his fist.

The explosion had damaged the lower half of the structure, tilting it enough that he could jump from the higher tier on to a ledge, and straight to the security who were scrambling after the explosion.

The guard dropped to his knees, and with a quick twist Kace snapped his neck. He felt no guilt, only fury. He had no patience for those that worked for the Vipers, and everyone who stepped in his way would get the same treatment.

A sharp burn in his stomach, blood warm as it spread across his skin. Reaching forward he yanked a gun from another guard, only to turn it around and tip it under his chin. "Where are the fucking Units?"

"Fuck you!"

Kace pulled the trigger, and his beast roared with exhilaration as he moved quickly, leaving body after body, heading towards the stairs. He spread his mental reach, hoping the connection reached his brothers.

'Update?'

Kace reached the top floor quickly, only encountering one more guard who he quickly disposed of with the gun. Emptying the clip into the twitching corpse, he threw the weapon to the side.

'Ten second warning,' Riley said, his voice strained.

'I need a fucking update!' Kace braced himself against the wall just as the second of three bombs exploded. They were small, easily disguised and planted around the arena to create maximum damage. The floor shook, dust raining down from above as concrete began to crack.

The veins of light carved into the concrete flickered in the walls, wild magic that hummed. Moving back the magic snapped out, and Kace tried to call his own arcane to help defend against the powerful whip. His tattoos glowed, the siphons that concentrated his magic straining past whatever blocked his chi.

'Fuck sake, I'm working on it!' came Xander's snarl.

Kace bit back his reply, concentrating on not getting shot. Bullets whizzed past, and bar the one lodged somewhere in his stomach they all missed. He moved faster than they expected, their human minds unable to track as he took them out one by one. Each death should have been calming his beast, but instead he fucking revelled in the chaos.

The last guard he grabbed by the throat, the man pissing himself as Kace squeezed. "The Units, where are they kept?" he growled.

The guard turned red, and releasing his grip slightly he began to choke. "I don't... I don't know," he managed to get out. "August... Augustine."

Kace dropped the guard to the floor as he turned down the corridor he had gestured to. The veins stirred in the concrete, pulsating the walls and beneath his feet as he stepped into a large open space.

'*Ten second warning!*' Riley's voice pierced through, but Kace ignored the warning as he met Augustine's gaze. He stood by a door beside his huge security guard. Dust smeared across his face, and just as Kace widened his stance the third and final bomb exploded.

The ceiling collapsed, large chunks falling between them as something ignited and a fire roared to life. Kace stared at Augustine through the flames, his memories of his time on the sands rushing to the surface. Every hit, every cut and every death at his hands. All because of the man who stood only a few feet away.

Augustine's lips curved into a slow smile, and every muscle in Kace's body tensed.

'*I've got them!*' Xander said, shouting inside his mind. '*Both Hunter and Eva!*'

Kace cocked his head, fists clenched as he stepped closer. The fire licked at his skin, but he didn't care, not when vengeance was only moments away.

Hunter was safe.

Eva was safe.

Which left Augustine to him.

Pressure coiled beneath tight skin, his beast ready to drown in blood.

'*Fuck K, she's hurt bad.*'

Kace's chest tightened, and Augustine's smile turned to a full grin at his hesitation.

'*Did you hear me? She's hurt bad,*' Xander repeated.

Riley pressed his mind. '*We have five minutes to get out, the exits are closing and some of the tunnels are flooding. Most floors have already been evacuated.*'

'*Hunter's shifted and is guarding her, Kace I need you down here now!*' Xander continued.

Kace had waited almost two decades to face off against the man who had thrown him to the sands, who had watched and laughed at his every win and fall. He wasn't sure when he would get the opportunity again.

'*Kace, we're running out of time!*'

And still he chose Eva.

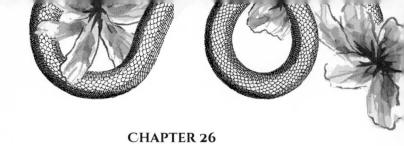

CHAPTER 26

EVA

E va didn't sleep. It wasn't that it was impossible, but she had found out pretty quickly that vampires didn't really require anywhere near as much sleep. She usually tried for an hour or two, but only if she felt safe enough to allow herself to be that vulnerable. When she was with Lucas he would become easily distracted, giving her the time to rest her mind, but since she had been with Augustine she hadn't been able to relax. Not even for a moment.

So why the fuck were her eyes closed, and something soft covered her?

Eva tore the sheets from her body, jumping over the side of the bed to crouch against the wall. It happened so fast she didn't even give herself a chance to open her eyes fully, and when she did the room was too bright, forcing her to squint. Her limbs moved without pain, her breathing calm and even as she blinked the grogginess away, her eyes adjusting far slower than comfortable to the light. She hadn't slept in so long, she was no longer used to it.

"Eva?"

She stilled at her name, recognising the familiar voice, but not her surroundings.

Kyra appeared at the foot of the bed, moving slowly with her hands held out and open. "Eva, it's only me."

Eva jumped up from her position, running over to her friend to wrap her in a hug. It lasted only a second, Kyra exhaling in a sudden rush. "Oh, I'm so sorry!" She had forgotten her strength. "I didn't mean..."

Kyra pulled her back, arms tightening as Eva collapsed into the embrace.

"Careful, Princess. She's a new fledgling," Xander commented as he hovered close, his icy eyes cautious when they met Eva's.

"Hunter? Did you find Hunter, he was this big cat... and Kace? Where's Kace?" The words rushed out in a jumble, panic causing her to stutter. "Hunter, I need to see Hunter." He had been covered in so much blood, his fur coated.

"We've got Hunter, he's been sedated in another room to help heal his wounds," Xander said. "But I need you to stay calm."

"Calm?" Eva's fangs ached, and she fought the urge to hiss, her arms instinctively closing around Kyra. "Hunter's only a child, he saw... and they hurt..."

"Hunter's strong, he will recover fine," he said with a forced composure that pissed her off even more. "But If you don't calm down you may hurt Kyra."

Eva scowled, no longer able to keep her voice steady. "I'm not going to eat her!"

Kyra pulled back to touch her face, her fingers hesitant. "Eva, I didn't know. I thought..." Tears burned down her cheeks. "You were still texting, saying you were busy. I didn't –"

"It's okay," Eva interrupted as Kyra's face crumpled. "It's okay. How could you have known? Lucas kept my phone and was messaging you. It's okay."

Kyra closed her eyes, taking a second to gain her composure. "Your control is so impressive. I can feel your hunger, and even this close it's not affecting you like it should in someone so young."

Eva blinked, eyes burning. "Kyra, he turned me... he took my humanity." It was the first time she had admitted it out loud, and once she heard it vocally, she finally broke. "I... I..." Eva collapsed to the floor, Kyra following.

Eva wasn't sure how long she cried for, minutes or even hours.

She cried for the pain.

She cried for the loss.

She cried for the woman she once was.

The sobs came, and with each one Kyra held her, rubbing down her back in soothing strokes. It must have been a while, the window on the other side of the bed that had glowed brightly was now a dark amber. Xander still hovered just over Kyra's shoulder, brows creased.

"I can't have children." The admittance came out a croak. "I'm so angry at all the choices he took from me."

"What was forced on you doesn't make you any less than before." Kyra said, her face just as wet. "This wasn't your fault."

A deep breath. "I know."

Kyra nodded, some of the tension bleeding from her shoulders. "Do you know how hard it is to knock out a vampire? We found the wood splintered in both your hands, we think it's why you weren't waking up."

Eva glanced at her palms, seeing nothing but perfect skin.

"The doctor said you're going to need more blood due to the pretty severe damage to your head. So we expected you to wake up ravenous, so I'm pretty surprised how relaxed you are considering." Kyra paused, hesitant. "And we decided to wait until you were awake before they could examine you... more intimately."

"More intimately?" Eva frowned, taking a second to understand. "No."

"I think you should be checked. After everything you've been through, and for how long..."

Eva sat back on her heels, licking the salt from her top lip. "Why? I can't get pregnant and can no longer suffer from the same diseases as humans."

"Eva..."

"Augustine didn't get that far," she said, not entirely lying. He hadn't used his dick, unlike Lucas, but that didn't mean he hadn't done other things. Things that have broken her. Things she wanted to forget.

Xander was a storm cloud in the corner, his presence alone drawing her attention. She couldn't look him in the eye, so she stared at the swelling just beneath, moving down to trace the bruises across his jaw. He looked like he had picked a fight with a steam train, and the train won.

"I have super healing now, so I'll be fine once I've fed anyway."

"There's more than just physical damage," Xander said, his tone so calm and careful Eva wanted to hiss at him.

"I said no," she said, closing her eyes to calm her spiked pulse. "No doctors. I'm fine, I promise. I don't want or need a pity party." She tried to smile, hoping it was warm and comforting unlike the intense cold that settled like a vice around her lungs. "Did Kace get out?"

Kyra and Xander exchanged a look, one Eva couldn't read.

"What?"

"He's recovering downstairs," Kyra said quietly.

"Recovering? Is he okay?" Pain fluttered, the urge to find him growing. "Did he get hurt?"

"He's fine, but you should stay away from him right now," Xander added, crossing his arms. "Kace is... volatile."

Eva flicked her gaze across Xander's bruises again, eye narrowing. "What happened?"

Kyra cleared her throat. "We have some of your stuff," she said as a distraction, and Eva pursed her lips to stop from pressing. Kyra's face was an open book, and something was clearly wrong. "Pictures and jewellery. Your car too, it's safe in the garage."

"My car?" Eva's smile was genuine. Some of her favourite memories were of her father teaching her basic mechanical skills on the same white BMW. He had bought it before she was even born, and Eva adored it. She had thought it was lost along with everything else, just something from her past life.

"There's clothes in the wardrobe, and once it's safe you can return to your flat if you want."

"Return? You know how the landlord was, he would have already sold anything he could get his hands on to pay the rent by now."

Kyra's smile was small. "Kace has been paying your rent."

Eva paused, the cold on her chest lessening. "Oh."

Why would he do that?

"I think we should leave Eva to rest." Xander gently pulled Kyra into his arms. "Come on, Princess. You can watch those terrible tv shows with her tomorrow."

Kyra's eyes brightened, her words aimed at Eva. "I'm so happy you're safe." She turned with Xander to the door, hesitating at the threshold. "You always had such a beautiful soul, even when you were human. Now it's even brighter."

Eva couldn't speak, so she simply nodded instead.

She found herself standing there for a while, the dark amber turning to pitch black outside the window. The room was bathed in a soft glow, the lamp in the corner left on. It was strange, she hadn't been left alone in so long, and she thought she would love it. Instead she was just surrounded in silence, trying to shift the uneasy feeling. She was out, safe. So why didn't she feel it?

Kyra had placed all her photographs on the dresser. Memories of her smiling, laughing and dancing. Memories of a girl that no longer existed. It made the uneasy feeling grow, expand until it was a hollow weight in the centre of her chest, as if her heart was missing.

The corridor was empty when she slipped outside, Kyra nowhere in sight. Eva was thankful, because while she didn't want to be alone, she couldn't face the expression in her friend's face. Not right then, not without breaking down into another fit of sorrow. And crying wasn't Eva's deal, not like that. No, she wanted to dance it out, allow her movements to portray her deepest emotions.

Except there was no music left in her soul.

They had taken that too.

Finding the stairs she descended, moving silently on bare feet. She wasn't sure where she was headed, unable to relax as she kept walking. She couldn't sleep again, and she couldn't sit still. She had all this energy, and nowhere to expel it.

She wondered if the wood would be warm against her feet as she found herself walking between the shadows, feeling herself pulled to the darkness. She had only ever played with the shadows, feeling them almost alive as they slithered across her arm when she reached into a darkened corner.

A pulse, deafening in her ears as hunger tightened her throat.

Eva pulled her arm from the shadows, an almost suction trying to pull her back before she hid the same arm behind her back, as if she had been caught doing something wrong.

"He's downstairs."

She looked up at the man who appeared in the door-frame, not needing him to confirm what he meant by 'he's.'

"Blueberry muffins," she said, remembering the man's favourite treat, despite his hair being longer than before. He had a face not many people could forget, and she had baked for all of the Guardians who had helped protect Kyra. Everyone except Kace.

The man bowed gently. "Through that door is the garage. Take the lift down one floor."

Eva hesitated, eyes cutting back to hers. "Thank you."

"But be careful," he continued. "Sometimes people can't be fixed."

"Who said he was broken?"

The man's smile was sad, personal before he turned away, and she was alone once more in a house she wasn't familiar with.

The garage was cold, not necessarily in temperature, but in atmosphere compared to the warmth of the house above. All shiny metal and white paint that showcased every car and motorbike parked. Eva gave herself a moment to just look across the impressive collection, cars she could only dream about driving parked only a foot away. She skimmed across them, from flashy sports cars and practical 4X4's until she settled on her old car in the corner. It was partially hidden, gleaming as if freshly cleaned. She brushed her hand down the side as she passed, the tension in her muscles releasing just a little.

The lift arrived quickly, a slim metal construction that matched the garage with open walls. She watched the scarred concrete as she descended the single floor, the white and metal of the garage turning into pale tiles beneath her feet, the surrounding rooms pitch black. Eva swallowed the panic as her eyes adjusted to the dark. Someone was close, their heartbeat slow and steady unlike her own jagged rhythm. There were no comforts down there like there were in her borrowed bedroom. Everything was metal, which seemed to be a theme, with a few benches set up with powders and crystals. Something acidic tickled her nose, stronger the closer she stepped to the bench. Ignoring it she found an open doorway, Kace breathing evenly atop a thin mattress and pallet of blankets on the floor, one partially covering his hips. His face was relaxed with sleep, his face just as bruised as Xander's.

Eva wasn't sure what she was doing as she stepped inside. He hadn't asked for her to be there, and she knew from experience how horrifying it was to have someone stand over you while you were vulnerable.

But she felt... safe. The weight on her chest had eased entirely with him so close, the hollow void not so obvious. So she allowed herself to stand there for a moment, for just a minute before she returned alone to the other room.

What's wrong with me? she thought, closing her eyes for a second. Her life had been turned upside down, and now she was seeking comfort from the brooding guy who had saved her?

There's a mental illness for that.

"Oh, God," she whispered, swiping a hand down her face. She needed to leave, but her body wasn't co-operating as she stood there in the darkness. She felt the shadows, a blanket that she could wrap herself in and disappear.

Disappear.

That would be easier.

Eva turned, ready to leave until her attention caught on an unframed photograph on his desk. She moved closer, carefully stepping over his long legs to touch her fingertips to the image of a woman, her head thrown back, eyes closed with a private smile as she danced.

The picture was taken by one of her parents, unbeknown to her at the time. There had been no reason for her to even dance, no audition or show. She had just wanted to, to move and spin just for herself.

Except the woman in the photograph wasn't her, not anymore.

Unable to look any longer she pushed the photograph away, finding drawings and sketches beneath. Kace had been replicating the image, drawing images of her over and over, capturing her movements in such delicate detail.

Kace's breathing hitched, and there was no warning as his arm struck out to grab her. She squealed, falling as his heavy body pinned her beneath him, her wrists held tightly above her head.

Kace growled, a rattling in his chest before he blinked a few times, but he didn't release her wrists. "What do you think you're doing here, Eva?" he asked, his voice husky from sleep. She had never heard him so relaxed, the rich rumble somehow calming, crushing her earlier panic as she allowed his voice to wash over her.

Eva cleared her throat. "I'm sorry, I didn't mean to wake you."

Or watch you like a weird stalker, she mentally added.

"I just didn't want to be alone."

"Alone?" Kace tilted his head, his beautiful hair

brushing over his eyes. "You can never be alone in this fucking house."

"You can let me go now." She looked up at her hands, pulling them. Kace only tightened his hold as another vibration rumbled up from his chest, tingling against her breasts. He settled more heavily against her, and she realised he had been naked beneath that blanket.

Very naked.

It also made her realise someone, probably Kyra, had dressed her in thin, silk pyjamas that did nothing to protect her from his growing erection.

"Sorry," he grumbled, finally releasing her wrists, bracing himself above her.

"Your tone says otherwise."

A smirk twisted his lips, the tattoos along his left arm brightening from his fingertips all the way up to his neck. His eyes were lazy, and Eva had to force herself to not brush the hair from his face as his attention drifted to her lips. She thought he was about to kiss her, his lips opening as his shoulders tensed, but instead he rolled off, landing on his feet.

Eva forced herself to stare at his chest, tracing the tattoos there that continued to glow as he grabbed a pair of jogging bottoms from the floor and tugged them up his legs and over his hips.

"What happened to your wound?" The cut from the sword had healed entirely, leaving nothing but a slightly pink mark. Bruises patterned across his ribs, a deep purple that she hadn't noticed before in the darkness.

Kace crossed his arms, staring down at her. "You shouldn't have come down here."

"I..." Eva struggled with the exposure, his attention always so intense. "I feel safer with you."

A growl. "No one feels safe with me."

236

"Yeah, that's probably because you're an arsehole that's as moody as the moon." Eva sat up, feeling the sting of rejection.

The rebuff burned, and she wasn't even sure what she was being rejected for. She hadn't expected anything from him, and yet she still found herself there.

"You paid my rent, why?"

"Your rent needed to be paid, and I had the cash. It wasn't a big deal." A shrug, his arms still crossed, closing himself off.

Eva curled her hands into fists, looking away.

"It was a big deal. I thought everything was gone and now..."

Oh, for fuck's sake, she thought. *Please don't cry again!*

Eva let out an angry huff. "Look," she said, concentrating so her voice didn't crack. "I just wanted to thank you. So, yeah, thanks."

Kace crouched in front of her, but Eva refused to face him. She yelped when he reached down to lift her into his arms, walking in powerful strides towards the lift. "Kace!" She smacked his arm away, and with a grunt he lifted her until she was over his shoulder. "Bloody hell, I'm going!"

"You shouldn't have come down here," he said once more. "You should have stayed away from me."

"Put me down," she hissed. "If you wanted me to leave so much, you could have just said!"

"Noted." His grip tightened a fraction.

"Kace!" Eva tried to wiggle free, but other than biting him she was stuck. "Ugh! You're insufferable."

She thought she felt him laugh beneath her stomach, but as he made no sound, she wasn't sure. He gave her no warning, settling her back on her legs in the corridor several floors above. Hoping no one else saw her humiliation, she turned without a word, moving back towards the room she had woken up in.

"You're hungry, I can sense it."

Eva paused, her hand pressed on the door. "I'm fine."

"Let me feed you, Eva."

The way he said her name caused butterflies in her stomach to flutter.

Fuck. Me. Sideways. What is wrong with me?

"Night, Kace," she said instead, not sure what she wanted when so emotionally drained. "Sweet dreams."

"I only dream about you." She didn't make it far before she felt his presence at her back. He stepped into her borrowed bedroom, closing the door behind him quietly. "And they're not sweet."

A hand brushed her shoulder, and she stilled to keep from moving. Kace seemed almost hesitant, his touch light across her skin.

"No, they're anything but," he continued, his voice dropping impossibly deeper to a rumble, a perfect juxtaposition to his soft caress. "I dream about your legs wrapped around me. My cock buried in your tight, wet cunt and your fangs bleeding my throat."

Eva's thighs clenched instinctively.

"I never dream, I've only ever had nightmares. Until you."

Unable to face away any longer she turned, but he had already moved back.

"Why do you sleep downstairs?" she asked, his gaze an intensity that electrified the air. He had always looked at her like that, like she had his complete attention.

She could hear his heart, beating harder than it was only moments before.

"It's safer."

"For who?"

His lashes dropped low to hide his expression, and Eva wasn't sure if he would answer until she heard his barest whisper. "For everyone."

She reached for him, his warning growl stopping her. "You think you're this monster," she said, his eyes holding something predacious, something dangerous when they steadied on hers once more. "But I've met monsters, and you're nothing like them."

"You have no idea what I am, or what I've done." Kace's lips twisted. "I'm exactly like the monsters who hurt you. Except I'm worse."

Eva couldn't help her flinch, and Kace stepped forward a single step.

"I've killed more people than you could ever imagine. I've bathed in their blood, and do you know what? I fucking loved it."

Another step forward, and Eva lifted her chin as she stood her ground.

"I can't bear to be touched, my anger so black that I crave the violence. I'm broken, Eva. So fucking ruined that I stain everything I touch." His fists clenched beside him, his jaw tight. "I'm dangerous, so much so I terrify my own brothers. It's why if you were smart you would stay away."

Eva trembled, unsure what to do. She was at a crossroads, and she needed to know which way to turn. Which way would heal.

Nobody was perfect, and Kace was a man who had placed himself into a dangerous situation to save a child. To save her. He wasn't a monster despite what he saw in the mirror.

"I'm not scared of you," she said. "You're nothing like them."

A warning growl, his final step bringing him so close they almost touched. "I'm not your hero."

"Maybe, but you're not the villain either." She strained her neck back, making sure to keep the eye contact. His height made it difficult, but she wanted him to see the truth in her gaze. "Kiss me."

A strangled noise escaped from his throat. "Eva."

She couldn't wait any longer, not when she had decided. She reached for him, pulling him down until she could place her lips against his. He tasted of rain, and it was exactly what she wanted, what she needed.

He was tense beneath her fingertip for the briefest of seconds, and then he took over, his fingers curling into her hair as he devoured her with such ferocity she moaned. He had her turned, her back pressed to the door with his hand around her throat in seconds, and all she wanted was more. He didn't take her breath away, the pressure a heavy presence that seemed to shake, pinning her as he tried to regain control.

She waited for a trauma reaction, but instead it only heightened her arousal.

Kace wasn't Lucas.

He wasn't Augustine or even Dutch.

He was safe.

"I don't know how to be gentle," he whispered as he pulled back, his chest heaving in quickened breaths. "Tell me to leave, Eva."

That was her chance to stop, and she couldn't think of anything worse. "I don't want gentle. All I wanted was a choice, and I choose you." His growl vibrated against her breasts when he picked her up, her legs wrapping around his waist as his lips came down so hard she felt hers bruise. He moved them a few steps to the bed, the sudden feeling of falling lasting only a second before her back hit the mattress. She bounced slightly, his expression like a man starved as he stood over her.

"You shouldn't have come to me Eva, because now you're mine. And I don't know if I'll ever be able to let you go."

Eva didn't get to process his threat before he was on her, his kiss consuming, a passion so hot she wanted to be burned, forever scorched and marked as his. He made her feel alive, as if she hadn't just had her life ripped apart.

His tongue stroked down her fang, teasing the sharp tip until she tasted a drop of his blood. Hunger shot through her, her fangs throbbing as she pressed into their kiss. Unable to wait any longer she tugged on her silk shorts, the fabric caught with Kace's weight on her hips. She moaned, the silk tearing and then his fingers were there, pushing at her folds with such blunt strokes that her back bowed. There was no teasing, just solid brushes of his thumb across her clit, his finger pumping inside so fast her stomach tightened as if she was ready to explode.

She tried to reach for him, but in one move he had her wrists pinned in one of his, his fingers leaving her empty.

"Please!" she cried, rubbing herself against him like a cat in heat. She had been so close, her release just a stroke away.

"Stay," he demanded, adding pressure to his grip before releasing.

Eva needed to touch him, to trace every single tattoo along the left side of his body until she had memorised every harsh line. She wanted to stroke along every hard curve of muscle, and know every inch of his skin. Her hands instinctively moved to his shoulders as his teeth grazed across her breasts in little nips, biting hard around a nipple through the silk of the vest. A mixture of pain and pleasure shot through her, and when he released it he licked the small hurt, wetting the fabric.

She needed skin on skin, her hands reaching down to

tug at the silk vest before Kace let out an impatient growl. He took over the removal of the vest, only to wrap it around her wrists, forcing them back above her head.

"Last warning, Sunshine."

Eva went to protest, but then his lips wrapped around her neglected breast, his stubble rough along her sensitive skin.

CHAPTER 27

KACE

He was trying to be gentle, his muscles so painfully solid as he forced himself to pull back. His beast was riding him, snarling inside his mind to take her, and take her hard until she had no memory of any of her other lovers.

Kace took a second to soothe his temper, his patience splintering with her every moan and wiggle beneath him. He made sure his bites were a fraction less than he truly wanted, even though her flesh was able to take more pressure now she had been turned. She wouldn't so easily break at his rough attention, but he needed to be softer, to not scare her with how much he wanted to mark her. The women he had slept with before were just faceless bodies, but with Eva it was different.

Mine, his beast snarled, and Kace had to agree. He was beyond broken, his mind a kaleidoscope that fractured at the smallest inconveniences. He was violent and dangerous, yet he was selfish enough to keep her anyway.

He had been in a dark place when they came back from the Pits, despite the plan being a success and Hunter having been rescued. He had attacked Xander when he had blocked him from going to Eva, his rage so black no one could have possibly stopped him if hadn't pulled back.

Her moans broke through, her eyes entirely black from both hunger and arousal as he released her nipple. Her fangs had lengthened further, grazing her bottom lip as she rubbed herself against his cotton cladded legs.

His cock strained, so hard it hurt.

"Last warning, Sunshine," he growled, wrapping the silk even more around her wrists before he released the fabric. He needed to stay calm, and if she touched him he wasn't sure what he would do while he was so on edge. She could easily break the fabric, which was the whole point. He didn't want her to feel trapped, because even on the edge he didn't want to panic her. In the back of his mind he knew what likely happened in all those months, and it took everything in him to remain in the moment, and to not hunt down every fucker who had ever hurt what was his.

Jumping up he removed the joggers, tossing them behind him before he was back, her skin cool compared to his hot. He flicked his gaze back to her wrists, her hands remaining pinned as she rolled her gorgeous hips, inviting him for a touch. Or a taste.

Kace's mouth watered, remembering when he first took her against her front door what felt like a lifetime ago. It had been his first experience in oral, and now he wanted to drown, to lick her pussy until she screamed his name.

His hands hooked beneath her thighs, bringing her slick centre closer to his mouth. His first lick was quick, her scream vibrating right to his cock so much he ground it into the mattress. His second lick was harsher, the flat of his tongue taking its time to taste her arousal that was his new obsession.

He traced every slick curve, slipping his tongue inside before flicking it up to the bundle of nerves at the apex of her thighs. His hands spread her wider, keeping her open as his fingers brushed down to press two fingers inside, curving them up in the exact way that had her panting.

She clenched around the digits, her legs tensing as he forced her closer and closer to a release. She shifted against his hand, riding his fingers while he continued to lick and suck, burying his face like a man starved.

He heard the silk tear, and he growled against her clit. He wanted to take his time, to savour every moan and cry but it seemed he was just as impatient as she was. He needed to be inside her, to fuck her so hard it would make her forget, even if it was for a single moment. She was his catharsis, and he would lay down cities for him to be hers.

"Mine." He didn't realise his beast had spoken that aloud until he felt the distinctive rumble from his throat, and Eva's eyes widened.

He flipped them, sitting up so she straddled his thighs, his cock seeking out her wet heat. The fabric was long gone as her hands went straight to his hair, tugging painfully at the strands as she took his lips in a kiss. There was a spike of fear, but he fought the darkness of his memories from pulling him under. He anchored himself to her scent, to her feel and taste as her little feminine moans throbbed against him, her body rubbing as she soaked his thighs.

He wasn't back on the sands, fighting, killing to survive. He was with Eva, it was her weight on his lap, her little fangs teasing with her kiss. He wondered if she could taste herself on his lips, and then he realised he wanted to feed her, her own orgasm.

Next time, he promised himself. Next time they will take it slower.

Probably.

His cock rubbed between her thighs, enjoying the friction as her fangs continued to scrape along his skin, his blood only adding to every sensation. He pulled her closer, his fingers digging into her hips as he positioned her right above where he needed to be.

"Feed from me," he grunted, the tip of his cock sliding along her wetness. "Take from me, Eva."

Her fangs struck at the same time he thrust up, impaling himself in one rough stroke. They both let out a scream-edged moan before she sucked hard, taking him inside her too.

Euphoria. The pain from her bite burned, turning into pleasure that only heightened every single ripple he felt around his cock. His hands clenched on her hips, lifting her up until only the tip was still inside before he forced her back down. He set the rhythm, remaining in control while she moaned against his neck.

He wanted to claim her, mark her as his.

"So fucking tight," he growled, moving her up and down, increasing his thrusts while all she could do was ride him.

Her teeth tore at his skin until she had no choice but to let go, her cries of pleasure forcing him to move faster, harder as she met him thrust for thrust. She flung her head back on a scream, pussy clenching so tight Kace almost blacked out. Red dripped from her luscious lips, down her jaw and neck before pooling on the upper curves of her breasts. The visual of bright red against her pale, pearlescent skin almost made him come.

"Mine," he grunted, no longer caring that she heard his possessive claim. She had a choice, and she had made it.

Eva let out a moan as she watched him through lowered lashes. Kace wrapped a hand in her hair, keeping her from bouncing on his cock so he could lick the blood from her breasts, following it up her throat, over her jaw until he could lick it from her lips. The kiss was violent, a clashing of coppery tongues and teeth, the need to dominate overpowering as he flipped her over once more, her golden-brown hair flaring out on the white sheets.

"Kace!" she screamed as he reached down to flick her clit, her attention on where they were joined. "Please!"

"Eyes on me."

She immediately looked up, and Kace expected a teasing twist of her lips like the brat she was. But she was too lost, her cries echoing around them so loud he hoped everyone in the house could hear. He loved that he didn't have to muffle her cries, and his chest swelled at the thought he could make her scream in pleasure.

She was so close, his cock trapped in a vice that he knew one more flick and she would explode. Electricity pricked against his chest, his chi alight along his tattoos. The sensation was strange, growing while his beast urged him for more.

Mine!

He felt his chi expand, stretch as it spread over Eva beneath him, covering her from head to toe.

Her back bowed, and he swore he could feel her chi, tingling as it merged with his. He had heard of such things between magic bearers, but never thought he would experience it himself, especially with a woman who had no access to magic. It was a full body orgasm, one that had him groaning, wanting more. Except the sensations suddenly stopped at a cliff, waiting for them to fall together.

"Look at me," he growled, slowing his thrusts, her pussy squeezing.

Eva licked at her lips, flashing her fangs. "Kace," she warned, hissing out his name. "I swear to fucking God if you don't..."

He slowed his hips even more, his finger teasing.

Her eyes snapped to his, glistening with attitude. "You're an arsehole."

Kace pulled out, her little gasp followed by an angry growl that made him grin. She thrust her head back into the mattress as she rolled her hips closer to his cock, begging him. He positioned himself back at her opening, his finger moving closer and closer to her aching clit.

"Eva, eyes on me."

She dropped her chin, and as soon as he had her full attention he thrust inside. Her mouth opened on a silent cry, and something snapped into place. Whatever had held them both under its thrall sent electricity over his skin, her pussy clamping around him so tightly as she screamed her orgasm, and he couldn't hold his own back as he roared.

EVA

What just happened?

Eva had had sex before, in fact she had had sex quite a few times. But it had never been like *that*. It had felt like a full-body experience, a tingling sensation that encompassed every inch of her skin. The feeling was gone, only echoes left, but now there was a warmth deep within her chest that wasn't there before.

Blood had spread across most of the bed, little drops of crimson that decorated the sheets, duvet and pillows in obscene patterns. Some still coated her breasts, as well as smeared along Kace's jaw. His eyes were reflective when he lifted his face, the tattoos along his arm pulsating, glowing a white light much brighter than it was before.

Panic creased his expression, his breathing laboured as he jumped from the bed, his body as rigid as a statue.

"Kace?" Eva scooted slowly to the edge of the bed.

The bedroom door smashed open, coming clean off its hinges as two men stood shadowed in the opening.

"You okay?" Xander stepped inside, eyes dipping to the blood smeared along her skin.

Eva sat frozen, horror tightening her muscles as she flicked her attention between the two men. "What...?"

"You need to back away, slowly," one said, his gaze hard as he stared at Kace. A scar split down his face, harshing his features. She recognised him as another one of the Guardians who had protected Kyra, but right then she couldn't remember his name.

Kace growled, his breathing rapid. "Mine," he said, his voice an impossibly deep tone that sent shivers down her spine.

Xander cursed, holding his hands up as he took a single step in the room. "K..."

"Get Riley," the scarred man interrupted. "I'll protect her."

Multiple colours burst from Kace's skin, blinding as Eva held her hand up to save her eyes. A howl echoed, rattling the walls as she turned to face the most terrifying, yet beautiful creature she had ever seen. Where Kace once stood was an enormous beast, its head shaped similar to a wolf's, but bigger with thick forearms closer to a lion. Grey fur covered it's body, slick with muscles and markings that glimmered down its entire left side. The same swirls and symbols that Kace had tattooed.

Holy shit!

"Kace?" she whispered, and the beast's head turned towards her, upper lip lifted to show impressive fangs.

"Get out of here!" the scarred man shouted at her, stepping further inside the room. A sword was in his hand, long and sharp that glinted against the lamp on the floor.

Eva jumped from the bed, placing herself between the beast and the man. She hissed, the sound unnatural as her hands tightened into fists. "Don't you dare touch him!" Her words became garbled through her fangs, which had elongated past her lips. Fur brushed her back, a snarl so loud she felt it along her naked skin.

"Eva!" Xander warned just as a dark-haired man entered through the door. "Get back!"

Arms wrapped around her waist, and before she could react, she felt herself being pulled apart with a static pop.

CHAPTER 28
EVA

E va's elbow connected to someone's face, hard enough she felt the crack. The arms that held her dropped, and she turned, her fist connecting to a solid chest.

"Fuck me!" the stranger growled, the words coming out slightly blurred as he rubbed at the skin she had just hit. "I think you've broken my fucking jaw!" He disappeared with a pop, appearing a few feet away with a scowl.

Eva took a second to figure it was soft grass beneath her feet, a deafening roar ripping through the house that glowed just behind, containing nothing but pure rage. "Touch me again and I'll shove something very large and sharp up where the sun doesn't shine." Wind rustled her hair, and she scraped it back behind her ears.

The dark stranger squinted. "Is that a promise?" He sucked at his lip before grimacing, reaching up to stroke along his jaw again. "This is the thanks I get for saving your fine arse."

"Saving me?" she echoed, another roar, followed by shouts getting louder. "Who exactly are you?"

Why the fuck does he have red eyes?

"The name's Lucifer," he said, clicking his tongue. "Or Lucy. Or sex god or even..." A window smashed, drawing both their attention. "Fuck me, he's on a big one tonight." He tore the t-shirt from his chest, throwing it at Eva's face. "Put that on before he catches you naked. Trust me, If I have to choose between you or me, I choose me every fucking time."

Eva tugged the shirt over her head, the fabric long enough to almost reach her knees. Except there was slits throughout the design, revealing so much flesh it wasn't much better than being naked.

"Who's on a big one? Kace?" The warmth in her chest seemed to crackle, tightening as she watched the shadows in the lightened windows move. "Is he okay?"

"'Is he okay,' she asks," Lucy said, replicating her higher pitched voice. "Of course he's not okay, it's Kace. Also, congratulations, you didn't puke after your first drift."

Eva stared at him confused, arms crossed to cover her exposed breasts through the gaps in the shirt.

"You know, teleport? You were in the bedroom and now you're... do you know what? Never mind." Another crash, louder than before and his head snapped to the side. "Fuck it, you're on your own. I'm not dealing with him, he'll try to eat me like last time."

Lucifer returned his red eyes to her, an almost apologetic gleam in them.

"Have fun with psycho boy. Don't die."

"Wait!"

He disappeared in a burst of smoke, just as a snarl sounded close.

Eva turned, Kace's beast crashing through the front door, leaving it splintered into pieces as he tore across the grass towards her. He moved with such speed she struggled to track him, and after a single blink he had curved his larger body around her own as he turned to face the Guardians.

"Eva, don't move!" one of them barked as they crossed the space in powerful strides, his hair long and blonde with just a hint of pink.

Cookies, she thought. He loved her cookies. He held a gun in a tight grip, and she saw red. "Don't come near us!" She instinctively reached back, stroking her fingers through the fur on his nape.

Six men stood across from them, their expressions a mix of horror, anger and a touch of sorrow.

The blonde who loved cookies whistled, stepping to the side. "I'll distract him while you guys get Eva to safety."

Kace growled as he leaned forward on his paws, sharp, serrated claws piercing through the wet earth.

Eva tightened her grip on his fur, tugging. "Kace, you're okay. We're okay." She noticed his ears flick towards her, but he still remained facing the men, showing them his fangs. Up close she noticed little sharp bristles along his back, laying parallel to his spine.

"Oh fuck!" Riley stepped closer, and Kace tensed as if ready to strike. "They've bonded."

"Now this is entertainment!" Lucifer chuckled from a safe distance away. "Does anyone have any popcorn?"

It was the one with the scar down his face that replied. "She was bleeding."

"I was feeding!" Eva shouted, frustrated.

"Riley, can we get him back?" Xander asked the dark-haired man beside him. "Or is he too far gone?"

"I don't know." The man named Riley cocked his head, his shoulders relaxing slightly. "If we all back off, he'll calm down."

"Kyra's going to kill me if he hurts her," Xander said, hand tightening on a knife.

"Stop talking like I'm not here," Eva snapped, stroking her hand down Kace's side in what she hoped was soothing, calming strokes. "Kace won't hurt me."

The Guardians looked between one another, disbelief marking their expressions.

"He won't," she growled, only for Kace to tense beneath her palm. Steadying her tone she continued her strokes. "Kace is fine. *I'm* fine."

Sort of, anyway.

Riley gritted his teeth. "Eva, he's..."

"You need to trust him," she interrupted, meeting every single pair of eyes, finishing with Riley.

"You can't be serious?"

"He hasn't been this bad in a while."

"He'll kill her."

Eva wasn't sure who had spoken, keeping her attention on the man who was clearly the leader. Riley nodded, lips pursed as he backed up slowly, forcing the other Guardians to follow. As soon as they were a reasonable distance away she turned her back, pressing herself against Kace's warmth. She wasn't sure how long they waited, the sky above still dark when a burst of coloured light appeared beneath her palm. Kace's transformation was instant, the beast one second and then the man another. He suddenly stood there, body slick with sweat as he turned quickly, ripping the t-shirt off her without a word.

"Hey!" she screeched. "Naked, remember?"

He didn't even glance towards her as he reached under her knees, lifting her into his arms as he left the ruined fabric behind. He moved them quickly towards the house, his face carved from stone as he ignored the concerned calls from the Guardians, climbing the stairs quickly. She expected him to take her back to her borrowed bedroom, except he turned left down the hall, kicking open a door and stepping inside.

The bedroom was similar to her borrowed one, the bed on the opposite wall. It smelt of both Kace and dust, which she assumed meant he hadn't stayed there in a while, everything undisturbed.

He kept moving to the bathroom, setting her down on the edge of the bathtub before turning to the large, walk-in shower. He quickly turned the water on, reaching for her hand as he pulled them both beneath the spray.

"Kace?"

He wrapped his arms around her waist as he placed his nose against her throat, taking in a deep breath as the water cascaded over them. The warmth in her chest intensified, and she relaxed into his hold.

Eva reached up to stroke his jaw, ignoring his flinch. Carefully he shifted back, watching her with such predatory intensity she couldn't tear her gaze away, his silver irises slowing returning to dark forest green. Without a word he grabbed the soap, lathering up his hands as he began to clean her skin.

"So," she began, uncomfortable with his silence. "You turn into this big, fluffy creature? That's cool."

Kace blinked, but his expression remaining hard.

"Is that... normal?"

Kace remained silent, meticulously washing along her skin as he removed every speck of blood and dirt. When he got to her hair he gently tugged her head back, his fingers brushing through the strands.

They were beneath the water a while, long enough for the tension to be released from his body. When she reached for the soap, placing her hands across his chest did he shut the water off.

"I'll get Kyra. She can..." He cleared his throat. "I need to go."

"Go? Go where?"

He ignored her question, offering her a large, white towel. "My brothers will be able to keep you safe."

"Kace? Where are you going?" Wrapped in the towel she followed him into the bedroom, and then into the walk-in wardrobe. Eva hesitated at the wall of knives, and the little pile of what looked like grenades. "Tell me what's happening."

Muscles bunched in his back as he grabbed a pair of leathers, pulling them up with a single tug.

"Kace!"

He spun so quickly she let out a squeak, his expression dark. "I'm not your fucking babysitter, Eva. I'm busy unless you want my cock."

"Excuse me?" Eva's mouth gaped. "Fuck you!"

His mouth twisted. "You already have, Sunshine."

Tears prickled her eyes, but Eva refused to let them fall. "You're such an arsehole."

"An arsehole who has shit to do." Kace stormed past her, collecting a black t-shirt and a few knives along the way. He paused with his hand on the door handle, his head turned so all she saw was his profile. "I told you I wasn't your hero. So don't expect me to be."

CHAPTER 29
KACE

K ace couldn't believe how hard it was to leave, his beast tearing at him inside to go back to her. But he wasn't safe, that had been blatantly clear when he lost control, and she was clearly attached to him because of her trauma, replacing one monster with another.

Fuck.

He had promised himself he would never find a mate, never bind himself to someone when he was so ruined, and yet now it had happened with *her,* the one woman who subdued his beast he knew he could never let her go without tearing himself apart.

Good thing he was a masochist.

Sweet pain was something he understood.

Kace clenched his jaw, the strange heat in his chest growing at the thought of Eva being his.

"You ready, Red?" Marshall smirked, leading him to the concrete dungeon below The Vault.

Kace shook himself from any thoughts of Eva, not wanting to distract himself when he had a job to do. A chain rattled, a rasping voice calling for help from deep within the darkened hole.

Eva's ex-boyfriend appeared from the dark, his black, dilated eyes scanning across the room, searching for help that wouldn't come. His skin was as pale as paper with deep bruises set beneath his eyes. All of his humanity had been stripped, leaving only his most primitive instincts as he snarled and twisted in the chains.

Kace crouched, bringing himself face to face with the man that had turned Eva. He smiled, reaching over to wrap his hand around his throat, trying to pull him to his feet. Except the chain attached to the metal chair beneath stopped him from rising fully.

"Lucas Whitlock," Marshall said. "Slimy fucker, but we've had some great fun over the past few days, haven't we Bud? Twat even has his initials carved into a ring."

Kace didn't care for his name, he just wanted his screams, his blood. Without a word he released Lucas's throat, only to grab a small knife and strike it down into his knee.

Lucas screamed as he sagged back down, and Kace closed his eyes, listening to the sound.

Fucking beautiful. It was what he needed, what he craved to calm his beast. Turning the handle he broke the blade, leaving it deep inside.

"Please!" Lucas rasped out a cry. "Please, I'll do anything. Just make it stop."

Marshall laughed. "We've discussed this, Bud. You're here because my friend wants something from you. And what can I say? I'm a people pleaser." He lit a cigarette, the orange glow creating cruel shadows across his face.

"I've got money, lots of money," he hissed. "Let me go and I'll make you rich!"

Marshall reached over with his cigarette, placing the burning end to Lucas's cheek. "This prick wasn't difficult to find. He likes to gamble, and is in a lot of debt to some big fucking players."

Kace reached for another blade, pulling it down his thigh to leave a trail of blood. He had fought many vampires, their bodies exceedingly tough and able to take more damage than any other Breed. He couldn't fucking wait.

"What do you know about the Vipers?" Kace asked calmly.

Lucas's eyes widened. "The Vipers? I... I don't know any Vipers."

Kace licked across his bottom lip, cocking his head. "Let's try that question again." He pressed harder, cutting up the opposite thigh and began peeling the skin back layer by layer.

"Please!" Lucas begged, trying to yank himself free, his hands curling to fists. "Please, the Lord will kill me!"

"Then you're useless to me." Kace pulled back, only to gesture to Marshall.

"Wait!"

Kace paused, hiding his smile.

"The Vipers run the Pits. The head is Augustine, he organises the events. I run the money sometimes. Please, I can help you with whatever you want, just don't kill me."

"The Pits have had a sudden... closure." Kace began, flicking the bloodied blade in the air and catching it again. "How can I contact Augustine?"

A strangled sound, the metal chair screeching as Lucas fought to be free. His strength had been zapped the longer they kept him from feeding, his remaining energy trying to heal the wounds that Marshall already inflicted. Kace swallowed the jealousy, wanting to be the only one to have hurt him. To have made him suffer.

"Last chance," Kace warned, trailing his blade up

Lucas's chest to press against the hollow of his throat. "How can I contact Augustine?"

Recognition flared in his eyes, mixed with confusion as a hiss spit from his mouth.

"Ah," Kace said, unable to control his smile. "So, you do recognise me."

"That bitch isn't even fucking..."

Kace cut him off with a punch to the face, his cheek cracking beneath his knuckles. It took serious power to break a vampires bone, and that was the one time he was grateful for his beast.

Blood splattered, surprisingly cold.

"My phone," Lucas wheezed. "You can call from my phone, but I don't have direct contact with Augustine, only Dutch."

Marshall disappeared, coming back a few minutes later with a jacket, searching in the pocket. "Number?"

Lucas mumbled the numbers, taking two times before he could clearly dictate the correct order. Once it began to ring, Marsh held it out to Kace.

He ignored the slight disappointment, wanting to punish Lucas for longer before he had broken.

The call wouldn't connect, and after three tries Kace crushed the phone in his hand. It had been worth a try, but he wasn't really there for the Vipers anyway.

Lucas's eyes bulged, his mouth flopping open. "No, wait! I can help you, I can..." Kace cut his words off with another punch, the rhythmic pounding of flesh on flesh so fucking satisfying as he kept going until his face resembled nothing but mush. But he didn't kill him, not yet.

"Feed him," Kace demanded, and Marsh immediately stepped forward, cutting his wrist and squeezing some of his blood into Lucas's wrecked mouth.

Kace needed Lucas to remain conscious, so he could truly suffer.

He was going to protect Eva the only way he knew how, and to do that he needed to coax the snakes from their hiding place. But not before he destroyed the man who had first killed her.

"Now," he began as he accepted the pretty-looking saw that Marsh held out, turning back to Lucas. "Where were we?"

CHAPTER 30
EVA

E va sat with her arms wrapped around her knees, looking out into the surrounding grove from the window nook. She could make out the city in the distance, the tall skyscrapers glinting with the early morning sun. A black cat curled by her feet, grumbling every time Eva dared to move.

"Kace swore he would never bond with anyone, and it's not something that's supposed to be so instant. It's a whole..."

"I don't remember asking for your opinion." Eva looked up at the man who had approached, the same man who had tried to attack Kace with a sword. He stood with his arms crossed, his expression just as closed off. She traced the scar down his face, able to see it more clearly than before. It should have made his face cruel, but instead it made him even more striking.

Jax, she thought, remembering his name. He liked her lemon tarts.

"You don't understand, he has always made it clear that he would *never* bond with anyone. It wasn't an option for him because of..." Jax cut himself off, a flash of pain across his expression. "My brother deserves an apology for last night, and so do you."

Eva turned back to the window, reaching over to stroke down the soft black fur.

"I just need you to know that bonding with someone is entirely new to us. It's part of our... curse." Jax cleared his throat. "Before you reject him, maybe you should talk."

"He said everything he needed to last night." A click as a door opened, and Eva carefully moved the cat before swivelling her body towards the doctor who had just stepped out into the hall. "Hunter, is he okay?" she asked.

The doctor was tall, a female with pale white hair and matching bushy brows. Lines wrinkled her face, her eyes a pale yellow. She seemed surprised to see Eva, recovering the shock with a professional smile. "He's healing well. Bruises and cuts will take time compared to his internal injuries, but as long as he continues to shift he should recover with no ill-effects."

"So I can see him?" Eva had already stepped past the doctor and into the room before she could even respond.

"Oh, Miss Morgan," the doctor exclaimed. "I didn't realise you were up and about already. I would really like to speak to you about..."

"No thanks." Eva shut the door, pressing her forehead to the wood.

"How comes you can ignore the doctor, but I can't?"

"Because I'm an adult." Eva smiled, happy to hear his voice. "You okay?"

"You should see the other guy."

Hunter lay curled on his side, his head raising as she hesitantly stepped closer. Bruises covered the entirety of his face, his left eye swollen shut and his lip split.

"So you got out," he said, sitting up. The sheet that covered his body pooled to his waist, showing off even more bruises along his chest. "My jaguar thought you were dead. When that man picked you up, the one like Red... you didn't move."

Eva pulled a chair closer, placing her hand on the bed, palm up. He looked at it like it was a scorpion. "I'm not dead. Well, technically I'm undead." She rolled her eyes dramatically, making him smile.

"Blood sucker," Hunter said, still eyeing her palm as if it were a trick. "That's disgusting."

"It wasn't something I chose, but it is what I am now."

"My mum always told me your type was evil."

Eva shook her head. "It's actions and morals that define someone as evil, not their Breed."

"Maybe." Hunter's eyes brightened, his animal teasing his irises. "You're the same chick from the Vaults, the one who distracted Red. Did Red know you were with those people? Why didn't he stop them? Why..."

Eva smiled, realising how young he looked when he wasn't so defensive.

"Do you think he will be angry with me? I fucked up, like really fucked up. He's done everything to help me, and I went against his training. Is he going to kick me out?"

"Hey, hey," Eva interrupted as she tried to soothe his panic. "It's okay, it's going to be okay."

The bedroom door opened, and Eva didn't need to turn to know who it was, not when she felt it in the warmth that spread like wildfire inside her chest. That at the distinctive scent of blood.

Giving Hunter one last soft smile she stood, only for him to finally reach for her hand. "Do what the doctor says, and I'll be back soon, if that's okay?"

Hunter nodded, nervously flicking his gaze to Kace who had approached silently to the bed. Blood covered the majority of his arms and chest, the liquid still wet.

264

What, the actual fuck?

"Don't worry, I was just leaving," she said as Kace muttered something quietly to Hunter, her ears unable to catch as she hurried out of the room.

She needed to go for a walk. Or bake. Or anything to distract herself from that man. Except fate must really hate her, because she felt his presence behind only seconds later as a hand encircled her upper arm, tugging her to a stop.

"I'm only going to ask you once," she said, refusing to face him. "Let me go."

He spun her towards him, her hands coming up to slap his chest, ignoring the blood. "Why were you in Hunter's room?"

"Because I wanted to see how he was." The words came out cold, clipped. "I didn't realise I needed your permission."

His brows dripped, scowl deepening.

"You have five seconds to release me, or I'll damage something you're pretty fond of."

He leant down, his breath warm against her cheek, and Eva fought the shivers that threatened. "You wouldn't, you enjoy it too much."

She wasn't cutting off her nose to spite her face. She wasn't.

A blush burned its way across her cheeks, and what was even more frustrating was the fact her body was only capable because of the blood she had took from him.

"Ah," he muttered, lashes dropping to cover the expression in his eyes. "There it is."

She frowned, Kace hard to decipher. "What do you want from me?"

He seemed to hesitate, head cocked to the side as he studied her. "I don't know," he whispered, releasing his grip.

"Hey, you guys coming?"

Blood squelched between her fingers when she clenched them into tight fists. Kace didn't pull back, but he did turn his head slightly to reply over her shoulder.

"Yeah, we're coming." He seemed to dip his head once more, his lips so close to her skin. "After you," he said with a hint of challenge.

She wanted to snarl, but curiosity won the better of her as she followed his direction towards what looked like a dining room. Six men sat or stood, each looking tense except for one.

Lucifer whistled, his chair leant back on two legs as he balanced with his feet on the edge of the table. "Family meeting!" he shouted, and many of the Guardians turned to pin him with a glare. "Firstly, Kace, why the fuck are you covered in blood? And secondly, why wasn't I invited?"

Kace moved until his side brushed hers, crossing his arms across his chest. "Where's Kyra?"

It was Xander who answered. "Kyra agreed she couldn't stay impartial when it came to Eva."

"Why would she need to remain impartial?" Eva muttered. "What's happening?"

Riley stood, eyes skimming across Kace's bloody chest. He tilted his head, and only when Kace nodded and the tension released a little from his shoulders did Riley speak. "So," he began, settling back in his chair. "You want to destroy the Pits entirely."

Eva stilled, feeling Kace's intensity prickle along her skin.

"I don't give a fuck about the Pits. I'm going to take out Augustine."

Eva flinched at the name, and only then did she glance up at Kace. He was ruthless, that was the word that came to mind as he concentrated every ounce of his attention on her. He invaded every one of her senses until she felt

266

consumed, and all she wanted was to surrender to his power despite the rage that radiated from him in waves.

Which was probably a pretty unhealthy reaction.

Stop it! she cursed herself. *You're mad at him, remember?*

Xander frowned, cracking his knuckles against the table. "You're going to initiate a territorial war."

"Like I give a shit?" Kace smirked, finally looking away long enough for her to breathe again. "Eva isn't safe until he's nothing but shit and dust that I can piss on. I'm also not asking, I'm telling you I'm going to destroy those snakes, and *everyone* who stands in my way."

"Is that a threat, K?" Xander asked, irises glinting.

"Oh brother, it's a promise."

"That's enough," Riley growled. "Kace is right, those fucking snakes have had it coming for a long time." He glanced at Alice, who smiled at him in return.

Jax grunted, crossing his arms to mirror Kace. "We're still currently under the radar to the majority of the Undercity, but it's only a matter of time before they take notice. It will make our jobs a lot fucking harder if we start making enemies of the Lords."

Riley sighed. "Like you said, it's only a matter of time, especially with the increasing Daemonic activity. Sythe, any information on the current position of the Pits?"

Sythe smiled with his teeth, the look feral as he brushed his fingers through his jet black hair. "I've heard whispers that the damage from the bombs you guys planted was extensive. They won't be operable for a while unless they move operations."

Xander sat down at the table. "Augustine and Dutch are probably scrambling, thinking a price is on their head."

"They're the Vipers, they've always had a price on their heads," Riley added.

"There's a silent partner," Eva said, pausing for the briefest of seconds when everyone turned to face her. "I've never met them, but both Augustine and Dutch mentioned someone called Bishop."

Sythe cocked his head, dark brow creased. "The Vipers have never had a partner, and I've not heard of a Bishop." He exchanged a look with Riley, his expression unreadable before he nodded.

The blonde with the pink tinge tapped the table. "The Pits have become a dead zone. All the entrances and exits have been locked tight, including the underground garage. A quake was felt throughout the market." He turned towards Kace. "Those bombs you created made a serious fucking bang."

"Which means they would have moved," Eva said. "Augustine owns a building in the city, it's designed like a giant safe house. The only way to go between the floors is a lift that only Augustine, his security guard and Dutch have access to."

"A safe house?" The blonde stood, rummaging for something behind him before returning with a laptop computer. "Do you know where this building is?"

"Yeah, I think I can find it." Eva bit her lip.

She was finally out, but she wouldn't ever be truly safe, not when Augustine was still out there as her master. The last think she remembered was the pain, but apparently it was Xander who found her with Hunter. Dutch hadn't been there, which meant he was probably still alive. She needed to see them both dead, otherwise she would never be able to stop looking over her shoulder.

"But, I'll only tell you if I go too." She felt Kace's attention once more, but wasn't yet ready to face him.

"I don't think so, she can…"

"She will be a liability. She will…"

"It's too dangerous, what happens..."

Some of the Guardians argued, and Riley silenced them with a single look. "Eva, you need to think about what you're asking. You've been through a serious trauma..."

"I don't think any of you can comment about what *I've* been through," Eva interrupted, anger kissing her bloodstream. "If you try and keep me here, you're all no better than Augustine."

Riley stiffened. "Eva..."

"My *mate* has already said she's coming," Kace growled. "Lucy can drift her out if it gets too dangerous."

Lucifer whooped, clapping his hands together with an audible slap.

A smack, followed by a grunt.

"What?" Lucifer moaned. "I'm always left at fucking home."

Riley exhaled, eyes twirling silver. "Mate, huh?"

Kace's scowl didn't fade. "Mine."

Riley's expression remained severe, but his voice softened to a whisper. "Fate sure knows how to fuck with us. I truly hope Eva will be what keeps you with us, brother."

Eva waited for Riley to turn before she grabbed Kace, pulling him towards the door. "I'm not some damsel in distress," she hissed. "I didn't need your help."

Kace smirked, his head dipping so his lips almost brushed hers. "Keep acting bratty, Sunshine. See where it gets you."

Eva let out a frustrated huff. "Careful, Kace. Someone might think you actually like me."

He moved closer, and she refused to step back. Without a word he pulled at her hand, turning it so her palm was open to the air. Gold glinted on his finger, and Eva frowned when she recognised the initials carved into the tarnished surface.

L.W.

"Kace, what have you done?" Something sharp landed in her hand, and she immediately closed her fingers around it. His eyes dipped down, and she hesitantly opened her hand one finger at a time. Two fangs sat in the centre of her palm, still covered in blood and flesh.

He had given her Lucas's fangs.

The man who had killed her.

"You should never have come to me Eva." Kace's free hand brushed her jaw, tipping her head back to meet his dark green eyes. "Because it's going to be really fucking hard to let you go."

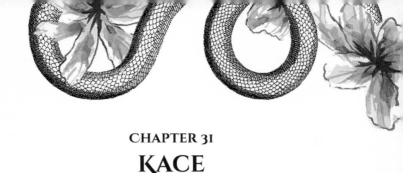

CHAPTER 31

KACE

K ace growled, Sythe and Axel's attention quickly skirting away from Eva's curvy arse.

Of course she had to wear leather, he thought, struggling to tear his eyes away either.

She moved, drawing his attention to her less than amused expression.

Fuck. Of course vampires could see in pitch black.

"Lucy ready?" he asked, going back to placing the explosives onto the concrete wall. The crystals hummed, and Kace was excited to try out his new little project.

Titus sat on the floor, a laptop balanced on his knees. "Two minutes," he said, typing away, the glow the only light in the room. "Apparently he's adding glitter."

"Of course he fucking is," Riley muttered, standing at the doorway of the estate agents they had broken into. The building Eva marked as the Viper Tower was in the human district, and cleverly disguised as an elite bank. Security was extensive, as was expected with a bank, but they didn't plan to go through the front door.

"You need to move the second one a few feet to the

right, otherwise the concrete is going to be too thick," Titus said, scowling at the building's blueprints.

The bank, according to the information Titus had found, was actually an officially registered bank with Companies House. The blueprints showed it took up half of the building, with the other half what they assumed to be the Vipers safe house.

"Kyra wasn't aware of the meeting, was she?" Eva asked Xander, who stood stiff beside her. He had removed his sunglasses, his eyes pale even when shifted to his beast. "She's going to kill you when she finds out."

Xander grunted. "Don't do something stupid, like die, and she'll be fine."

"We both know she won't be." Eva laughed, shaking her head as Kace stepped back, pushing her tighter into the corner.

"Ready to go." He waited for her protest as he touched his new trophy gold ring on his finger.

"Hey, I don't need..."

Loud pops and crackles echoed, followed by blinding bursts of multi-coloured light that brightened the entire street just outside the door. The noise wouldn't be as loud as his bombs, but they were enough to distract.

Clicking his fingers Kace released a burst of arcane, the heat a catalyst that ignited the small devices in sequence. The crystals ruptured, the concentrated energy cracking the concrete perfectly.

"Titus?" he asked, waiting for confirmation.

"CCTV is looped."

With one kick the wall connecting the two basements crashed, allowing them access into the underground garage.

The air shifted, and Lucifer appeared beside Eva, who almost jumped out of her skin. "Holy shit, those fireworks were fucking *awesome*," he chuckled, rubbing his hands together. "I knew it was a good idea to add the extra powder."

"And the glitter?" Eva asked.

Lucifer turned his smirk to her. "Because, my little bloodsucker, the world needs more fucking sparkle."

Kace pulled Eva closer to him, and Lucifer's grin widened. "Let's go, we don't want to risk someone calling for help."

"What's the point of Alice playing nice with The Met if we're still going to have issues with the police?" Axel muttered. "Breaking and entering isn't even that big of a deal."

"She works for Spook Squad, I don't think they're going to be much fucking help unless we find a dead body," Sythe said. "Unless you would like to volunteer?"

"Fuck you." Axel flipped him the finger.

One by one they climbed through the space in the wall, the garage lit up by strip lighting along the floor.

"Look at this beauty." Sythe let out a low whistle as he brushed his hand down the side of a flashy yellow sports car. "Aw, K, you dented her."

Eva smiled at Sythe's pout, and Kace fought the snarl that rattled his chest. He didn't want her to smile at anyone but him.

Which was fucking ridiculous.

"Er, guys," Titus said as he swept his gaze across the room. "There's three lifts. There's only supposed to be one."

"And they're the wrong colour," Eva added. "The lift that connects to the upper floors is gold, not silver."

Xander grunted. "Well, where the bloody hell is the correct lift then?"

Footsteps echoed, and Kace cocked his head as he pulled one of his throwing blades from the sheath on his chest. Closing his eyes he turned, the blade releasing from his hand just as the first guard stepped through the hidden door, gun pointed. His knife hit him dead between the eyes, and he fell like a sack of shit.

Bullets pinged, and Kace threw himself towards Eva. Wrapping her in his arms he grunted, feeling one stray bullet slice into his back.

"Clear," Riley said as Kace quickly swept his gaze across Eva, making sure nothing else had ricocheted.

"Did you get hit?" Eva pressed her hands gently to his stomach, fingers sweeping down his abs before she pushed gently for him to turn.

"No," he grunted, the bullet lodged somewhere inside. It ached, but it wouldn't kill him.

Eva's fingers hesitated at the wound, coming away red. "Oh my god Kace, let me..."

"It's nothing," he interrupted. "Keep your head in the game, or I may start to think you like me."

The echo of her own words did the trick. The panic that had edged her lips lessened as her head snapped up, eyes narrowing.

"Don't come to me when you're all hurt and bleeding," she said with a warning that made him want to see how far he could push. "I won't help you."

"We both know you love me bleeding, don't we, Sunshine?"

Eva let out a frustrated scream, her fangs teasing white against her lips. "You're insufferable."

Kace chuckled, pulling out a second knife to hand to her. "Noted."

Eva paused, fingers twitching as if she wanted to hit him before she grabbed the offering.

"You're welcome," he said before she could thank him, just so he could see a little aggravation flash in her darkened eyes. He loved her blue irises, thought they were so serene and pure compared to his own taint. But he was also fascinated by the predatorial hunger that glinted when they turned obsidian.

In those eyes he saw himself. Corrupted. Dangerous.

The stairs beyond the hidden door lead into the main auditorium of the bank, the floor black and white tiles with dark wood panelling behind the numerous desks lined up by the walls. A larger desk was in the centre back, in front of the same three silver lifts that must have been connected to the basement. The desk was gold, and not just simply painted, either. Directly behind were the same three lifts.

"Do you think they keep real money here?" Lucy asked. "Asking for a friend."

"What do you even need money for? You live at the house for free," Axel said.

"Oh, I don't know fuckface. Maybe I want to buy a puppy? Or a nice whore who will suck my juicy co..."

"Enough," Riley hissed. "This is not the time, or the place."

Lucifer clicked his tongue, a smile teasing his lips. "There's wild magic here, black."

"They had a faerie," Eva said, absently brushing her fingers down her tattooed arms.

"Had?"

"Yeah, I err... killed her."

Lucy let out a whistle through his teeth. "Seems the little bloodsucker has a darker side. Yum."

"I can't feel any magic," Kace said, trying to cool his sudden spike in temper.

"That's because I'm better than you," Lucy said. "But there's definitely something..." He took a step forward, and the white tile clicked. "Oh fuck."

The lights brightened, illuminating the entire area in

crimson. Symbols glowed on every white tile, unfamiliar swirls that whined a high-pitched tune.

Eva gasped, and as Kace stepped towards her, keeping to the black tiles, her body seemed to flicker.

"Eva?" He reached forward, but his arm swept through her form entirely. "What the..." With a blink she had disappeared, and so had everyone else but Titus. "Fuck."

Another blink, and the edges of the bank turned to shadows, quickly sweeping closer until he was no longer in the bank, but a hallway not much different to an office block.

Titus had already lifted his gun, shooting two of the guards while Kace knocked the third out with a heavy fist.

"Well, hello to you too," Titus muttered, placing his pistol back on his hip. "Do you think this is real?"

Kace reached out to the wall, feeling every groove of the wood beneath his fingertips. The carpet was brown, threadbare that released dust with every step. "Feels real." His stomach twisted, panic tensing his muscles until he felt the heat of Eva in his chest. She was still there, somewhere. Hopefully not alone.

"I don't think it's glamour," Titus said with a frown, stepping over one of the guards. "I think Lucifer accidently activated the intruder mechanism. I've been reading online forums recently that specialise in leaked Fae war tactics. Rather than take an enemy head on they would split them with a short portal spell."

"Making it easier to pick us off one by one. That's clever," Kace added. "So we're still in the same building, but a different floor."

"Seems to be." Titus slung his laptop over his back with a strap. "Which is either good, or bad."

"Well, which one is it?"

"Oh, I don't fucking know, K. Let me just look up all of

the Fae war tactics, oh right, they keep their secrets tighter than a nun's knickers."

Kace braced as he kicked open the closest door, the room empty other than a dust-covered shelf. The window that was once there was boarded from the outside, and Kace remembered the entire front of the building was covered in black, shiny cladding.

"Can your beast sense anything?"

Kace quietened his breathing, drawing on his beast to stretch his senses. He couldn't feel anyone other than himself and Titus. "Those three are dead, so where the fuck is everyone else?"

"I don't like this, let's try and find a way down. Or up."

The next room was just as vacant, as was the third and fourth. At the end of the hall was a lift, the mirrored surface tarnished. Nothing adorned the walls except shadows where pictures or paintings were once placed. The wood panelling had broken, revealing raw plaster beneath.

"This floor only has one lift, so where have the other two gone?" Kace asked as he carefully dipped his fingers into his back. He felt the bullet, his body already pushing out the foreign object. Coated in blood Kace brushed his finger across the cool surface, drawing a random glyph. He knew many glyphs, having drawn and tattooed every single one on himself and his brothers.

The blood boiled, disappearing altogether within seconds, but it did exactly what Kace expected. "There's glamour." There were three main magics that operated on Earth Side, with witches that was either black, nature or arcane based. Druid magic, which was both glyph and natural arcane based, and lastly the wild magic of the Fae. The different magics mixed as well as oil and water, and they frequently repelled one another.

Titus frowned, pressing the call button. The doors

opened with a pained squeak, the inside just as worn as the outside. There were no more buttons, just smudged mirrors that held a spiderweb of cracks. "I think you're right. Hand me a blade, please."

Without hesitation Kace handed over another blade, and Titus immediately popped off the surrounding case of the call button. "The thing with glamour is it only affects the appearance, and not the function." Kneeling down he pulled his laptop back out, along with several wires which he attached to those inside the button. "This lift is on its own internal server, which is pretty efficient, actually."

"You able to hack it?"

Titus shot him a dark look. "Of course, but it's going to take some time."

"We don't have time." Kace touched the blank wall to the left of the lift, trying and failing to call arcane to his fingertips. The wall rippled, and he was sure he saw the outline of one of the other lifts. "The entire wall is covered in glamour. It's..."

A gentle beep, and Kace stepped back just as the wall split open like doors, revealing a large fucking bear.

CHAPTER 32

EVA

Eva crouched as the whoosh of air subsided, quickly taking in her new surroundings. The entire room was open from one side to the other, the walls having been ripped out. A rectangular semi-transparent glass partition creating a meeting room in the centre, with a table that could easily fit twenty.

"What in the fuckery is this?" Lucifer shook his head like a wet dog, the movement quivering down his body. "Have I hit my head? You could probably host a rugby game in this space."

"I told you it was built like a safe house," Eva whispered, touching her hand against the boarded over window. "They clearly only needed the top floors and the bottom, so the middle has just been left."

"I'm sorry, but what sort of safe house uses Fae portals?" He stuck a finger in his ear, as if trying to clear pressure. "Bloody uncivilised swines, that's who. Wild magic is so fucking unpredictable."

He stretched his arms into the air, clicking his back. Eva followed the line of his arm, stopping when she noticed two horns protruding from his dark hair. Horns that definitely weren't there a minute ago.

Lucy raised a brow, and Eva quickly dropped her eyes as he jumped towards her. "Boo!"

She hit out, her fist missing his jaw to hit his shoulder. "What is wrong with you?"

"Okay, ow!" he grunted, rubbing the hurt. "Honestly, is no one scared of me anymore? I miss the time where people fucking pissed their pants when I walked into the room. Honestly, living on Earth Side is killing my street cred."

"What do you mean?" Eva asked.

Lucifer blinked, pouting his lips. "How can someone so innocent get involved with a group of spicy barbarians like them?" He placed his hands on his hips, staring down at her. "I used to reside in The Nether, you know, some human cultures refer to it as Hell."

"Hell?"

Lucifer smirked. "Well, where else would you find a Daemon?"

Fuck. Me. Sideways. He was a Daemon. Like a real fucking Daemon.

"Don't worry, little bloodsucker, I will protect you from this strange building and its contents. I respect the fuck out of Kace, even though he's a raging psycho. He doesn't take shit from anyone, and you seem to be the calm to his storm. He's chosen his mate well."

Eva tried to swallow the slight panic. "I'm not his mate." The word felt wrong on her tongue. She had been brought up thinking about marriage and babies, not being soulbound to someone she barely knew.

"Then it's really going to fucking hurt, for the both of you." Lucifer shrugged, rummaging in the hot pink bag he had slung over his shoulder. "Not everything in life can be planned." He pulled out a small ball, the surface a pale pearlescent cream. With one throw it cracked against the wall, bursting into a cloud of powder.

"Glitter, really?"

Lucy let out a whoop. "Your mate is a fucking artist with these things, although he's super boring." He rushed over, pushing the powder with his boot. "And yes, I sometimes sneak some glitter in there when he isn't looking. You would too if you had lived more lifetimes than you can ever imagine in the dark. You learn to live for the light."

Eva watched as Lucifer frowned, his head tilting to the side. The horns had completely spread though his hair, the tips curling down towards his sharp cheekbones.

"The room is real, it's not a glamour which means there's stairs in the corner. We should see if we can find the others on another level."

"Can't you just... poof us?"

"Poof?" he snorted. "It's called a drift, and no, it's not how it works. I need to be able to visualise the destination and I don't know where the fuck we are." He stormed over to the doors, pushing on the metal that didn't budge. "So I haven't lived here for that long, and even I know that bolting closed the emergency exit is a serious health hazard."

Eva pushed the door too, even with them both it didn't move.

"Step back." Lucifer clicked his fingers, frowning at his hand. He stretched, rolling his shoulders before trying again, staring intensely at his palm.

Eva pursed her lips. "Are you having performance issues?"

Lucy snarled, the veins along his arms darkening to black. Curling his fingers he punched the metal door, it denting beneath his strength. "I didn't want to alarm you, but it seems I can't access my chi, something is blocking it."

"How can something block it?" She knew of chi's. Kyra

having explained before that access to one's chi was the difference between a human and a witch. Or in Lucifer's case a human and a Daemon, although she was sure there were many more differences.

Lucifer hit the door again, his fist straining against the metal. "It means I can't 'poof' us out of here."

"That's..." Eva turned at a familiar ding. "Lucy, I thought you said there was no glamour?" At the back of the room, behind the glass partition was a single lift that definitely wasn't there before.

Lucifer turned in the same direction, red eyes glowing. "I take it back, your mates exploding balls are shit."

The lift doors parted, and Eva froze, ice sinking into her lungs.

"Hello there, pretty lady," Dutch said with a grin. "How nice of you to come home."

Lucifer snarled, forcing Eva behind him.

Dutch's smile widened, and Eva noticed that he was missing his left eye, the skin around it smooth and unmarked. His attention flicked to Lucy, and then he was gone, blurring his speed far faster than she had ever witnessed.

"Shit!"

She reached for a wooden stake, having stored one in her boot. Her fingertips touched the smooth surface before she felt a solid weight hit her, her grip slipping as she fell heavily to the floor. Dutch's fangs sliced across her shoulder, and before she could scream, she stabbed up with her knife, catching between two ribs.

She was sure Lucifer hadn't expected Dutch's speed, his hesitation evident before he seemed to explode, his shirt ripping as he grew to almost seven-foot, the muscles in his back flexing as black wings shot out from discreet little slits. The skeletal frame was covered in a thin membrane, the high arches curved with sharp spikes. He yanked Dutch away, throwing him across the room, and through the glass in the centre of the room.

Skin tore, and Eva grunted as Dutch took a chunk of flesh with him. She raised herself on her arms, freezing when she noticed Lucy's sheer size.

Holy shit. She understood why cultures from around the world dictated Daemons as evil, because Lucifer looked terrifying.

Dutch jumped to his feet, his smile turning frenzied, his black eyes far from sane. "My uncle's pretty distracted right now. I bet he wouldn't be even that mad If I fucked you before him. That's fair, right? Considering you killed my mate."

His words broke her from her stupor, her hand scrambling around for the stake that was missing from her boot. "Shit," she said through clenched teeth. It was gone, having disappeared in the scuffle.

Lucy let out a pained grunt, and Eva turned just as Dutch attacked, ripping down one of his wings as if it were paper. "You dirty little bastard," he screeched. "I'm going to shove your head so far up your own fucking arse..."

"Lucy!" Eva threw the knife Kace had given her, Lucifer catching it without even looking. The silver came down in a flash, scoring Dutch hard enough for the vampire to let go, barely saving his wing.

Eva pushed herself across the room, the shattered glass crunching beneath her boots as she reached for the table. "Fuck!" The top was plastic, a wood-like texture covering the entire surface while the legs were metal, rusted.

She needed wood. Except there wasn't any wood.

Fuck my life!

She yanked on a leg, and due to the erosion it broke off in her hand, the inside hollow. Gripping it firmly, she raced to the two men, careful to not get caught by Lucifer's sharp wing. They were a shadowed smudge in her vision, their movements like lightening that crashed from one side of the room to another, their combined snarls blurring into a dissonance.

It took all her concentration to tear them apart, both their expressions contorted into pure rage. There was a second, a break of the two and she hit out with the flat of the table leg across Dutch's back. The metal warped, reverberating back up at her arm.

But it didn't slow him down, and with a hiss Dutch reared back to grab the weapon, only to turn and thrust it straight through Lucifer's chest.

Eva didn't have time to react, Lucifer's eyes widening with shock before Dutch was on her, hand encircling her throat to squeeze all her air. He lifted, and if she didn't reach up to grab his outstretched arm her neck would have broken.

"I always knew you would be so much fun." He moved her across the room, throwing her into the lift as if she were a ragdoll. Her head cracked against the mirrored panels, the pain a quick shock but didn't break skin.

The lift dinged, the doors beginning to close as he stepped inside with a grin. Fear forced her to her feet just as a thunder rattled the room, and Lucifer was suddenly there, a creature of pure darkness and fury. His horns had grown, reaching his jaw while his wings stretched out three times his height. His shirt was long gone, revealing a wide chest that was covered in red markings and a gaping hole, the bloody table leg held in a hand turned claw.

Dutch barely had time to turn, and just before the doors closed he was yanked back, blood splattering across her face as Lucifer ripped Dutch's head clean off his shoulders.

Eva stood there, staring at herself in the mirrored

surface sucking in staggered breaths. The lift began to ascend, and in a panic she reached for all the buttons, pressing so hard some began to crack.

Except nothing stopped her rising, so she braced herself as the lift finally came to a stop, knowing who stood on the other side of the doors.

Waiting for her.

CHAPTER 33

KACE

Shifters were fucking arseholes. Especially bears.

"How much longer do you need?" Kace snarled, barely dodging a paw the size of his head.

"I'm sorry," Titus said with a hum of impatience. "Did you want to do this while I take care of the fucking bear?"

Kace bared his teeth, his attention split with making sure the bloody shifter taller than his six-four didn't disturb Titus doing his thing, and taking down the random guards who were appearing out of thin fucking air like magicians. Add that to the fact he couldn't feel his chi, they were in a total shit storm.

"Stop toying with him!"

Kace gripped the bear's bottom jaw. "I'm..."

His other hand closed around the top, fingers precariously close to sharp teeth already covered in his blood.

"Not..."

With a grunt he pulled, the skin between his snout splitting as the jaws dislocated, leaving them attached by a single piece of flesh.

"Toying with him!"

The bear gave an ungodly screech of pain, rearing back

and Kace savoured the slight resistance as his knife impaled deep within his skull. In any other situation he would have loved to have gone hand-to-hand with a bear, that type of shifter being exceedingly rare in the UK.

He was almost a little disappointed.

A loud pop, and another guard collapsed behind him with a bullet hole dead between his eyes.

Titus dropped his pistol back to the ground, his fingers moving fast over the keyboard once more. "We both know you could have taken him within minutes. Which means you were definitely toying with him."

Kace checked the wound on his thigh, the claws having done some serious damage, not to mention the chunk he was missing from his upper arm. Okay, so he was playing with his prey a little. Anyone who had a hand in hurting Eva had it coming.

The light above the lift glowed, and Titus unattached his laptop.

Adrenaline pulsed through Kace's veins, trepidation overshadowed as he waited with a patience that was rapidly wearing thin.

A clang, the bullet that was lodged in his back hitting the floor.

Titus raised his pale brows, but didn't comment as the lift finally arrived, the inside glass smashed with specks of blood dotting the metallic floor.

The warmth in his chest that appeared around the same time as his beast forced their mating was still there, helping him keep calm, keeping him sane as the red mist of rage teased at the edges of his vision. His beast was a heavy vibration beneath his skin, content for him to lead. At least, for now.

The lift closed around them, ascending immediately to

the next floor. Kace turned to pin Titus with a glare, his nostrils flared with the force of his exhale.

"I got the lift operating, didn't I?" Titus grunted, a muscle in his jaw twitching.

Axel, Sythe and Riley were on the next floor, their expressions surprised when Kace held the door open for them to run towards the lift, shots ringing behind them. A few floors later Xander stood amongst a pile of dead men, chest heaving.

He snarled when they appeared, feet stomping as he pushed inside. "I swear if any of those spooks follow us home." He stroked his fingers down his abs, checking several bullet holes along his stomach. "Motherfuckers."

The vibration beneath Kace's skin strengthened, his hands tightening into fists. The lift moved smoothly, and after each empty floor he felt his muscles stiffen until he was wound so tight he felt coiled to snap. The adrenaline tingled, the need to fight, to kill almost as essential as oxygen.

After ten empty floors, the doors opened and Lucifer lay on the floor, a hole the size of a fist in the centre of his chest.

"Oh fuck," someone whispered, but Kace couldn't concentrate on anything else.

"Eva?"

Lucifer panted, each breath a rattle. "She went up." He tried to climb to his feet, his legs unable to take his weight as both Riley and Xander rushed out to grab him, quickly followed by Titus.

His brother turned, clicking a button on his keyboard. "Go, I'll send the lift back down when we're done here."

Sythe and Axel nodded, but Kace was beyond any communication as the lift moved once more, his beast so prominent he could feel claws at the end of his fingertips, felt a phantom tail ready to split into sharp whips.

Sythe unsheathed his sword as Axel rolled his shoulders, hopping from one foot to the other. Tension was palpable between them, Kace's heart thumping painfully in his chest as he shot out of the lift doors as soon as they began to open, the room beyond completely dark.

Pulling on his beast he blinked into the void, able to make out the shape of furniture. There was even more blood, smeared with clear evidence of a struggle that only worsened the angered snarls and growls inside his mind.

Sythe froze beside him, his brother's eyes widening before he disappeared into the dark, wrapping shadows around his body until he was invisible to the naked eye. Kace could still sense him through his beast, and was able to track him across the room until he appeared by the opulent sofa, his blade flashing as it sliced straight through the neck of a man crouched.

As soon as the first head rolled, the men who had been hiding in wait stood, their goggles allowing them to see in the pitch black.

Sythe disappeared once more, only to appear a few feet away behind another guard.

"Go, we will handle these," Axel said and Kace took no time to move across the room. He knew the guards would fall quickly, their reactions slow, even though clearly trained. Humans, or maybe a shifter or two.

Weak.

The giant fucking penthouse was built with thick walls and locked doors, forcing Kace to take his time to sweep the areas, fighting against his instinct to just destroy everything in his path.

Movement above his head, and a blade left Kace's hand without thought, sinking deep within the guard's chest. His gun fell through limp fingers, dropping down beneath the gap of the bannister.

Bracing himself along the wall, he ran, using the momentum to launch himself up, and over the bannister to the mezzanine above to find a light hum, a glow beneath a door.

The door shattered against his kick, the room empty but for a seven foot mirror, symbols pulsing around the edges. The surface shimmered, glowing brighter as he stepped closer.

A dark voice whispered through the glass, the words muffled.

Kace touched his fingertips to the mirror, passing through with no resistance. His hand disappeared, and then his arm before the sensation of hooks piercing into his skin, pulling him through. Kace pulled, able to free himself from whatever had caught him. He landed into a crouch, the smell of ash and death tickling his nose.

"Turn around and put your hands up."

Kace slowly raised to his full height, following the instructions to find Augustine standing there, one hand wrapped around his mate's throat and another hidden from sight.

Mate.

"Well, if it isn't the infamous Red." Confusion flashed in Augustine's obsidian eyes, quickly clouding over with rage. "Do you really believe I would trap myself so easily?" he said, gesturing to the mirror behind Kace. "It's a waking glass, and you have no idea how many faeries I had to kill to get one."

Kace let out a growl, taking a step forward before Eva's face twisted with pain, her lips opening on a gasp. The bite on her throat had stopped bleeding, but he knew it was fresh.

"Careful," Augustine warned, "there's a stake perfectly placed against her heart. One wrong move and she's nothing but dust. You wouldn't cause her harm, would you, Red?"

Flames crackled, an orange blaze deep below the unsteady platform on which they stood. The sands of the Pits lay in ruins, much of the surrounding arena beyond recognition. Kace thought he would have grinned at the sight, except all he cared about was the woman in the master vampire's grip.

"It was a mistake to hire only humans."

"Breed generally cannot be trusted." Augustine cocked his head, his grip tightening on Eva. "It took me a while, Red, but I finally recognised you."

Kace waited, heart a heavy thump that he knew both could hear.

"You were such a weak, pathetic child. You sobbed when your grandfather left you with me, so much you puked." Flames reflected in the darkness of his eyes, his smile a smirk. "But then you survived, a fucking artist on the sands."

Kace reached for another blade, fingers finding nothing. *Fuck.*

"You were my star, a child able to take out men three times his size." Augustine continued. "It all makes sense now, why you would be sponsored by Riley Storm. It was his father, Mason who bought your freedom. Offered me more money than you could ever have made me. Everything dies, and you would have fallen eventually."

Fur brushed beneath tight skin, Kace's eyes sweeping up to meet Eva's, her own calm and as blue as the ocean.

"Looks like that was a big fucking mistake," Augustine chuckled. "Together we could make the Undercity bow at our feet."

. . .

"The only thing you're bowing to is death." Kace let his beast shadow his features, his irises shifting to liquid silver.

Doubt glistened in Augustine's dark eyes. "What are you?"

Kace tried to keep a stoic face. "I'm the monster who eats monsters."

CHAPTER 34
EVA

Heat licked across her skin, Augustine's grip ice in comparison.

"Just couldn't stand to be away from me," he whispered against her ear, and she fought his hold as he pulled her further towards the edge.

Eva scratched down his arm, but his hand only strengthened, the other wrapping around her hair to pin her neck at a painful angle. Fangs pierced, and her scream echoed in the carnivorous room.

His head shifted to the side, only for his tongue to tease the edge of the wound. "Who are the friends you've invited to their deaths?"

The surface of the mirror rippled, and Eva shook as Kace fell into a crouch.

"Turn around and put your hands up." Augustine stiffened behind her as Kace rose to stand. "Well, if it isn't the infamous Red."

Pressure on her back, a sharp tip piercing her skin to radiate a shock of pain across her muscles. She let out a gasp, unable to keep it inside before she breathed through the burning ache, regaining her composure long enough to meet Kace's tightly hidden violence.

"What are you?" Augustine asked, his voice losing its authority.

There was no emotion on Kace's face, no pain or excitement. "I'm the monster who eats monsters."

A second of hesitation.

She felt it in the grip on her neck, and on the slight release of Augustine's fingers. It was enough for her to twist from his grasp, to strike out with her own fangs. She put everything in shredding and tearing, his blood a cascade down her lips that burned as hot as the flames that surrounded them.

Augustine screeched, and suddenly he was torn from her grip, the stake slicing into her stomach as it broke in two. Eva crashed to her knees, blood leaking from between her fingers as she pressed to stem the flow.

Kace moved in graceful strikes, Augustine stabbing out with the other half of the stake as he tried to defend himself against Kace's sheer force. The movements were mesmerising, a vicious dance that radiated such intense fury that she couldn't tear her attention away, not until black edged its way in to her peripheral.

The burning pain was nauseating as she slowly pulled the wood free, her hand shaking as she tried to grasp the sharp edge. The ache moved slowly, spreading across her body with every pump of her heart. It started in her stomach, radiating from her wound until every breath sent agony across every limb, her muscles rigid.

The wood slipped, sinking further inside.

Kace turned at her gasp, and Augustine used the opportunity to stab him with the other half of the stake. She had torn Augustine's throat, his entire jaw and chest a bright red as he grinned.

"You're not here for you, you're here for *her*." Augustine gripped his weapon, eyes flicking between Kace and Eva as he laughed. "Beautiful isn't she, even covered in blood, dying."

Eva concentrated on her breathing, not wanting to make a sound as she finally got a steady hold on the wood. It finally slipped free, no longer than her hand, and no thicker than a pencil. Releasing her grip on the weapon she fell forward, stopping her fall with the flats of her hands. With all her strength she looked up through her hair, Kace ripping his shirt to reveal a large hole in his left shoulder, slicing through his intricate tattoos.

He stretched his arm, expression revealing no pain. Instead he looked terrifying, an avenging angel surrounded by flames.

Augustine snarled. "She's mine, I own her."

"Enough," Kace growled, stepping forward.

Augustine moved back, foot slipping slightly on a piece of debris. "You don't want her, Red. She's nothing, a pathetic fledgling who willingly dropped to her knees for me."

Eva's voice was weak. "Stop it."

Kace growled, moving slowly closer.

"I must say, she sure knows how to suck a cock." Eva sucked in a pained breath as Augustine grinned. "She moaned, begging for it. She's nothing but a whore who spread her..."

Kace shot forward, and at the exact same time Augustine threw his weapon. Eva could do nothing as she watched the stake soar, aimed straight for her.

KACE

Kace let out an almighty roar, twisting at the last second to move in front of Eva. The stake caught him in his chest, skin and muscle ripping as he tore it from his body.

Breathe.

Lightening through his veins, the red mist that had teased the edges of his vision descending until he was at the cusp of the abyss.

Breathe.

He could hear Eva, her breaths coming in shallow, almost silent pants. He needed to remain calm as he faced Augustine, the vampire's mouth gaping like a fish.

"She isn't worth your life," Augustine said, his bloody hand raising as if it would stop Kace from stalking closer. He stumbled back, the grace he had only movements before absent as terror stiffened his limbs. "She's just a whore."

Kace finally let a cruel smile spread across his face, the rage a ferocious vibration beneath his skin.

"We can get out of this, together." Augustine's foot caught the edge of the platform, a chunk of concrete falling below. "You, me and her." His throat had almost entirely healed from Eva's bite.

There was nowhere for him to go, so Kace waited with a predatory patience. He wanted to savour the moment, forever imprint Augustine's fear in his memory. Augustine collided with him like a fucking train, the vampire trying to blur past.

Kace felt nothing as he knocked Augustine to the floor, the vampire slightly weakened from his blood loss. He was beyond words, almost beyond thought as he pressed closer, forcing Augustine to his knees.

Breathe.

Augustine hissed, fangs long past his lips. "You can have..." His words cut off as Kace slowly pressed the stake into his chest, watching Augustine's eyes as the realisation of his death slowly sunk in, and then stopped a mere centimetre from his heart.

Kace would have preferred to have done it himself, to watch his life drain from his decrepit gaze. He would have bathed himself in the blood, consumed it.

But it wasn't his vengeance anymore, it was hers.

Keeping the stake exactly where it was he dragged Augustine towards Eva, who had her entire weight on her shaking arms. Kace carefully positioned Augustine in front of her, the vampire unable to move with the tip of the stake kissing his heart.

She looked up, determination creasing her brows as she sat back on her heels. He helped lift her hand, wrapping it around the wood.

Augustine snarled, fangs so long they almost reached his chin.

Smoke and dust had settled on her skin, a single tear dropping down her cheek to leave a clean trail. With a scream she pushed forward, and Kace finally let himself release his rage. The stake had pushed through to the other side, and reaching down he snapped it free, leaving the wood trapped inside Augustine's chest.

He pulled Augustine up by his throat, the Vampire already starting to die as the skin around his eyes began to slowly decay, turning back to his true age. His mouth was agape, tongue already blackened as Kace walked him to the very edge of the platform, making sure he met his widened, obsidian gaze.

His beast tightened his vocal cords, but Kace needed Augustine to hear his final words. "You're wrong. She's worth everything."

Fear twisted the vampire's features, all sense of superiority disappearing as his weakened arms flayed to stop from falling. With a surprised gasp he collapsed backwards, disappearing into the flames that cleansed the deaths of hundreds, if not thousands on the sands.

A heavy pressure lifted, and he wasted no more time on the man who had destroyed his childhood, turning back to his mate. Except she was motionless, collapsed on her back.

"Eva." Kace's voice was no longer his own, his hands shaking as he rushed to his knees beside her. He tore at the flesh of his wrist, pressing the wound to her mouth and waited for her to bite, to take his life for herself.

His blood fell on frozen lips, her lashes dark against pale skin. Pulling her up he cradled her on his lap, pressing her limp head against his throat. With a pained scream he cut his own skin, silently begging the fates to feel the sharp pain of her fangs, and then the deadly pleasure of her venom.

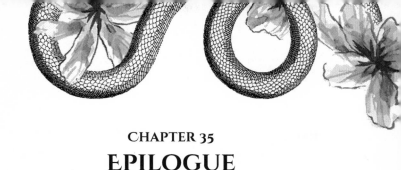

CHAPTER 35

EPILOGUE

KACE

Eva was immobile beneath the sheets, so pale with her golden-brown hair spread across the white pillow. He knew she was alive, her body taking it's time to heal the wound that had almost killed her, the stake splintering inside her stomach.

She had been poisoned by the wood, and his beast hadn't once relaxed as he watched over her, letting no one close as she rested, healed. No one would see her so vulnerable, never again.

Wake up.

It hadn't even been a day, and already his patience was non-existent.

Come on, Sunshine. Wake up.

Slipping in beside her, he pulled her against his chest, her skin as cold as ice. She didn't react at his touch, and his heart clenched at her so still. Eva was fire, passion and pure attitude, not a lifeless corpse.

Wake. Up.

A vibration rattled, his beast just beneath the surface.

He had accepted long ago that he would never find a mate, never allow himself to be that exposed to another being for their souls to be bound together with magic.

He was ruined, beyond repair.

A man who feared touch, and yet all he wanted to do was bury himself against the woman who argued as passionately as she kissed a monster. There was no dread, nor panic at being bound, their souls connected forever.

And yet, she could never be his.

He had to let her go.

EVA
FOUR WEEKS LATER

She was a master vampire, able to live her life as her own, now London's vampire Elder had approved it. Yet the butterflies in her stomach were wreaking havoc as she hesitated at the thick door. It had taken her weeks to gain enough courage, chickening out twice before she finally decided enough was enough.

Eva Morgan didn't chase after men. Ever.

Except one.

She nervously brushed her fingers down her arms, pausing as her thumbs touched the head of the snakes that should have been a horrific reminder. Except they were no longer the markings of the Vipers, the blunt lines and crude runes long gone. Her left arm had been transformed, the scales turned into the silhouettes of flowers with highlights of white, a sun blazing on the snake's head. Her right arm was the opposite, the flowers shadowed dark in each scale, the head a crescent moon.

'We both know what it's like to be trapped, to be a prison-

er.' The words Kace had said as he pressed the tattoo gun so gently against her skin. *'I would never do that to you.'*

He was an artist that kept her nightmares at bay, the overwhelming need she had for him dangerous, her emotions confused in the following week of the Pits collapse.

She had needed time, and he hadn't fought her when she returned to the life before she was murdered. He had given her what she needed, her freedom.

But she couldn't forget about the connection that warmed her skin, even when the heat of the blood had long cooled. It was like being near a blazing fire, a comfort she sought that had weakened the longer she had stayed away. It was a pain she couldn't describe, as if she was missing a part of herself.

Their joining had been different, more raw and violent. And after several sessions of therapy, at Kyra's insistence, she knew in her heart that it wasn't a trick. It was as if fate knew they needed each other, and the only way for either of their stubbornness to see it was to force the bond. At least, that's what she had decided to believe anyway.

Forever a romanticist.

Laughter escaped as she pressed the door open, silently walking inside. Kace stood with his back to her, carefully moving from one transition to another, holding each position for a few seconds for the kids to match. It heightened her nerves, because she knew he must have sensed her, and yet he didn't turn, the muscles along his bare back tensing.

Oh shit. Maybe he didn't want the bond?

A glint of gold, her eyes dropping to the ring on his left hand.

"What are you doing here, Eva?" he said, his deep voice flowing over her like rough waves.

Eva cleared her throat, ignoring the curious stares from the kids. "You're still wearing the ring."

Kace touched a thumb against the flat surface, turning to fully face her. She had braced for the full force of his gaze, deciding she wanted to drown in the deep green of his eyes.

"You never answered my question," he said, face unreadable.

"Oh." Eva tugged on the hem of her shirt. "I wanted to ask you to dance."

Kace raised a single brow, his face carefully composed. "Dance?"

"Yes, dance." An awkward pause. "You know, with me."

Okay, this was definitely a stupid idea!

Kace cocked his head, arms crossing as a teasing smile parted his lips. "I can't dance." His eyes darted to the vampire fangs that she hung from her ears, and she knew he approved.

"Good thing I can." She hadn't noticed they were now alone, the kids gone and for some reason it made her feel even more nervous.

"Careful," Kace said, a heated gleam in his eye when they steadied back on hers. "I may start to think you like me." He closed the distance, tension strung taut as he kept a cushion of air between them.

"You told me to stay away," she said, voice dropping to a whisper.

"And look how well you follow orders."

Eva licked across her bottom lip, and Kace traced the movement. "Maybe I don't want to stay away."

Silver glinted in his irises. "Eva... I'm not what you need."

"No, but you're what I want. If you'll have me."

Kace blinked, his eyes returning to forest green. His lips

crushed to hers, and she opened for him without hesitation. He tasted of steel, rain and embers. A violence so tightly concealed she couldn't wait to coax it out.

Mine, she thought as his hands brushed down her sides to settle heavily on her hips. *He's all mine.*

His breath came out in a growl when he pulled back only to rest his forehead against hers. "The ring," he said, hand tightening as if he was scared she would pull away. "I keep it as a warning to anyone who ever thinks about hurting you."

"Don't you think he was my revenge?"

"Yes," he said with a smirk, unrepentant.

"Ugh, you're insufferable!" she laughed, smacking him against the chest.

"Always." His smile strained, his lashes dropping to hide his expression. "I believed I never had a heart, having been ripped out long ago on those claret sands. Then there you were, my beast stunned into silence as you threatened me with a fucking frying pan."

"It was a wok."

"Brat." Kace nipped along her lip. "Eva, it's not just me anymore, it's Hunter too. He needs..."

Eva silenced him with a kiss. She had dreamt of a white wedding, and a large house with children playing in the garden. Instead she has a broody barbarian, who kissed her with such intensity it was like she was the only other person in existence, and a just as moody teenager.

What more could she ask for?

Happiness pulsed in her chest, her cheeks stretched to the edge of pain. "So, will you dance with me?"

His eyes were a brand, voice a dark rasp. "Eva, you're the light to my darkness. You were always mine, and I will dance with you now, forever and always."

The Pretty Boy

Their tension twisted like an abrasion, a rope wrapping around his throat until there was no air left. The attraction was violent. A compulsion that he fought with every breath.

He was losing control of his own body. Of his beast.

He couldn't have a distraction, even one as tempting as *him*.

Not when he was weak. Pathetic. Broken.

No one understood the pain that trembled along his skin, the need for poison to numb the discomfort. But it wasn't working. He needed something stronger. Something that could destroy him. It wasn't an addiction, despite what everyone believed. Despite what *he* believed.

But it wasn't working, the pain all consuming.

He had nothing left.

No life. No strength. Nothing...

Except, maybe *him*...

He's tried everything to make the pain go away... except *him*.

Dark Paranormal Romance - Found Family - M/M - Fated Mates - Who Hurt You?

Read **Whisper of Fate** for a dark, and twisted friends to lovers romance featuring Axel and Sam.

Want to see Eva finally bake for Kace?

Enjoy this free sexy bonus epilogue!
Download >
https://BookHip.com/XBTHAPZ

Please leave a review of Touch of Blood on Amazon! Reviews are super important, and help readers discover this series and allows me to continue writing these stories.

Thank you from the bottom of my disturbed heart, Taylor

P.S. Want a fun, safe place to chat about my books with others? Join my exclusive reader group, Taylor's Supernatural Society!

Books by Taylor Aston White

Curse of The Guardians

Kiss of Darkness
Touch of Blood
Whisper of Fate

Alice Skye Series

Witch's Sorrow
Druid's Storm
Rogue's Mercy
Elemental's Curse
Knight's War
Veil's Fall

Alice Skye World

Witch's Bounty
(Newsletter exclusive)
Chasing Shadows
(Website exclusive)

Keep in touch with Taylor Aston White

Instagram
@taylorastonwhite
TikTok
@taylorastonwhite
Facebook
/taylorastonwhite
Website
www.taylorastonwhite.com
Bookbub
www.bookbub.com/profile/taylor-aston-white
Goodreads
www.goodreads.com/taylorastonwhite

Sign up for Taylor's newsletter mailing list to receive updates, exclusive content, giveaways, early excerpts and much more.
Plus there's a free short story!
www.taylorastonwhite.com

ABOUT THE AUTHOR

Taylor Aston White loves to explore mythology and European faerie tales to create her own, modern magic world. She collects crystals, house plants and dark lipstick, and has two young children who like to 'help' with her writing by slamming their hands across the keyboard.

After working several uncreative jobs and one super creative one, she decided to become a full-time author and now spends the majority of her time between her children and writing the weird and wonderful stories that pop into her head.